DNA NEVER LIES

You kept a secret for sixty years. It won't be secret much longer.

SUE GEORGE

PI P

PALMER LEWIS PRESS

Cover design: The Cover Collection

PROLOGUE

He always thought he knew better than she did. Always.

Furious, she unclipped her earrings and threw them into a corner of the unkempt room, shaking her brown hair out of its tight set, and ruffling it back into its usual mess.

Men don't always know best. Husbands, boyfriends, fathers – all think they know more than you do. But this time at least, she had been the one who'd been right.

The event – the evening itself, as well as what came before and would come after – had developed as she'd predicted. She had warned, repeatedly, that it would be a disaster, and it had been.

So why did on earth had she gone along with it, giving in to his relentless pressure? She'd opposed it for months. She should have carried on saying no. Aargh! She tore off the elaborate crepe gown that he'd thought appropriate for the occasion and screwed it up, deliberately treading on it and kicking it towards her earrings.

Crowds of people had shown up, probably attracted by the free alcohol, but they had not enjoyed themselves. No, they'd laughed at her, they'd grumbled and complained, as she stood apart and watched them.

But now it was over and, exhausted, she fell onto the divan, pulling the thin scratchy blanket over her face. He blamed her for everything going wrong – tonight and always – but surely most of the fault lay with him? Oh, it was all too much.

What happened to the person that she used to be – confident, with an eye for what worked and what did not? Determined. Focused.

Just as she was dropping off to sleep, she heard the jiggling of the key in the lock, followed by the splintering of the rotten doorframe. He wasn't a man with enough patience to figure out how to open the door. Now, off its hinges, the door banged against the wall, and the man let out a stream of expletives she was too tired and drunk to decipher.

Bile rose in her throat; he was coming exactly as he'd said he would. His eagerness to punish her, to make her pay somehow for something, had overcome those kinder parts of his nature that she remembered from long ago. She had exhausted his patience and now she would suffer for it.

Another worry sprang into her mind: how much would she have to pay the landlord for this mess? Maybe the creep would throw her out. He hated her too. Never mind that the rotten wood was already crumbling, any damage would be her fault. The contract said as much.

'Why didn't you wait for me,' the man growled, not pausing to turn on the light. The room seemed icy. She hadn't bothered with the heating; it barely worked anyway. He shivered and pressed his chilly body against hers, only slightly warmer, as the narrowness of the divan allowed his weight to pin her easily against the cushions.

Her body went rigid but she did not feel terror or disgust as he pressed between her legs. No, she felt a profound indifference, so detached from her skin and her flesh, her heart and her soul, that she was not sure that it belonged to her anymore. In ways that she did never – could never – explain, she had somehow left herself behind. She passed out and, some time before the sun rose, he grabbed his clothes and slipped away from her disgust.

Next morning, after he had gone, she noticed marks from his fingers livid on her shoulders. It was only then that the impact of what had happened hit her. She ran into the bathroom and vomited.

Still, that would never happen again. It was over and done with.

Wasn't it?

PART ONE

CHAPTER ONE

In millions of homes across Britain, the day started in much the same way. The Pendleton family sat in a bright suburban living room with their after-breakfast coffees, the TV on mute in the background, a seasonal scented candle with cinnamon and spicy notes disguising the fact that the Christmas tree didn't smell of anything.

Barbara, almost but not quite ninety, looked at the tree dispassionately. She preferred the tinsel one they had used for years, rather than this messy, smell-free, *real* tree whose needles would lurk under the rug for months. Lynne, her eldest daughter who had moved in with her 'just in case', had thrown it out, pronouncing it 'not fit for purpose', though it wasn't clear exactly what that purpose might be.

Her great-grandson Danny, dressed in sweatpants and T-shirt, scrabbled under the tree, sorting through the shiny foil-wrapped parcels. As the youngest, he was more than happy to distribute the presents.

At sixteen, Danny retained a child's excitement towards the day. He suspected his elders weren't experiencing quite the same levels of anticipation but he still reckoned that his gifts would be a bit of a laugh.

'I want to go first,' he said, 'so I can give you oldies all of yours at once.' Danny wore his light brown hair long on top and shaved down the sides, his blue eyes smiling with the confidence of a much-loved boy who hadn't yet shown any sign of acne.

He handed out four rectangular packages, each the size of a box of chocolates, to his great-grandmother, his grandmother, his great-aunt, and his great-uncle. His parents had gone to his sister's in Portugal; she was so pregnant that she might pop at any second. Danny had no wish to spend an unspecified period of time in a tumbledown house in the middle of nowhere, especially when there would soon be a baby yelling its head off. With his grandmother Cathy he was being, as his father so rightly put it, 'spoilt rotten'.

'What's all this then?' Barbara's son Nick wondered, turning the still-wrapped package over in his hands. 'Same things for all of us?'

'You were telling me how Great-Grandad had been researching his family tree, but when he was still alive, you couldn't get your DNA tested to tell if you were descended from Vikings, or royalty, or rich people. Or even famous mass-murderers or something.'

Danny grinned at them; he had their attention.

'So, me and Mum figured that it would be fun for you to get those DNA tests that are being advertised.' He smiled, confident that his gifts would be appreciated and laughed over. Which part of the world would the family have come from? Would they be Norwegian or Russian or, as his mother predicted, mostly from England with perhaps some native American from Barbara's side.

'That's fun! Thank you, love,' said Cathy, unwrapping hers and looking at the cover. 'Maybe we'll find some rich relatives we don't know about.'

'It's always possible,' said Nick dryly. 'So what do we do now?'

Lynne opened her box and started reading the instructions.

'Oh, right, we spit in the tiny bottle and then post it off. The company processes it and we get emails with the results. I expect they'll be telling us we aren't Vikings after all, but we're all from the same boring bit of southern England that we live in now! Even Great-Grandma.'

'No, she won't be!' said Danny. 'Remember that her parents went from Scotland to Canada a hundred and something years ago. So at least we'll all be a little bit Scottish!'

'What do you think, Mum?' Lynne turned to her mother who was turning the box over in her hands, not having opened it yet. 'Do you expect we'll discover anything interesting?'

Barbara had a faraway, detached look in her eyes. While this detachment wasn't entirely unusual in nearly ninety-year-olds, Barbara wasn't like others of her age. No one still teaching yoga at her age could be considered unexceptional.

'I suppose a bit of saliva can't do any harm,' she said slowly, painstakingly unwrapping the package and staring hard at the instructions.

Barbara watched Lynne as she pulled the cushions away from the chairs, then the sofa, then began delving into the wastepaper bin full of wrapping paper.

'Mum, you haven't seen them, have you?'

'What's that, dear?'

'Those DNA kits. Yours and mine. Nick and Cathy must have taken theirs home now, but I can't see ours anywhere.'

'I haven't seen them since Danny gave them to us earlier.'

Barbara's attention seemed to be focused on another gift – a National Geographic book of luscious photographs – and she watched surreptitiously as Lynne cast her eyes over the picture of a beach surrounded by palm trees.

'We can't have *lost* them. They must be *somewhere.*'

'Well of course they are *somewhere*.'

Lynne wrinkled her forehead, screwing up her eyes and sighing in exasperation.

'It will be such a shame if we can't take the tests together. It will take the fun out of it.'

'Fun!'

Barbara spat out the word with such contempt and vitriol that her daughter thought she must have misheard.

'Perhaps Cathy or Nick took them home by mistake,' Barbara continued in a more normal voice.

'Yes,' sighed Lynne. 'That could well be it. They all look the same so perhaps they didn't realise they had ours as well as theirs. I'll call them tomorrow when they've had a chance to unpack.'

Barbara nodded, once more turning the pages of her book.

'It will be interesting to see what our DNA shows, won't it, Mum?' said Lynne anxiously. 'I'd love to see if there are any interesting connections on your side of the family. You've always said you don't really know anything about them.'

Barbara, looking into the mid-distance, said: 'I've made it to eighty-nine and a half without thinking about it much. I'm not sure what I've missed.'

'But most people want to understand where they came from.'

'Do they? But we already know where we came from. It isn't very interesting or unusual. You could even call it boring.'

Lynne sighed. 'Why are you being so awkward?'

Barbara said nothing, focusing on her book.

'Well, I want to know more about you, even if you don't,' Lynne continued.

Barbara sighed. 'You must have heard of Pandora's Box. When you open it, all the demons in the world fly out and you can never put them back in again.'

'Mum.'

'Hmm?'

'Don't be silly. We're ordinary people. You said so yourself only a moment ago.'

Barbara was quiet. When you're young – like Danny – you think old people have always been old, that only conventional and predictable problems have ever occurred, and that everything to do with history is firmly in the past. Even Barbara's children, not at all young anymore, thought her life had never pushed further than the boundaries of the obvious, despite their lack of clarity as to the details.

In response to teenage problems, or watching the news on television, Danny, sweet boy, often said that everything happens for a reason. When did that stupid saying become common currency, she wondered? Such harmful nonsense. Besides, if that were true, then whoever invented DNA must have done it to torment people like her and destroy the stability that they had spent their entire lives constructing.

CHAPTER TWO

Karen's mother once had a mirror engraved with the words 'Today is the first day of the rest of your life'. Now it would be incorporated into a meme, a lightweight prod towards positive thinking. But back in the 70s, when young Karen dropped her mother's mirror, breaking it in three, the words signified loss: loss of the pretty mirror, its pink plastic handle still in one piece. Loss of hope, though about what she didn't know; maybe about her mother, who had abandoned her, yet again, with her grandparents. Seven years' bad luck it was, then.

Nevertheless, some days mark a positive turning point, the first day of something new and better. When Karen groggily woke up to a slightly sunny Thursday morning and pulled her laptop across her bed, she had no expectations that this would be anything more than the usual tortuous drag. The endless hassle for small amounts of money. She did not realise that today might finally be the day that she – failed journalist, failed academic, failed partner, almost failed genealogy and probate researcher – found something that was actually going to work.

Because this morning, rather than endless spam from companies she had signed up to in the grip of some now-dead enthusiasm, there was an individual email, subject line: *Family tree query – can you help?*

Unlikely, Karen sighed, opening it anyway.

Dear Dr Copperfield,
I saw your advertisement in Find My
Family Magazine, and I wonder if you'd
be able to help with a mystery I have
uncovered. This is both painful and highly
confidential so I'd like to visit you at your
offices, or at least speak to you on the phone
before we start. Would you also give me a
note of your fees?
Yours sincerely,
Lynne Pendleton

Karen had not worked in a university for several years; had cast the whole experience, both the good parts and the bad, to the recesses of her mind. So she was always taken aback when someone addressed her as 'doctor'. Of course, she had earned that title – had sweated blood in the archives – and for what exactly? Thousands of pounds worth of debt, which she had only just paid off? Nightmares over the viva at which, as she had been told, she had performed 'not too shabbily'? Whatever that meant. In any event, she only needed to make minor changes to her thesis, and there she was: Karen Copperfield, PhD, and the start of a time in her life she now tried hard to forget.

Nevertheless, she responded.

Dear Ms Pendleton,
Thanks for getting in touch. I work from
home but would be glad to meet anywhere
in central London that suits you. I often
meet clients in the Festival Hall on the
South Bank, so I suggest we meet there.
What about 11am on Monday?
We can discuss my fee at that time as it

depends on what you are asking me to do.
With best wishes,
Karen Copperfield

Work from home; that was a laugh. Work from bed, more like. She barely had a table to work from, let alone 'offices' suitable for meeting clients. Fees... well they were a joke too. Still, this morning she hadn't run out of coffee, and there was someone out there who believed her expertise might be worth paying for.

Karen dragged herself towards the kettle and toaster. Nine am. She was still not operating at the level she used to. What she wanted to be was a super-fit, determined researcher, willing to uncover hidden truths and right all types of wrongs. By her own reckoning, she had never managed any of that, although she had tried and tried. Still, her running had improved (Faster! Further!) and she was getting back to her old levels of fitness. That was what the doctors prescribed these days as a cure for so many ills: exercise. They could be right.

Her keenly priced flat – London was never cheap – was located a bus trip from the Underground, in the farthest end of far east London, an area close to the motorway. It was isolated and isolating, the hum and pollution of the traffic ever-present, the situation and apartment itself almost designed to encourage depression. Still, she had a purpose now, a client, someone likely to pay her so that she didn't need to ask her ex-partners – either of them – or her sister, or her credit card, to help her pay the rent that month.

She texted Lisa:

A client! Amazing! See you Sunday? Kiss, kiss, I miss my sis. x

Her phone pinged straight away.

Remember that I am in Scotland with Keith till Wednesday. Sunday after? Miss you too. xx

Karen always considered that her sister was never quite as close, geographically or in any other way, as she should be. But still, Sunday week would do and she knew that, in the scheme of things, husbands took priority.

Two coffees, two slices of strangely doughy wholemeal toast and cheese, and she was ready to start the day at the gym. Achieving so many minutes of cardio and so many minutes of resistance training... those statistics helped her remain grounded. They gave her the sense of achievement that she used to have when she had taken an exam and been awarded high marks. Karen Copperfield was someone who amounted to something; without achievements, who even was she?

• • • ● ● • ● ● • • •

At eleven on Monday morning, London's Festival Hall was just getting going. There wouldn't be any performances for a few hours yet and it almost seemed designed for ad-hoc meetings: freelance journalists waiting for interviewees to show up, retired people looking for somewhere central to gather in case one was delayed, two students chatting and spreading their books over four-person tables, handily situated next to electrical sockets for charging their devices. But fortunately for all of them, there were plenty of places to sit where they wouldn't be disturbed.

Amongst the gathering bustle, Karen picked out her client immediately. Lynne Pendleton was a silver-bobbed woman somewhere in her sixties, mid-height, mid-weight, wearing a pale blue padded coat that was entirely right for the weather. As Lynne turned towards her, Karen could tell that the coat matched Lynne's eyes. The pale blue eyes which also said: 'I don't want to trust you, but what choice is there?' The soft-coloured coat was a camouflage, far more than a style choice.

'Ms Pendleton.' Karen held out her hand. 'I'm Karen Copperfield. Thank you so much for coming to meet me. Did you travel far?'

Ah, the necessary pleasantries designed to put them at ease; Karen as much as her client. She waved towards some tables set slightly apart from the others.

'Swindon,' Lynne replied. 'Not such a long way.'

That was probably an easier journey to central London than Karen's had been, she reflected.

'Great!' said Karen breezily, going into the protection of professional performance. 'Shall I get us a coffee?'

Lynne nodded. 'Thank you.' She sat down, draping her pretty coat on the back of a chair. Underneath, Lynne was wearing a navy and white patterned tunic which Karen registered as elegant.

Two cappuccinos in hand, Karen shuffled in an ungainly manner around the table making the chairs shift with a screech. The two women exchanged a grimace as she plonked herself down. Were her trousers too tight, Karen wondered? Did she seem scruffy? Maybe this was the wrong suit. Calm down, she thought, calm down. The ever-present background hum of clashing cups and laughter grew slightly louder.

'So, what can I do for you?'

Karen sat on her hands, willing her nervousness not to show. How many clients did she need before this anxiety quelled? There had been a few of them, and she had done all right, but there were not enough of them for confidence.

She would have been surprised to find out – disbelieving even – that her appearance belied her feelings. Rather than someone nervous and flaky, Lynne saw a confident, professional, middle-aged woman. Her light brown hair was cut in a feathered style, its tips slightly golden as if highlighted, but not enough to scream 'bleached', her understated earrings and matching necklace just right. Karen's pleasant, welcoming face was accentuated by some very subtle, well-applied make-up, and her lips – a few shades darker than her pale skin – smiled encouragingly.

Lynne began pulling folders and sheaves of paper out of her shoulder bag and set them in front of her, piling them up neatly. Then, with her hands marking the sides of them, pushing them into a neater pile, she sighed heavily.

'I've come to the horrible realisation that my dad isn't my biological father,' Lynne said, pressing her lips together. She moved them against each other for a few seconds before continuing. 'I don't know who I am anymore.'

She looked up, as one tear made its way slowly down her cheek, appearing embarrassed as if this was far too early in the proceedings to express emotion.

'I'm very sorry to hear that,' Karen replied, out of her depth with this crying stranger, and hoping that her own experience of counselling would soon kick in to help. 'How did you find this out?'

Lynne slid a tissue from the sleeve of her tunic and held it against her cheek.

'My great-nephew bought several members of our family DNA tests for Christmas, and when we got the results back it soon became obvious that my brother and sister aren't entirely related to me.'

'Not entirely related?'

'When you get the results, they give you suggestions about distant cousins and so on. Theirs were identical. Mine were quite different.' She breathed deeply and slowly. 'They showed up as brother and sister to each other, and I was merely...' she paused again. 'Close family. And I thought that perhaps there was some mistake.'

Lynne paused, emotions running across her face. She blinked rapidly.

'So I rang the helpline to talk through what had happened, and the operator... said she was very sorry but it seemed that we had different fathers. My brother and sister had the same father, and I had another one.'

'And is your mother still alive?' Karen asked softly.

'Yes. She won't talk about it at all. We bought a test for her, but she lost it. I think she threw it away. As far as I can tell, she threw away mine too but I decided to buy myself another one. I suppose I realised something was up. Anyway, she has now completely clammed up on the subject, except to say that she doesn't believe in DNA. Now, I don't know what to do. She's nearly ninety. And she's fit and well, unusually so, but still.'

Lynne stared off into space for a while. She ran her fingers through her hair, smoothing it behind her ears for a few moments, then nervously pulling its too-short ends towards her chin before she continued.

'There are some people we are all three related to, others that Cathy and Nick are related to and I'm not, and some that I am connected to and they aren't. Oh, God...'

Karen nodded at her to go on.

'My aunt, my father's, well not my father but you know, his sister Ann, she was very keen on genealogy and so we know all about his side of the family, going back goodness knows how many generations. Her children have tested and they come up as first cousins to Cathy and Nick. But I don't. The people I have thought were my cousins, they aren't mine. I'm not connected to them at all.'

Pressing her lips together, Lynne shook her head. 'I just don't know what to do, how to go forward.'

She put both her hands around her white porcelain coffee cup and pulled its comfort towards her, sipping.

'I'm throwing myself on your mercy. I can't do this myself. I don't have the knowledge. About the DNA especially.' Lynne inhaled, then seemed to stop breathing before she continued. 'All the details are so confusing and the more I look at them, the more muddled I feel. Then there's also a mental block.

Whatever secret it is that Mum has been keeping from us all these years, well I don't want to know. Except I do. You understand?'

'I think so, yes.'

Lynne looked to Karen for reassurance, for affirmation. Karen, in turn, had a very unprofessional desire to stroke her hair, to promise that everything would be all right. But everything would probably be far from all right. Nor was she in a position to promise anything.

'You will take me on, won't you?' There was pleading in Lynne's voice, whining even. Karen pulled herself together, almost physically. She shuffled and settled on her pale wood chair before she smiled:

'Do you want me to find out the identity of your birth father? If I can.' Karen hoped that her voice sounded soothing, confident. True confidence was beyond her, but soothing – perhaps she could carry that off.

'Yes. I do want that. This is all too much for me.' She pushed her pile of papers across the table towards Karen. 'There's a lot of information here, photocopies and print-outs. My sister has the originals.'

Karen nodded. 'I'll also need management access for the site where you have tested your DNA so that I can contact the people who come up as your matches. Yours and not your siblings', that is. You need to set me up for that. I can do it for you now on my laptop, if you like.'

On top of the papers, Lynne had put a print-out of a basic family tree. While Lynne logged into her Ancestry account, Karen cast her eyes over the tree, seeing that it only went back two generations from Lynne, as well as two generations forwards.

'Danny, my great-nephew, he's the one who gave us the tests for Christmas. Poor boy.' Lynne shook her head, dejected. 'He had no idea what he was doing.'

The women smiled sadly at each other before Karen edged back into professionalism.

'Look, Lynne. You wanted information about my fees. With previous clients, they were straightforward cases. They generally lived outside of the UK, wanting me to look at archives, or gravestones or baptismal records, things that aren't available online. Or they wanted their easy-to-investigate family tree packaged nicely as a coffee-table book with local history and photographs. I have a price for those services. But this is detective work. It may be easy to find out the answers you need, it may not. I must warn you about that.'

'I realise that,' Lynne said forcefully. 'But I have to do this. I can't tell you how deeply it has affected me. Money is not a problem: I sold my house to move in with my mother because she's old. Perhaps I shouldn't have done that. She didn't ask me to and maybe she didn't need me to. But I did, I needed it.'

Karen paused again. 'I also have to tell you that there are plenty of volunteers online who help with just this sort of situation. Search angels. They don't charge anything.'

'They could be anyone! Who knows what their agenda is? Or how good they are!' Lynne shuddered at the idea.

Karen nodded. 'I'm going to charge you by the hour, then. Let's see what I have discovered after a few days.'

'I've Googled you.' Lynne smiled. 'You've done heavy-hitting journalism and your academic work is well-respected. Most people working on genetic genealogy taught themselves, I understand that, but you have intellectual rigour and I trust that. Those are the reasons why I wanted you.'

'Thank you,' said Karen, blushing. She didn't believe a word of it and neither did her ex-employers, no matter what Lynne had found on the internet. 'I'll draw up a contract and send it to you later today. But before I start,' she continued, 'you need to tell me everything you can about your family.'

CHAPTER THREE

Barbara was out when Lynne got back; Monday afternoon, so it had to be choir at the Wellbeing Hub, and then she would be having tea with someone or other. Lynne was tired just thinking about it. Why did her mother seem so much more energetic than she was? She had given up work now, whereas her mother still taught chair-based yoga for heaven's sake. Lynne felt briefly envious – she wouldn't be like that at going on ninety – and a growing irritation. Who was this person? She had never really asked.

The emptiness of the house reflected the emptiness of Lynne herself. She glanced towards, and then away from, the cocktail cabinet, where she could see the whisky she suddenly craved. What the hell, she thought, pouring herself a glass and swigging the contents.

Like all the rest of the furniture in her childhood home, the cabinet was in a style now called 'mid-century modern' which Lynne still thought of as 'old tat'. It was the sort of thing many people had bought on hire purchase when they married in the 50s and then lived with for the rest of their lives. The sort of thing she had rejected in favour of Habitat or Ikea. Until now, when she was glad of its familiarity.

The front door clicked, before banging shut. Here she was then. The bus had been prompt.

'Hello, Mum. How was choir?' Lynne moved into the hall, almost surprised that her mother continued to function just as she had before *that day* when the DNA results came through.

The small, slim, white-haired woman carried on unbuttoning her red duffel coat as she looked up and smiled. Her black-framed glasses were a perfect match with the red and white patterned jumper and black trousers. For a woman who always claimed to have no time for or interest in clothes, Barbara exhibited an innate sense of style. She took her time hanging the coat neatly on the coat rack.

'Oh, the usual,' Barbara said. 'Songs from the sixties. I know more of them now than I ever did at the time.'

'No Rogers and Hammerstein? Wasn't that what you wanted?'

'One day, I expect. Anyway, let me put my feet up for a while and get my breath back.'

Ah, Lynne thought. Her mother was tired after all. She needed a rest to recover from the exertions of the day and wouldn't be offering to make supper as she so often did. Lynne recognised a bizarre sense of relief. It made her mother seem more normal, less like the sort of person who might be able to keep a significant part of her life secret for more than sixty years.

Lynne would never forget the morning she opened her email and saw the message: Your DNA results are in! The email promised ethnicity estimates – well she never cared about that, considered it a bit of a joke even if Danny and his mother didn't – as well as connections with long-lost relatives and tracing your family's journey. And so on and so forth.

Were secrets better? Maybe. If she had never found out that her DNA separated her from everything and everyone she knew, they could have carried on just as before. They might have bickered from time to time, feeling both understandable and more baffling resentments, but generally getting on the same as any other extended family.

So when she looked at her DNA notification, she wasn't expecting anything unusual. Her DNA matches were grouped under headings, with the top one reading *Close Family – First Cousins*. Under that, there they were: Catherine Mortimer and Nicholas Pendleton. Lynne had burst out laughing. Close family, well, that's obvious! What else do you call your sister and brother? What an anti-climax. There were figures and percentages indicating shared DNA next to their names but she didn't understand what they meant.

Under the next heading down, she had one unknown person listed as a first to second cousin, then another listed as second to third cousin, and after that, more headings and many more distant connections. What were fourth or fifth cousins anyway? She neither knew nor cared. There were other things she had to do that day. It would have to wait until later.

Except that it didn't. An hour or so later, she spotted an email from Nick. She remembered the subject line all too clearly: *DNA mistakes LOL*.

Have you looked at your results? I think we have different parents! (And here, she remembered sadly, he had added laugh-till-you-cry emoticons).

Look at this screenshot. I'm going into a meeting now but speak later. X

Such a short email, but Lynne felt side-swiped as if Nick had taken the flat of his hand and slapped her hard on the face, leaving her reeling. Nick had always been a thoughtful and kind man. Yet, unthinkingly, he had done this.

The screenshot made it clear. The top of the list, under siblings, was Cathy – announced as sister under a firm, bold headline. Listed below Cathy... well there she was. On her own list: *Close Family – First Cousin* Lynne Pendleton. But his list had people hers did not. Charlie Trussell was listed as a first cousin, and on a list below that, as first to second cousins, two people with the user names GennieM and Felicity Trussell90. There was, though, one connection that she shared with Nick: a first to second cousin with the user name Jazzbabe260.

She started to shake. If this was a mistake, then what kind of mistake could it be? Lynne paced back and forth, starting to wonder. Why had her mother's test 'gone missing'? Where had it 'gone missing' to? The tiniest tapping grew louder to fill her brain with unaccustomed noise. What did it mean? Something was wrong. She could feel her breathing growing ever more shallow.

After a few hours, she sent both her siblings a text. To Nick, she wrote. *What does this mean? Call me. Please? ASAP.*

She trusted that he would be able to see her underlying panic. Oh please, she begged the screen on her phone. She needed him to get back to her right now.

Cathy needed a different approach. *Hey Cath. Not sure if you have seen the DNA results yet. What do you reckon? xxx*

Nick texted back straightaway. *On the train with colleagues. Look later. x*

Nothing from Cathy, though; unsurprising really.

In the meantime, Lynne stared at her results, trying to make sense of them. There were around half a dozen people listed as connections closer than fourth cousin but – apart from her siblings – she recognised no one. They must be people she had never met, great-grandparents' descendants, or something. Few of their user names seemed real, just bits of names or numbers joined together. For instance, Jazzbabe260. Who on earth could that be? And as well as her downgrading to 'close family', their cousin Charlie and his daughter Felicity, and their other cousin Lorna's daughter Gennie had not shown up on her list at all. Just on Nick's.

But why was this bothering her so much when it was clearly a strange anomaly?

Nick was good at calming his sisters; he always had been. And Lynne's assumption that he had sensed her panic was correct, as he called her again before he got back to the office.

'Nick, oh I'm so pleased to hear your voice.'

'Don't worry about it.'

'What does this mean, Nick? I don't have Charlie or the kids on my list at all.'

'It's strange, isn't it? They must have contaminated the samples. Who do you have?'

'No one close. I mean there's someone with the user name Jazzbabe260.'

'Yes, I have her too. Whoever she is.'

'I suppose that's a relief. That there are some mutual connections, I mean. What is your ethnicity estimate?'

'England, Wales and north-western Europe, sixty-seven per cent. Ireland and Scotland, twenty-seven per cent. Then a few odd bits, one per cent Sweden and so on.'

'Oh. Well, I got Ireland and Scotland sixty per cent, England, Wales and north-western Europe twenty-five per cent, southern Europe ten per cent. But I never believed in that. It seems so arbitrary. How do they differentiate between England and Scotland?'

'Give customer services a ring and see what they suggest.'

'Maybe I should wait until I speak to Cathy.'

'No.' Nick said firmly. 'Don't do that. She may not look at her phone. Not until the planets are favourably aligned anyway.'

Lynne laughed; she was always someone who acted, rather than thought about it. Cathy reversed that. 'Okay,' she said and hung up.

Lynne would never forget that helpline call; not the details of it because some of them shifted and changed in her mind and she could never remember the exact words either of them spoke, or in which order. How had she explained her problem, that her brother and sister had different matches from her, how they were only listed as close family? The words themselves were flexible. But the message wasn't.

She had been ready to complain, to tell the helpline woman that her sample had obviously been contaminated, because this was the most likely explanation. But when the woman on the other end of the line spoke, Lynne just poured out her anguish. 'Why are my brother and sister listed as close family to first cousin,' not as my siblings, when they are listed as siblings to each other. We definitely aren't cousins, they are my brother and sister, so there must be something wrong here. Why would they be listed as my cousins?'

Lynne remembered her voice rising; she already knew what she was implying.

'I'm so sorry, ma'am. DNA doesn't lie. It's very unlikely that the sample was contaminated. Your biological father was not the same as your brother and sister's.'

For the first time in her life, she knew exactly what 'having the rug pulled from under your feet' meant. One minute, she was standing upright, her phone pressed to her ear, the next, she was leaning against the wall, dizzy, the room swimming around her, like the floor itself had dropped away.

'Cousins' in familial DNA tests didn't necessarily mean that two people were the children of their parents' siblings, she heard the woman say from somewhere that could have been a cloud, another dimension, so unreal and distant did it feel. Instead, it was the amount of shared DNA that indicated what sort of relationship it might be, and she didn't share enough of it with Nick or Cathy for either of them to be her full sibling.

She knew the woman had been gentle in her telling; there was embarrassment, sadness and regret in her voice. But she was not the one staring at herself in the mirror, wondering who she was *really*.

Lynne pushed these recollections back into the past and decided to ring Cathy while their mother was having a brief lie down. She answered with a quick 'Yup'.

'I saw the genealogist today. She seemed very nice,' Lynne said while thinking, nice, that's not right. Capable? Trustworthy? Intelligent? She bit her lip, as she heard Cathy tut.

'Well, it's all very well for you, making appointments on a Monday morning. Some of us have a living to earn.'

'I know,' Lynne said soothingly, although she didn't feel like soothing Cathy then or ever.

'Still, I suppose you have to do it.'

'I do, yes.'

'And you can afford it.'

Lynne sighed. 'Well, let's see what she finds out. I'm sure there will be something.'

She clicked off. Hopefully, their mother wouldn't have heard any of that. But at some point, they would have to return to that awful conversation of some weeks earlier. The conversation where she suddenly realised this is my mother and I don't know her anymore. Everything about her is a mystery to me.

CHAPTER FOUR

BARBARA: SWINDON, ENGLAND, 1958

The district nurse turned around and smiled a reassuring goodbye, as Victor clicked the front door behind her. He bent down, looking tenderly at his daughter. 'Now you must be very good and quiet, Lynne. Mummy is poorly.'

'Is that Cathy's fault? She never stops crying,' Lynne asked.

Barbara knew whose fault it was: hers. The 'she' who never stopped crying could be Cathy but it could equally be herself. It didn't matter which of them Lynne meant. They were both drowning in a sea of misery, and Victor was already out of his depth.

'When I was a baby, I didn't cry a lot.' It was a statement, an unassailable fact. Lynne presented herself as a solid, unshakeable child, stubborn and easy to comfort. Barbara looked at her in wonder. How could this little girl, so at home in the world, be hers?

'Not really,' Victor curled his hand softly around Lynne's shoulder.

Nurse Benson had spoken quietly to Victor but Barbara still heard the barrage of questions he tried to answer: how did Barbara seem when Lynne was born? Did she have any history of nervous complaints? Did she take after her mother? And, finally, did she have a female relative whose own responsibilities might allow her to take care of the children? Victor cleared up just two of them: after Lynne's birth, Barbara was absolutely fine, tip-top, ecstatic. So full of energy, she shimmered.

And while her female relatives remained in Canada, he supposed his mother would be more than happy to help. Besides, Lynne had recently started school so she would be out of the way. If only Cathy didn't cry so much, if only. Barbara looked on helplessly as they decided their fate.

Several days later, Marjorie Pendleton bustled through the door, set her brown suitcase down by the front door, and marched straight up to the bedroom without even taking off her hat and coat.

'Barbara, dear!' Marjorie kissed her damp cheek. 'What a to-do this is!' She shook her head as Barbara turned her face to the pillow in humiliation.

'Here's Cathy, Mum.' Victor came into the room holding the baby, who was half asleep, making tiny whimpers while she decided whether to wake up.

'Two weeks makes such a difference!' Marjorie exclaimed. She reached out for Cathy and grasped her close. 'There now. What a big girl you are.'

Marjorie seemed thrilled by her new role. Her daughter Ann was expecting, but she lived hundreds of miles away in Scotland, on the isle of Lewis, where her husband's people had farmed for centuries. It was already obvious to Barbara that she relished being Lynne's grandmother, even though she had to realise that there was no biological connection. All of them could add up; Barbara was around three months pregnant before Victor even reached Canada. She had noticed Marjorie's quizzical glances at Lynne, relieved that they were never put into words.

'Now, let's feed and change this baby, and I'll take her for a little walk.'

Defeated, Barbara sank back onto the pillows.

'I think Mum will be really good with Cathy,' Victor said confidently.

'Because in their different ways, both of them complain and grizzle?'

Victor looked shocked. His mother was indeed petulant and irritable, but Barbara was never normally unkind and would not say such things out loud.

'I'm sorry, I'm sorry.'

She shook her head.

'This is for the best, you'll see.' He smiled.

When Victor's jolly father Fred arrived at the weekend, things felt even worse for Barbara. There was no point to her, was there? She watched as Marjorie cuddled and soothed Cathy, calming her down through effortless and understanding love. Fred tickled and laughed, coaxed and encouraged, with Cathy as he had with his own children.

The doctor expressed his satisfaction with this arrangement but was less reassuring about Barbara's condition, which he described as 'concerning', and arranged for her to be admitted to hospital. Victor had explained to her, sitting on the bed and taking her hand, that this would happen; they had all decided it was the best possible course of action. She started to cry, slowly, at first, then sobbing.

'I'm no use. I'm a terrible mother.'

'Buck up, old girl,' he said helplessly. 'Hospital's the right place for you. You can get better there.'

'What will Lynne think?'

'She's only four, too young to know what's going on. Let me worry about her.'

'I can't do it. Why can't I do it?'

Barbara held out her arms as Victor wrangled them into her warm chenille dressing gown and helped her down the stairs into an ambulance. She did not resist at all, but this lack of resistance was only physical. In her mind, to herself, she said no, again and again, methodically shaking her head back and forth.

'What is wrong with me?' She muttered the phrase once, twice, three or more times.

Victor looked panicked, shushed her. She seemed barely aware that – for everyone's sake – the neighbours must not see her being taken away.

Once in hospital, Barbara complied with everything asked of her. She knew she had a nervous condition – remembered it from what seemed like, and was, another life. She simply fell short of the demands of the job and this hurt her so very much.

She wanted, needed desperately, to not be this way. So she acceded to electric shock treatment, which allowed them to call her a 'good girl' – a phrase that pulled her straight back into childhood. She didn't struggle or beg in advance of the treatment, although she knew that she did thrash about during the shocks, while this terrible thing was being *administered*. When they put a gag in her mouth and tied her down. In fact, afterwards, the experience slipped from her conscious memory. There was a dim awareness that she had been in pain but when she tried to grasp it precisely – it slipped through her fingers. But the forgetting... well, that was something different. The reasons for her presence in hospital escaped her; her brain filled not so much with fog but thick, dark clouds. They would say to her, the nurses, wasn't she looking forward to seeing her little baby again?

But her recollections skirted her conscious mind. Which little baby? But gradually, when they spoke of Cathy, she remembered that, yes, Cathy was the baby and Lynne, well, Lynne was a big girl. They needed her back with them but she had to be good. This ill-defined 'goodness' would improve her health; she would get better.

Eventually, the grey clouds grew lighter and dispersed until everyone around her – hospital staff, Victor, his parents – agreed it was time for Barbara to go home. The district nurse would visit regularly to ensure she was on the mend. Further improvement, everyone said, would not come about until she was at home, a healthy and active wife and mother.

So back she went, with drugs from the doctor helping ease her path through any temporary difficulties. The culprit was her hormones, they agreed. Probably best not to get pregnant again if she could avoid it.

Victor and Barbara thought this was something they could, and would, avoid, without too much difficulty. Marjorie and John stood firmly in their roles as doting grandparents, the girls showed no signs of harm and all of them thought the family had weathered the storm.

As they had. This storm, at any rate.

CHAPTER FIVE

LYNNE: SWINDON, ENGLAND, FEBRUARY 2018

She could not wait a moment longer.

'Look, Mum, we need to talk.'

'Oh yes?'

'Let's sit down, shall we?'

Lynne was shaking as she walked over to the sofa, taking hold of her mother's icy hand. Barbara knew what Lynne wanted to discuss. Of course she did.

'Those DNA tests we did, Mum. Me and Cathy and Nick. They showed us – and we checked with the company – that Dad wasn't my biological father. He was theirs, but not mine.'

Now. There it was. Lynne had said it, and she made a triangle of her hands over her nose and mouth so that she could breathe steadily. That way, perhaps, she would not have a panic attack. But her mother took her time in answering; so long, in fact, that Lynne's breathing was almost back to normal.

'Why couldn't you have left it, Lynne? You must have realised that I'd thrown my test away?'

Lynne nodded. Though she didn't understand why Barbara had thrown the test away. She wasn't the missing one; it was Vic, her father. Or, as she now knew, her not-father. Her half-siblings' father.

'It's all nonsense, DNA. Pseudo-science.'

'Oh come on, Mum, you don't believe that.'

'Yes, I do,' Barbara said firmly. 'Why would you want to think your father was someone different? Wasn't he a good dad, a loving dad?'

'Of course he was. The best! I will always love him and miss him. But see things from my point of view, Mum. Someone else was my biological father and I have to know about him. Who was he? I need to know.'

'No, you don't. You know who your father was. Don't shame his memory. He was a wonderful husband. He saved my life. You should remember that.'

'I'm not shaming anyone or anything. I just want to know the truth.'

'No, you don't,' Barbara repeated coldly. 'The truth has never helped. Some things need to be left in the past.'

She withdrew her hand, rubbing it slowly where Lynne had been holding it.

'Was it horrible, Mum? Is that the reason? Did some man attack you?'

Barbara appeared to be gulping for air. Lynne felt cruel, like she was torturing a helpless old woman. What about her own needs, though? Her very existence? This all seemed crushingly unfair. But what had she expected? Lynne had absolutely no idea.

'Who was it, Mum. Did you have an affair or something?' Lynne's voice rose higher, more desperate, as Barbara struggled to get up from the deep seats of the sofa.

'Stop it, Lynne. Stop it now. Leave me alone.' She stood up and walked steadily to the doorway. 'I have never and will never talk about this. If you don't accept that, then you need to leave this house which, you may remember, is mine.'

The glass in the door rattled as Barbara shut it with a near slam. Lynne leaned back on the sofa, as exhausted as she had ever felt in her life, sick with a revulsion towards her mother that she had never felt before.

Nick and Cathy had not supported her decision to confront – or even talk to – their mother about the DNA results. They would not come to the house to be there while Lynne and Barbara talked. They wanted more research, more waiting, more thought; for Lynne to take her time. Unusually, they were together on this. Lynne was not sure when, if ever, that had happened before.

There were arguments – in person, in texts and emails, and in three-person WhatsApp chats – about what Lynne should do and when she should do it. The answer was always *not now, not yet.*

But Lynne was too angry with them to care. Fury towards them came far more readily than towards her mother. *Who am I?* Lynne needed to know. It's not that just the rug has been pulled from under my feet, she thought, but that there is no floor and I am falling forever with nothing to grab on to.

'Can I really call myself Pendleton?' she asked Cathy.

'But that's what's on your birth certificate. Don't be ridiculous.'

'He can't be my father though! Not my real father.'

The fierce look in Cathy's eyes was quite different from her usual pity, for herself and sometimes others. 'Of course he is. DNA doesn't matter, does it? Remember when he spent hours driving you around to swimming events? Or when he used to sing that song 'Yes, my darling daughter' to you? You were the one winding him around your little finger. Not me. Don't you remember...?'

Lynne had to close her mind to all the family memories Cathy was serving up. They were tainted now. She shuddered with disgust. It was all a con. Perhaps her father had not known she was not 'his'.

'I've got to know who I am!'

'For pity's sake, Lynne, you're who you always have been.' Nick was now joining in. He usually shied away from conflict. Cathy was the angry one, the all-round flaky member of the family. 'Also, Mum is old. She's nearly ninety. Let her die in peace.'

'Come on! She's the healthiest ninety-year-old you could ever meet. Been doing yoga for half her life. Fitter than the three of us put together.'

'It's not that unusual to be ninety these days,' Lynne continued at the top of her voice. 'Lots of people are over ninety. David Attenborough. Betty White. The queen. Dick Van Dyke. And lots and lots of Mum's friends. I don't expect they have people protecting them from everything just in case they can't handle it. Not everyone has dementia or needs to be protected from themselves.'

Nick and Cathy were trying to talk at the same time.

'And lots of people who would be ninety are dead,' he said. 'Dad, for instance. So cut it out.'

'But they aren't her,' Cathy shouted. 'They aren't our mother. They didn't have all those terrible periods of depression. She *does* need protecting from herself.'

The three of them fell silent, the air shimmering with anxiety and insecurity.

'She's been better for ages though,' Lynne replied sullenly.

'Has she? I doubt that,' Cathy continued with equal resentment. Lynne turned to look at her in confusion.

'Mum hasn't been depressed at all for forty years. That was what she always said, wasn't it? And that yoga had saved her. Do you understand that? I don't. I sometimes think I didn't know her at all.'

'Oh come on! You've always known her. Surely she meant she was saved from depression?' Nick looked as though he was angry with both his sisters.

'There is so much about her I don't know,' said Lynne.

'Well, I don't know it either. Neither does Nick. None of us knows.'

Nick sighed. 'Maybe Dad knew.'

The three of them pondered the implications of this, turning it around in their heads.

'We can never know one way or the other, can we?' Cathy said in tones of extreme weariness.

'Amber would suggest that we try to contact him,' said Nick. 'I expect she can put us in touch with one of her more loopy friends. She is in touch with the spiritual, as she never tires of telling us.'

They laughed, as they were meant to. Cathy's granddaughter Amber lived in a sustainable eco-community in Portugal, set up to be self-sufficient and in harmony with nature. She was the sort of person who'd name their offspring January. But Amber didn't know this bomb had been thrown into the peace of their family and there was no way, at present, that anyone would tell her. They had too much to sort out themselves first.

Chapter Six

She couldn't stop herself from starting immediately. There was no way Karen would wait to reach her so-called office before going through Lynne's great stack of papers. Instead, after the two women had said goodbye, and Karen had promised to email a contract later that day, she went around the corner to another coffee shop. Right then, she sat down to go through the documents. She was well aware of her instant enthusiasms; nevertheless, this project looked particularly enticing.

Wow, so much paperwork! Still, she supposed, it made a difference from staring at a screen for hours, and Lynne had said that her mother's family tree was not online, not as far as any of them knew. Only her father's family had public trees with any of the genealogy websites.

First, she looked at the birth certificates. There was Lynne's. October 1, 1954, Vancouver, British Columbia, to Victor Pendleton, twenty-eight, sports coach, and Barbara Pendleton, nee Thompson, twenty-six. So far, so straightforward. Lynne had also included copies of her siblings' certificates: Catherine, who was born in 1958, in Swindon, Wiltshire, by which time Victor was listed as physical education teacher; and Nicholas, born 1962, also in Swindon.

Under that, there was a copy of the Pendletons' marriage certificate and the very first paper clue. They had married on September 6, 1954, when Barbara would have been eight months' pregnant. They were both listed at the same address in Vancouver, and there was no occupation given for Barbara.

Karen started an email: *Questions for Lynne*
Why was your father in Vancouver?
You told me that your mother was pregnant with you when she got married but I didn't realise how far along she was. Do you know what she was doing before she married your father? What was her address before they lived together?

Her phone started vibrating its way around the table; it was a message from Ben, reminding her they were having dinner together, and it was her turn to pick the restaurant. Nothing fancy or expensive, just something a step up from the many chains that were filling central London. She picked an East London Thai restaurant, where the food was comparatively healthy and the tables not so packed together that conversation was impossible.

It would be good to see him; it always was. Also, she was pleased that, finally, she was earning some money again. In the reasonably near future, she would be buying dinner. Just not today.

Lynne had also included photos of herself as a tiny baby – the obligatory infant on a rug pose – plus others of her sister Cathy and brother Nick at similar ages. Then there was one of the whole family together, from the mid-60s. Barbara, her hair in that fixed cauliflower style worn by middle-aged women of the era, looked exhausted. Her eyes seemed almost shut, as though she wasn't quite there. It was impossible to imagine her teaching yoga or living so many decades longer. Victor, on the other hand, was tall and athletic-looking; he could certainly have been a sports teacher. Karen, who had loved team sports when she was at school, could imagine him shouting encouragement and running up and down as he did it.

There were also photocopies of marriage certificates, death certificates, and more birth certificates from people who she had not even heard about yet. There were also family trees compiled on a manual typewriter that paternal aunt Ann had done back in the 80s. Probably none of them were even relevant. But this conundrum would not be solved by looking at paper documents. Instead, Karen needed to get down to whatever the DNA would tell her.

The response to her email to Lynne came back quickly. Karen wondered whether she, too, was in a café rather than going home, and what she was thinking now that she had taken these first steps towards... some unknown future.

> *Hi Karen,*
> *The first answer is easy. He was a coach at the British Empire and Commonwealth Games (there's lots about it online) and he was working for the English cycling team. We have always known that. But what I don't know is when he arrived in Vancouver.*
> *As for my mother, she told us very little about her life before Dad. I know that her parents were farmers and died in a fire when she was in her teens. But I don't know if she had a job, or where she had been living. Sorry.*

Funny, Karen thought as she sent Lynne her thanks for the quick reply. People only know what they want to know, not what is written in black and white. If he was a coach for the England team, then he would have been with them training in the UK. Perhaps the teams would all have been in Canada for a while beforehand, but not (and Karen quickly looked to see when these games had started) as long as six or seven months. So they couldn't have known each other for long before they married in the September unless they had met before somehow. And as they both seemed to be intelligent enough people, he would have known she was pregnant. He had to have been helping her out. That wasn't a good time to be single and pregnant... anywhere really. But why did he do something that seemed so generous? That was asking a lot of someone, especially if you didn't know them very well.

But the one thing she just couldn't comprehend. How on earth did the family ignore those dates for so many years? It wasn't so much putting their heads in the sand as deliberately substituting the year 1954 for 1953, or something equally damning. Hmm. Anything she wrote to Lynne at that moment would be too critical and she didn't want that.

• • • • ● • ● ● • • •

Karen gathered up the papers and set out to walk across London. It was shivery cold and growing dark, but she had spent too many hours sitting down.

She was right on time for her early evening dinner with Ben, who worked just around the corner from the restaurant.

'Your face!' Karen laughed. She hadn't seen him for a couple of weeks and his facial stubble had turned into an identifiable beard and moustache. Ben rubbed it mock-thoughtfully.

'What do you think?' he asked with a smile. 'Too young? Too hipster?'

'Looks good. Anyway, you aren't as old as all that and who isn't a hipster round here now?'

The answer was, a lot of people in that once-poor part of London, but they glossed over that. Ben's look matched his lean physique, honed by all the cycling he had done over the course of his life. Presumably, Victor had also cycled a great deal. She was briefly reminded of his photograph, taken some fifty years earlier; they both had a full head of slightly floppy hair, well past the age when many men had gone bald. Ben, though, would not be using the Brylcreem Victor surely had.

'I have some promising news,' Karen said happily. 'A proper genealogy project.' She picked up a prawn cracker and stuffed it into her mouth, crunching.

'And this is a different sort of genealogy,' she continued. 'Not the sort I've trained in, the archives stuff. This is a DNA issue. Someone's asked me to find out the identity of their biological father. He's an NPE.'

Ben burst out laughing. 'What's that when it's at home?'

Karen pouted slightly, rolling her eyes. 'It's the acronym for a non-paternal event. Meaning that the man named on the birth certificate is not the man who *is* the father. Biologically speaking. Now, though, it's used to mean 'Not Parent Expected' because – at least in theory – the mother could be someone else too.'

'Not parent expected, eh? Well, whose is?'

'Ha-ha, you know what I mean. You *expect* your biological father is whoever is named on your birth certificate. But now, people are finding out that he isn't. Wasn't. And I wonder how many people will discover this now, both fathers and children.'

They fell silent. Both of them knew that writing in-depth articles on topics like this were what Karen had loved when she was a journalist.

'You know how much I enjoy research,' she said. 'This is research. A solving of puzzles.'

'Oh, Karen, be careful.'

Ben shook his head.

'How long have we known each other? Come on! I know where the 'solving of puzzles' got you. Beaten up and out of a job, that's where. Please tell me this isn't connected with criminals!'

Karen sipped her wine.

'IS IT?'

'Not as far as I know. I'm not doing investigative journalism. It's genealogy, historical research. People have secrets.'

Ben's scepticism shone out of his eyes.

'We don't know why they have them or what they are. We take people at face value, especially those we have known all our lives. Until we can see things aren't adding up.'

Putting his head on one side, Ben raised his eyebrows at her.

'Sometimes it's easier for relatives to get an outsider to make sense of these secrets, to find out what they mean, than it is to do it themselves.'

'Not crime then?'

'This is nothing like investigative journalism.' Karen sipped her wine again, hoping that she was telling the truth.

'Because even after you left journalism to do your master's degree, I remember how much you liked watching true crime documentaries.' He opened his eyes very wide. 'I don't entirely trust you to leave well alone.'

'You know,' she continued, 'There is an actual site called Websleuths, for amateurs trying to solve crimes, helping the police, giving theories on why people are missing. Can you imagine a site called Web Engineers?'

They both laughed. Ben was an engineer, specialising in transport planning. People usually glazed over when he started talking about his work because they didn't understand it. Nor was he good at explaining what he was doing. Instead, his discussions with strangers centred around his many and various hobbies.

'But you know that most of the people who are working in genetic genealogy taught themselves,' Karen continued. 'I mean it's a new thing. There wasn't anyone *to* teach it. They are citizen scientists, apparently.'

'Really? You are one of those now? But you stopped doing science when you were how old?'

'Yes, sixteen, I know. But this is different, isn't it? It's an add-on to the history that has been my discipline for the past few years. Anyway...'

'You never know what you might find out. Who might be out there.'

'Right.'

Karen turned the stem of the wine glass round and round in her fingers.

'But you will take care of yourself – physically, I mean. And you won't hold out too much hope, will you, that you'll find this person? Please?' Ben put his own hand over the hand that was fiddling with the glass.

Karen smiled and shook her head. 'Don't worry.' She was both irritated by, and grateful for, his concern.

'Now,' she continued. 'You've got to tell me about the trip to Mexico you're planning. It sounds wonderful.'

They hugged warmly before they got on trains going in opposite directions. It was so strange to think they had been married to each other, Karen thought. He had been in her life for so many years, but the thought of them making the vows to each other that they had now seemed surreal. He was a member of her family; her real family, one tied together by a bond that meant far more than shared DNA. He was her father, her brother, and her son all together in one person. How could they ever have been lovers?

Back in her flat, Karen knew she needed to put the brakes on her impatience. Everything would still be there in the morning, but she wasn't ready to switch off yet, even though she surely couldn't charge Lynne for anything she did this late in the evening? These were her own issues, not a paying customer's.

Nevertheless, she went into Lynne's DNA results on Ancestry and had a look at her connections.

First, Karen needed to exclude all Lynne's matches that were on the Thompson, maternal, side of the family.

This was not too difficult. Simply looking at what she shared with Nick and Cathy meant ruling out more than half of them.

What was left? Well, that was a puzzle all right.

One second to third cousin, who had not logged into their account for a year: MerryD. Nice username, Karen smiled. Hopefully she, at least, would give Lynne a warm welcome. There was a third to fourth cousin: DeeDee Swanson. Then there were a few fifth to sixth cousins at the higher end of that shared DNA spectrum – Oliver Prior, Kristen Harrop, Weston Wainwright – along with many others who had an increasingly tiny amount of overlap with Lynne. They all sounded so implausible, not like real people at all. But they were, surely? MerryD was unsearchable without more information, and DeeDee had no Facebook account under that name, but Oliver's, Kristen's and Weston's names were beside a range of middle-aged white people. There were Oliver Priors across various continents. Kristen Harrop could be a college professor in Maine or a personal trainer in Adelaide. There was only one Weston Wainwright, however, and he seemed to be in Toronto. He was strongly Christian; his public posts were of religious memes and photographs of smiling people inside, outside, and next to, various churches.

It was past midnight and Karen had to go to sleep, or at least try to. In the morning, she needed to be a pulled-together professional and that didn't come without cost, which meant going to bed right now. Karen turned off her laptop and started her wind-down night-time regime. As she got into bed and consciously closed her eyes, she willed her thoughts to move away from the genealogy puzzle and back into the go-to-sleep bedtime breathing patterns that she had so painstakingly learned.

CHAPTER SEVEN

LYNNE: SWINDON, ENGLAND, FEBRUARY 2018

One week since Lynne had told her mother she knew about her father. Just one week. Lynne had never experienced a personal life full of shouting and arguments; generally speaking, people got on well. And if they hadn't, like Cathy's passive aggression, ready to show up at any time, or her own brief marriage thirty years before, they brushed it aside. Pretended. That was just the way it was. But now, it was as if the anger and disagreements that could have happened in all that time appeared in full force over just seven days. She and her siblings had been shouting at each other and she could no longer rely on her mother's love. It was now contingent, though on what she was not sure. Obedience? Perhaps it always had been; Lynne no longer knew.

Nevertheless, she wanted to tell Barbara that she had visited a genealogist. More than that, she *was going to* tell her. As well as disappointment, a kind of numb thudding that things weren't as she had always thought, there was a fury in her that she was determined *would* be let out. The more Lynne thought about it, the more this sensation bubbled away. Maybe some of them, all of them, even she, had known. Explaining to Karen that her parents had married so late in her mother's pregnancy, that her father was probably in a different country when she was conceived. There was the anger against herself. How *could* she have not realised? How could any of them have been so stupid?

Barbara had barely spoken to Lynne – or any of the family – since Lynne told her about the DNA test. She had gone out, taught her chair yoga, and come back. She had eaten a few simple meals Lynne had made, but mainly she had taken cereal and put it in a bowl, or taken meals from the freezer, and put them in the microwave. She had taken them into her bedroom and shut the door.

'Mum. Listen to me. Mum.'

Barbara, who was standing looking through the glass kitchen door, turned her gaze on Lynne, who was tugging at her mother's cardigan.

'What.'

'Come and sit down, Mum.' Lynne took her mother's arm and dragged the reluctant woman a few feet towards the wooden chair. Barbara sighed and allowed herself to be dragged.

'Now,' said Lynne decisively, about to begin the conversation. But then she stopped. The two of them sat facing each other, both hostile. Lynne's anger suddenly dissipated and she began to cry.

'I have hired a genealogist to sort out this mess,' she said. The colour drained from Barbara's face.

'You did what?' she whispered.

'I don't know what secrets you're trying to hide, but I can't live with them. This is my life too, you know.'

Barbara was pale, quiet and still. For an instant, Lynne worried that she'd had a stroke but then her mother said, 'You selfish woman. How dare you? I told you that if you did this, you would have to leave my house. So leave. Leave now.'

'No, I won't. I have to have answers. It's not all about you.'

'It isn't all about me. That's right. But you have no idea what you are doing. I told you not to and I mean it.'

Barbara leaned back against the chair and closed her eyes.

'If you won't stop this, then I repeat. You need to leave. Go. Get out.'

'No. I shan't.'

Barbara got up, slowly, and hauled herself up the stairs as though the effort were almost beyond her. Lynne heard her door shut decisively. The fight had gone out of her now; she felt drained, empty. Was this really the right thing to do?

Chapter Eight

Barbara walked boldly up four steps to the front door and rang the bell. The home, sitting in a nice suburb, with roses round the door and a burnished plaque announcing 'Elizabeth House' was more like a small hotel than somewhere to keep women who had Gone Bad.

The woman on the telephone had sounded comforting and was, Barbara thought, the same person who opened the door. Tall and thin, probably in her thirties, she seemed pointed, angular. Her grey suit had never been stylish or smart.

'Yes,' she queried, looking Barbara up and down, disapproving of what she saw.

'I'm Barbara Thompson,' Barbara said uncertainly. 'I was told to ask for Miss Francis.'

'Ah yes, won't you come in?' It was only her voice that appeared pleasant, Barbara thought. Nothing else.

She opened the door wide enough for Barbara and her small brown case to pass into the entrance hall. Barbara had not been sure what to expect but perhaps this was it: dark brown, heavy furniture, deeply scuffed and linoleum on the floor, washed and bleached until the pattern had faded. There was a Union Jack and a Canadian flag, leaning together against the wall, and framed homilies from the Bible higher up, near the ceiling. The white roses filling the vase on the hall table had clearly been cut from the bush outside.

Miss Francis unlocked another door into an office, where she motioned Barbara to sit on an upright wooden chair, as she moved around to the other side of a large desk and sat down herself. She took a large ledger and opened it, settling her pen at the top of a new and empty page. The symbolism of this struck Barbara, and she began to tremble.

'Barbara Thompson.'

'Age?'

'Twenty-six.'

Putting down her pen, she looked Barbara straight in the eyes.

'And how far along are you?'

'I, uh, I'm not sure.'

'Have you not seen a doctor?'

Barbara shook her head.

'I have only recently known for sure that I am pregnant,' she continued. 'But, perhaps, five months.'

The woman, pursing her lips, began to write in another column.

'Religion?'

'Methodist.'

Miss Francis seemed not displeased by that.

'What about your parish? Did you ask them for help?'

'I'm not... I haven't been...'

There they were again, the pursed lips.

'And your parents? What do they have to say about this?'

'They don't know.'

'How many years of education?'

Barbara looked puzzled.

'Did you attend high school?'

'Yes, I did.' Barbara felt trapped. She must not suddenly come up with details she would never remember.

Miss Francis wrote a little more and then reached into a drawer under the table before looking back at her.

'You will only be known as Barbara here. We need to keep our girls' details confidential so you must not ask their surnames.'

Barbara nodded in confusion. Miss Francis handed over a thin, folded leaflet, an illustration of Elizabeth House on its cover. The colourful drawing made it look very cheerful and homely. A happy place.

'Please read this. It tells you what to expect from us and, in turn, what we expect from you.'

Barbara nodded again. What else could she do? Too much energy flooded her body, and she clasped her hands together so Miss Francis could not see them shaking.

'The nurse will examine you tomorrow.' She replaced the cap on her fountain pen. 'Of course, we will need to talk to you at much greater length about the circumstances that brought you here. But in the meantime, I will show you your bedroom.'

They walked upstairs to a small room at the front of the house, containing two single beds. There was little space for anything else. Like a student dormitory, Barbara thought, before any young hopefuls had moved in to add personal touches. Yet her roommate must be in residence, as there was an alarm clock next to one bed and slippers underneath.

'The lavatory is next door. And you may take a bath on Wednesdays and Sundays. Please use our towels and bed linen, not your own. However, we allow you to wear your own clothes, as long as they are suitable.'

Barbara shuddered. 'All right. But I don't have much.'

Miss Francis's eyebrows raised higher. She looked dubious.

'There are some maternity garments for girls who have nothing. Who are indigent. Are you indigent, Barbara?'

'I don't know. I'm not sure what you mean.'

'Oh well, never mind. We'll consider that later. Now,' she continued. 'I will draw up a list of your chores and let you have them at tea. You don't have any medical concerns?' Miss Francis's voice grew higher and lighter.

'No. I am fit and well.'

'Good.' Miss Francis was growing brisker and more cheerful. 'Unpack your suitcase and come to the dining room at half past five. We don't normally allow rests here during the day for healthy girls but there is nothing for you to do until then so you may as well take advantage of the situation. Please don't wander around the house without permission, or go into the garden except during recreation periods.'

With a sharp nod of her chin, she opened the bedroom door and shut it behind her. Barbara sat down on the bed, and the springs creaked. How many women had slept on it before her, she wondered? Would it give her backache? She had not experienced such a feeling before but as soon as it came to her mind, there was a sudden nagging, and she leaned back slightly to counteract it. She sat upright, which was better, but there seemed to be so much more of her stomach than there had been just yesterday.

Barbara picked up the leaflet and unfolded it. It was comprised mainly of photographs, all of the backs of young women – none identifiable – sitting in a classroom; working in a laundry, pushing bed linen through a mangle; placing cutlery on a table, while dignitaries looked on. Another was of a nursery containing half a dozen white babies, each in wooden cots, firmly barred from each other and from the women who had given birth to them. Then, there was another photograph of an unrecognisable couple bending over one of these babies. The woman's suit reminded Barbara of Miss Francis's costume. Perhaps she was that very woman. The caption directly under it read: *Baby completes a happy family.*

She felt sick. Had there really been no other option? No, she reminded herself, there had not. This was a good place to wait until she could make plans and she would not allow herself to feel guilty. Barbara stiffened her body and breathed deeply.

Elizabeth House wasn't what it seemed to be in the brochure: a kind place where you and your baby would be cared for. In the abstract, Barbara had suspected this but here was the confirmation.

'Better equip the girl for her future role' she read. That would mean becoming a wife and mother. Before that, it would be domestic service or, if not, some kind of factory work. The word 'God' appeared – she counted – six times. They had to be guided away from sin. The only sin she wanted to commit at that moment was sloth. Later, she was sure there would be wrath, but she had no interest in that yet.

An hour later, she was roused by the door opening and a woman, slightly older than her, progressed slowly into the room, her stomach far out in front of her. Sadness came off her in waves; there was a greyness in her lank hair, and her olive skin too seemed grey, along with her clothes.

'Hello,' Barbara said, pulling herself up from the bed. 'I'm Barbara.'

'Winifred,' the other woman said nervously. 'But we need to be quick into tea or they will give us the worst chores later.' She did not look directly at Barbara, her eyes seeming to dart everywhere else instead.

'All right.' Barbara hauled herself up from the bed and put on her shoes.

'They won't like you wearing those,' said Winifred, glancing down at her feet. 'You're bringing in dirt.'

'Would sandals be better? I have these, and I have sandals.'

'Oh, no, I don't know.' Winifred frowned, her face turning in on itself, her eyebrows coming to meet in the middle. She put the knuckle of her left index finger into her mouth.

'Well never mind then,' said Barbara. 'It's not your fault.'

'They'll say I should have told you.'

'I'll tell them you did,' Barbara said curtly. 'Please don't worry on my account. My footwear is my responsibility.'

Winifred hung her head, unconvinced. Nevertheless, she ambled onto the landing and towards the staircase.

Downstairs in the dining room, the atmosphere was less sombre. Part of the reason for that was the sheer noise. The cacophony of it. Eight pregnant girls, all talking at once, some of them screaming with laughter. Then, there were two or three sitting quietly, not speaking, looking absent and broken. All noise suddenly stopped as the room turned towards Barbara who was wondering where to sit. She expected there would be allocated seats and perhaps hers was next to Winifred.

They were so very young, Barbara thought immediately. Fifteen, sixteen, a couple in their early twenties. Calling them women would be pushing it. It was only Winifred and Barbara herself who were older than twenty-five. Perhaps older women found different ways of dealing with unwanted pregnancies. They married, for instance, though Barbara wondered immediately who on earth would marry Winifred.

'Sit here, sit here,' said one young woman, whose red hair still retained the memory of a fashionable style. 'I'm Doreen.' She smiled at Barbara. 'This is Trixie and this is Mary. You must have taken Alison's place,' she continued.

'Must I?'

'Yes, she was sharing with Winifred until yesterday and now she's gone. Were you waiting long for a bed?'

'No, no time at all. I telephoned to make an appointment yesterday.'

The three girls looked at each other.

'Well, that was quick! Perhaps they have taken you because you are old and look sensible,' said Mary. 'But we're in moral danger.' They all thought this was a terrific hoot. 'They probably think you were just unlucky. That you might be a good influence.' Barbara thought this was unlikely. 'They talk a lot about good influences.'

'Ah, but it's not so bad here,' said Trixie. 'I had one friend in that big Catholic home, you know the Sisters of Mercy, and they had to do laundry morning, noon and night! Her hands bled! And her backache! Her legs! They said she had to pay her way. And ten girls to each room. The girls whose parents paid didn't have to go through any of that.'

'What about her baby, though?' Barbara asked.

'Someone took it, I suppose. I don't know.' Trixie shrugged. 'Don't go thinking like that. Where will it get you?'

None of them spoke; she was right.

Trixie continued. 'The food here is not so bad. There's more than when I lived with my parents, anyway. Each time my mum was expecting, she never had enough. She felt ill all the time. The food here isn't always nice but at least there is plenty of it.'

'I expect they want our babies to be healthy,' Barbara said. 'They won't be healthy if we aren't.'

They looked at her suspiciously.

Doreen gestured with her chin towards a wraithlike girl, sitting alone at another table. 'That one there, Christine, just wants to marry her boyfriend. She goes on and bloody on about how much she misses him. He wants to marry her. But her father won't let them and she needs his permission.'

Christine's cheeks were hollow and her eyes huge. She looked skeletally thin, as though her limbs could snap, but her stomach was vast.

'Because she is so young?'

'She's not too young to get a bun in the oven! She's sixteen and the stupid law... Christine thought her dad would say yes because being an unmarried mother is worse, but he hates Sonny Jim, as he calls her boyfriend, and he thinks she should forget about Jim and the baby. Says that she has ruined her life enough already. But

Christine thinks having her baby given to a *nice family* means that her own life is over. Poor kid.'

'So how did you get into trouble, Barbara?' Doreen looked at her steadily. Barbara had thought about this. While she could not create a tissue of lies that would satisfy the people running this establishment, she had at least to say *something* to the other women in the home.

'A married man,' she said. Well, it was true enough, and she hoped that would do for the moment. 'But tell me, why are you all in moral danger?'

'I was in the reformatory,' said Mary. 'And the guard there, he gave me venereal disease along with this little inconvenience. But they caught us at it so at least they threw him out.'

'Men can't keep their hands off me, and I can't keep my hands off them,' Trixie said enthusiastically. 'After I get out of here, I'm going to find a rich one to marry. Just you wait.'

'I'm a good girl, I am,' Doreen laughed. 'But I just won't do what I'm told. They think that being on the streets at night means men will have their way with me, though as it was my brother made me pregnant, I don't see why being at home will make me safe. The people on the streets are good to me, much better than my family have ever been.'

'But she...' Doreen pointed to Winifred. 'She won't be here again. I think they'll tie her tubes.'

'Really?'

'This isn't her first baby. She'll show you the photographs, I'll bet ya. There's two of them, maybe three, maybe four. Who knows. Every time they take away a kid, she falls pregnant with another one.'

Barbara had thought she was a woman of the world; she had been wrong. Life was full of terrible dangers that she had never imagined, and this realisation made her dizzy. She sipped some water.

'Ah, food!' Trixie looked happy.

Two women Barbara had not seen yet came in bearing rectangular metal trays containing plain food – white fish, white mashed potatoes, and white sauce. Another woman carried bowls of chopped carrots. Their stomachs seemed comparatively flat, though the bumps were definitely there. They put the food down in front of the others and then sat down at the same table as Winifred.

'Girls.' Barbara had not noticed Miss Francis coming in, but everyone fell silent as her voice rang out steadily. 'For what we are about to receive, let the Lord make us truly thankful.'

'Amen,' said everyone. Including Barbara, who remembered what to do without even thinking about it.

One girl per table – on Barbara's table, it was Mary stood up and served the food onto the plates of the others.

'Barbara.' Miss Francis said crisply, coming towards her table before she started to eat. 'This is your timetable,' she handed over a typed page. 'Given that you have some while to go yet, most of your chores will be connected with cooking or food preparation. I can stand down one of the others.'

Barbara ran her eyes over the list. Prepare and serve breakfast, wash up after lunch, prepare and serve tea. At least, it seemed, this would not be every day. But she was such a terrible cook. How long would it be before they realised this? She finished eating and then went to lie on her bed once more. Resting in the evening was acceptable.

They would not bring her down, they would not. Barbara knew staying at Elizabeth House – in fact, everything she was doing – could be a mistake. But what was the alternative? She didn't have the money to rent anywhere to live, even if she spent everything she could lay her hands on, and anyway, what would she say about the baby? Widow? Divorcée? Too many questions. Unmarried mother? They wouldn't let to her anyway.

For tonight, for the week, for the month, this had to be her sanctuary.

She had a date in the future. October, probably. It loomed ahead of her as if that was the date of her death, not a time for new life. She was hurtling towards the edge of an abyss, and there was nothing she could do about it. She would free-fall to nothingness, never reaching the bottom.

While they were not prisoners, almost every part of their lives was organised by somebody else. The most onerous parts of this were their chores. Barbara sleepwalked her way through the making of tea and toast, the washing-up, the mashing of potatoes. The girls had to have lessons in whatever was deemed appropriate by those in charge. Barbara was not considered to require any further education; she was too old and possessed the basics of literacy and numeracy. She could have done some office work, of course. Still, it was considered unlikely that any employer would award a woman like that a secretarial position. Nor should they ever expect one. It was far more probable, desirable even, that such a woman would become a wife. Eventually, and in the fullness of time, and in partnership with the right man, a proper, suitable husband. He would not be one of their juvenile, feckless or married boyfriends.

They could walk into town on Thursday and Saturday afternoons, partly for exercise and also to show that Elizabeth House was doing a good job in rehabilitating them. They had to behave themselves and give their 'word of honour' that they would not meet men, or boys, or 'people of other races' or anyone undesirable who might lead them into any kind of temptation. They were strictly forbidden to drink alcohol or stray outside of certain geographic areas and they were supposed to go out in pairs, or small groups. They were not meant to be on their own.

Then there was church on Sunday, where they had to behave like good girls – schoolgirls rather than women with a will of their own – and walk in crocodiles and sing with the lust that they could not direct towards their fellow human beings. They wore hats, of course, hats with bands that had been given to the home by the church congregation, members of which looked on them with pity, curiosity or once – but that was enough for Barbara – disgust.

She not only hated it but she was also frightened. It felt as though she was slipping away, losing herself. What she had hoped would be a perfectly manageable and safe place to stay while she worked out what to do next, was spiralling into something she definitely could not handle. It was like a boarding school for adults, a voluntary jail. Her transformation into almost-inmate was too much. Yet she had only been there for a few weeks. There were months before the baby would arrive.

In the midst of all this anxiety, she was dimly aware that Vancouver was beautiful. Parts of it, anyway. She could just about see the mountains outside the city, their grandeur and permanence in such contrast to the crushing conformity of the home. Then there were the vast expanses of water, with so many trees visible right up to the edge.

She needed to be alone, not always surrounded by teenage girls determined to giggle their way through a thoroughly bleak time in their lives. Without considering where she was going, or whether she would be 'out of bounds', Barbara walked away from the nice suburban area with its manicured gardens and net curtains.

Distracted, she almost walked into a huge banner stretched right across the road:

1954 British Empire and Commonwealth Games
A Week You'll Remember For A Lifetime
Vancouver July 30—Aug 7

Yes, she knew it was 1954 – she could hardly forget it, could she? But she wasn't likely to remember that week. Other weeks were far more likely to stick in her head. She thought, suddenly, about different times, innocent activities. She thought of her high-school boyfriend and missed him, wincing as the sharp sensation hit right up at the top of her diaphragm. She sat down on a bench.

'Miss. I say, miss. Are you all right? Can I get you some help?' A tall, thin man of around her own age stared down at her with a mixture of concern and curiosity. His blue eyes were kind, helpful.

'No. I... I...'

Perhaps it was the feeling that someone was looking at her and seeing something real, not judging her but looking with genuine concern. That was what made her sorrow turn to sobbing.

'Hey, hey, hey,' he sat down beside her and proffered a clean white handkerchief. 'It can't be that bad, can it?'

Barbara leaned back against the bench and pulled her dress taut over her stomach. Her face was pitiful; she could sense it.

'Oh,' he said. 'Oh.'

'Yes, I'm in trouble.'

Barbara felt she had already said too much, but what did it matter. Really, what did it matter?

'Don't say that! It's a baby, a new life no matter how it came to be.'

Too shocked to speak immediately, Barbara glared back at him.

'That's all very well for you to say,' she responded curtly. 'I can see your stomach is still as flat as a board! No one's saying you are damaged goods.'

'Not exactly, no,' he said warily as if that might have been a possibility.

Barbara picked at the threads of her maternity smock. It was chartreuse, a yellowy-green colour that was starting to remind her of vomit.

'I hate Vancouver,' she said. 'It's backward and suburban. It feels like we're falling off the edge of the world. And it rains all the time.'

'Is that what you really think?' He laughed.

'Yes,' she said. Then, with an exasperated sigh: 'Oh, I don't know. Just a moment ago, I was admiring it from a distance. I don't like the place where I live. I guess that's it.'

'You could move then, couldn't you? If not now, then some time soon?'

'In this condition?' Barbara harrumphed.

'After the baby's born. You could go somewhere that isn't, I don't know, backward and suburban. Because people are suited much better to some places than others, aren't they?'

'Yes, they are. And for a long while, I'd found somewhere I was really suited to.' She paused. 'Until I wasn't.'

Barbara was surprised to find that she was no longer crying.

'Well, thank you,' she said standing up, not yet far enough along in her pregnancy to be unsteady. 'You seem to have stopped the tears.'

'Not at all.' He smiled. 'Shall we have some tea?'

Barbara didn't even think to say no; a friendly companion, someone unconnected with her past, or her present, who was offering to take her somewhere? Of course she wanted that. It seemed so long ago that she had walked anywhere pleasant, accompanied by someone congenial, to have a drink of any kind. Two months, she reckoned it had been. That wasn't nearly as long as it felt. The fact that she probably was not permitted to drink so much as a cup of tea with an unknown, unapproved-of man, made the situation even more enticing.

There was a café just across from the bench. Victor asked the waitress for a pot of tea and a selection of cakes.

'I shouldn't be having tea with a man when I don't even know his name.'

The man laughed. 'Over here, they call me 'string bean'. Back home, it's Lofty. Or sometimes Daddy Long Legs. But my real name is Victor.'

'You're English?' she asked, registering his accent. He smiled.

'I've been here for the past few months, preparing for these games.' He waved his arm towards the billboard.

'And yours?'

She swallowed hard.

'Barbara.'

'Pleased to meet you, Barbara,' he said with amusement, reaching out to shake her hand.

Barbara felt a little shudder of happiness when the cakes arrived. The last time she had eaten a cake had been... possibly February. Before she started feeling the morning sickness that she had mistaken for stomach flu or some kind of long-running food poisoning. It tasted so good, so sweet. Why had she not wanted to eat sweet things for all this time?

'Are you interested in sport?' Victor asked. 'Everyone here seems to be.'

'Perhaps a little,' she said. 'I was interested in it at high school but that was a long while ago now.'

'Not so very long.'

'It is to me.'

Victor nodded. 'Why don't you come to see a game or two, my treat. I have an allocation of tickets and no one to give them to.'

'You haven't brought your wife with you?'

'No wife.'

Barbara's eyes moved swiftly up and down what she could see of Victor, as he sat across the table from her. She noticed the navy jacket, white shirt and dark tie.

Nicely dressed, she thought. She had spent too many years with men who looked like they spent the evening being tossed out of bars before spending the night face down in a flowerbed.

'No husband,' she replied, and they both laughed together.

'I would like to do that very much,' she said. 'But we are under a strict curfew.'

Victor's eyebrows raised so high that it looked as if his face would take off. Barbara sighed.

'I am staying in a home for unmarried mothers. The sort who need their morals watching. But I have free afternoons on Thursdays and Saturdays. The inmates are allowed out then. Under strict rules, but the prison doors are open.'

Victor smiled. 'I think, in this neck of the woods, that counts as a date.'

Victor was sympathetic to her living situation. Who wouldn't want to escape such a place? He had been to boarding school; he knew what it was to be subject to other people's petty rules. And all to uphold a moral code that no one really believed in.

'You could always marry me!'

Barbara fell about with laughter.

'I do mean that,' he said, his voice tinged with hurt.

'But I don't know you!'

'Look. I want a wife. More to the point, I *need* a wife. I like you, you like me – at least you seem to – and if it all goes wrong at a later date, well. We can think about that if it happens.'

'Oh, Victor.' Barbara took his hand and began to stroke it. 'What a sweet man you are.'

'No.' He withdrew his hand quickly, harshly. 'Don't call me sweet.' He paused and said evenly. 'I know that I'd be doing you a favour, but you'd be getting me out of a jam too. A potential jam at any rate.'

He picked up her hand again.

'I'm nearly thirty and that's far too old to be a bachelor. It's not that I don't like girls – I like them very much...'

'But not in that way.'

'Sometimes in that way, occasionally in that way. But perhaps not enough.'

Barbara stared.

'You are disgusted. I'm sorry.' He stood up. 'Never mind, then.' Victor began to move away.

'Come back, Victor. Don't be silly.'

He turned towards her.

'I don't mind about that sort of thing. It makes far more sense than marrying me because, say, you need a housekeeper. Any husband of mine would have to put up with my housekeeping rather than expect to be looked after. But see, there are things about me you don't know, that I don't ever want to talk about, that might make you think I am a very bad bet as a wife. Any kind of wife.'

She looked at him apologetically and was surprised to see the pain on his face. It did not align with what he had just told her.

'Thank you for your proposal of marriage,' she said. 'I am very moved by it. But no.'

Barbara reached out her hand again and squeezed one of his. Victor bent down slightly, and she noticed one side of his short hair seemed not to have enough Brylcreem. Wisps were sticking up into the air, and the sun made them glisten.

'I need to be in love before I marry. Even in this condition,' she said, patting her stomach. Every day there was more of it. 'But I do desperately need a friend, and perhaps you could be that person. I am alone here, but with you, I don't feel such terrible loneliness.'

He sat back down next to her and they held hands intensely, in a way that Barbara had not held hands since high school.

'Then that is what I will be,' he said firmly. 'Because heaven knows I need a friend too.'

• • • ● ●• ● ● • • •

'Miss Thompson, won't you come in?'

It was a demand, albeit a polite one. This was not a request with a possibility of saying no. Barbara stood up and walked into the office where three suited women, two dressed in grey and one wearing blue so dark it was almost black, sat behind a large desk. Her father had just such a desk and it was designed to make him look important. No doubt the same attempt at intimidation was happening here.

'Do sit down.'

Barbara had never before heard the sort of English accent she imagined being spoken by the Queen. The woman who was talking, a kind-eyed person of around forty, with no make-up and no hairstyle to speak of, smiled at her. Barbara had had one proper interview in her life so far. This interview, she suspected, would be rather different.

'My name is Miss Warren,' the woman smiled, 'This is Mrs Laing, and that is Nurse Helvin. This meeting is for us all to think about what will happen to your baby after it is born, and also what might happen to you. The needs of you both are uppermost in our minds.'

Barbara stared at them blankly. She wasn't really there, was she? It was someone else. Perhaps, if she could genuinely convince herself that she was somebody else, then it would be easier. They might say they cared about her, but they did not. At least, not in the sense of having any interest in what she would have to say.

Miss Warren continued. 'Most of our girls are referred here through the church, or members of their family, or social workers. You simply turned up on our doorstep.' She laughed lightly, sympathy in her eyes.

Mrs Laing, who had no sympathy in any part of her body, said, 'Most irregular.'

'To know how to help you best, we need to know a little more about you. Where are you from? How did you find yourself in this predicament? In short, why are you here?'

Clearly, these three women were waiting for her to supply answers. She would say nothing.

Mrs Laing spoke next, her voice harder and clearer. 'Elizabeth House is a charity, supported by local churches. As a result, we need to find out where you come from so we can apply to your parish for assistance.'

Nurse Helvin, who was older than the other two women, nearer Barbara's mother's age, continued. 'I have examined you,' she said sternly, 'and I am sure that you have already had a child. Where is that child now?'

'I don't...'

'Did the baby live?'

Barbara appeared to be swaying, about to fall from the chair. Nurse Helvin poured a glass of water and handed it to her.

'We need to ask these questions, dear. This is for the benefit of everyone.'

Barbara nodded, sipping the water. She was Barbara, she had no child, there had never been any child.

'I am your main welfare officer,' said Miss Warren firmly. 'And with these other two ladies, I will need to think about where we will place your child for adoption after it is born.'

Barbara pulled herself together to speak.

'I was thinking about perhaps keeping the child.'

The expressions on the faces of all three women suddenly hardened. She could see them almost as sculptures, cast in pale clay.

Miss Warren seemed distressed by the idea. 'We really can't have that,' she said.

'But why not?' asked Barbara.

'Don't you see that it is selfish to keep your child, bringing it up in shame and poverty? You should not make yourself a martyr, an unmarried mother. You'd be depriving the baby of the love that it would gain from being part of a proper family, brought up by a respectable married couple, a mother and father. You'll be fulfilling a sacred duty by helping create a family. If you really love the child, you will give it up.'

'Oh,' said Barbara, unsure how to proceed and shrinking into the floor.

'Now obviously we are also interested in your moral welfare. Once you have given up your child, you can return to your old life if you want to, or move on to better things if you do not. You will forget that you were ever here.'

Mrs Laing spoke next. Her task was to find work for the mothers after their babies had gone. 'You are much older than most of the poor girls here. They were led astray and I daresay some of them are moral degenerates. But what happened to you? How on earth have you found yourself in this situation?'

Barbara had no idea what to say.

'Did a man lead you on with promises of marriage? Was that it?'

Barbara looked down, shaking her head. She could feel tears coming to her eyes.

'Were you deserted?' said Mrs Laing carefully. 'You are clearly an educated woman, you knew what could happen, both morally and physically, when you sinned. Sex before marriage is wrong for a reason, whether or not the couple loves each other.'

Barbara could feel her mouth turning into a smirk, so she blinked hard as if to stop tears of shame. In fact, the lecture was so absurd as to stop her tears in their tracks. She was not sure whether she had ever felt sex was a sin, or whether sin was something she believed in at all, but she was certainly not going to accept any judgement these ridiculous women were pronouncing.

'No,' she said. 'It wasn't that.'

'Because if that were the case, we could contact the man and ask him to accept his responsibilities.'

'No,' she said, shaking her head firmly. 'No.'

'Well now,' said Mrs Laing. 'Where did you live before you came here? Whereabouts were you born?'

'I was born in...' Barbara sighed. 'I was born in the Fraser Valley but I haven't lived there since I was a small child.'

'Ah, yes,' said Miss Warren. 'You also said that your parents are deceased.'

Barbara nodded.

'But it is many years since you were a small child. Where have you been all that time?'

Barbara said nothing, merely shaking her head. Perhaps they would think she had undergone some terrible trauma. Or maybe that she had been in prison for something heinous.

'Have you ever married?'

'No.'

The three women behind the desk put their heads together and whispered. Why was she being treated like a naughty schoolgirl, Barbara wondered? She had always behaved extremely well at school, but perhaps this was something she needed to accept about her new self.

Miss Warren spoke for all of them.

'I wish we could make you trust us, Barbara. I'm sorry that you don't. We will be making investigations into your background but in the meantime, this meeting is over.'

'Thank you,' whispered Barbara, as insincerely as she could manage without actually swearing.

Not one word Barbara had said to the three witches had been the truth, she realised. She would never, must never, tell anyone about her past. Still, she could feel the dread of a deadline hurtling ever closer. And sooner than that, it was always possible that they would find something true about her that would lead them back to the life she had left behind. She could not let that happen.

• • • ● ● • ● ● • • •

Barbara had forgotten the tautness of athletes' bodies. Every bit of them seemed to be muscle. None of the men she had seen semi-naked had been quite as sinewy as this.

'Do you look like that?' she asked Victor, laughing.

'Well, if you won't marry me, you'll never know, will you!' he laughed back.

England had done splendidly in the cycling and the team had many medals between them. Victor had not invited Barbara to any of their events because he needed to give them his full attention. But the participants were all staying around until the games had ended. The mile run was right at the end of the week.

It was in the athletics events that so many records were being beaten and Barbara followed them on the radio. At least, they had a radio in the kitchen when she was preparing the food and being interested in something so self-evidently wholesome as the Commonwealth Games was allowed. Barbara realised that there was joy and excitement to be had in things that she had written out of her life as being childish.

The mile run – the Mile of the Century as the publicity had it – was one of the last events at the games, and Victor had tickets. This would be their second date and could be their last if he was going back to England. They would make the most of it.

The Empire Stadium had recently been completed and it looked – and smelled – bright and new. Thirty-five thousand spectators were looking on with anticipation. This was a special event, she knew, because over the summer two men had run faster than people had ever run before. Roger Bannister – from England – had done it first, running a mile in a second under four minutes; six weeks later, Australian John Landy had run it one second faster. Barbara could see the eight men gathered on the track, shaking hands and shifting from foot to foot before some crouched down. The anticipation! Then, a shot, and they were off.

For the first few minutes, the eight ran steadily, in white and black tops, and white, black and red shorts, the numbers on their backs harder to see as they ran into the distance. They lapped the stadium, with the man from New Zealand heading the pack. Then, halfway through, the crowd started to shout and cheer. The gap was still there, but soon Landry and Bannister were in front, way in front. Barbara could hardly breathe. Landry was ahead and seemed to be staying that way. Five feet in front of Bannister.

The spectators were shouting and cheering, even those who looked so prim and proper in their frocks, hats and gloves. Barbara could feel her blood fizzing in her veins. Without even being conscious of it, she grabbed Victor's hand, and they both stood – fully alive right there – thinking of nothing but watching the runners.

There they were. Two men, young men, going faster than anyone had thought possible. How could human beings do something so extraordinary? She was overwhelmed with the sheer joy of it.

Suddenly, Landry, who had been ahead for much of the race, turned to check on his opponent. That tiny gesture allowed Bannister to overtake him, and the crowd roared. The Englishman won – he was just one second faster than Landry.

Bannister, exhausted, and flopping like a rag doll, was lifted high above the other runners on the track. Barbara and Victor both stood among the crowd, clapping and cheering. She was breathing so fast she could hardly bear it. This was wonderful. The complete heart-stopping exhilaration of it.

After a few minutes, they sat back down on the benches. That was it, then. The marathon was still happening in another part of the city but they couldn't be in two places at once. What's more, Barbara felt exhausted. She was, after all, seven months pregnant and it was surprisingly warm.

'I need a drink of water,' she sighed, leaning back, happy. So happy, she could hardly believe it. Victor came back with a cup quickly, looking at her with concern. But not too much concern; just enough.

'Ah,' she sighed. 'That water was wonderful. The absolute best.' Barbara smiled.

'What a marvellous race that was. I had forgotten that sport could be quite so... thrilling. Not that any race could have been as exciting as that one.'

She stood up.

'I suppose I should get back to prison.'

They took their time in getting out of the stadium; the crowds were enthusiastic and seemingly not keen on going anywhere.

'You could always come to the closing ceremony, you know. The Duke of Edinburgh will be there.'

Barbara turned to him.

'No. I think I have to ration my excitement. I can't have too much happiness because it will be so dreadful when I lose it again. When you go back to England.'

They walked for a short way and then sat down at a café. There were too many people and the queue was long, but they were both putting off the day's ending. Eventually, a waitress came over to the table, a pot of tea and some cups already on the tray. Victor took Barbara's hand and gazed into her eyes.

'The offer's still there, you know. I'd be thrilled if you'd be my wife.'

She smiled.

'Do you really think you could put up with me?'
'Of course I do! Please say yes!'

Barbara smiled, surprised that her eyes were filling with tears. How could she, *why* would she, say no? It didn't even occur to her that those harridans, as she thought of them, would disbelieve whatever story she told them.

CHAPTER NINE

Just as Karen came back from the corner shop with some coffee and part-cooked croissants, her phone began to vibrate. 'Too early,' she thought. At least let a night owl drink her coffee.

'Karen,' said Lynne urgently as she answered the phone. 'I've had a message on Ancestry from someone. You need to tell me what to do.'

'Right,' Karen said, in what she hoped was a calming voice. 'So what does it say?'

Lynne took a deep breath.

> *'Greetings! I have just seen your DNA results and it says we are related! This is wonderful for me because I keep hitting brick walls in my family tree and the few relatives I know in person just aren't interested in genealogy. I see that you don't have a family tree online, but if you were able to get in touch with me to discuss any connections, I would be forever grateful. In hope, Meredith Dyson.'*

Karen reeled in surprise. 'Wow. That's a significant possibly maybe,' she said.

'Yes, it is.'

'But there aren't any Dysons you know of in your family tree.'

'Not that I know of. Is this the first connection to my mystery birth father?'

'Could be, could be.'

Lynne paused.

'Could you reply for me please, Karen? I'm in a panic just thinking about it.'

'Of course. That's part of what you are paying me for. I just hadn't gone online yet today.' Because it is only 8am, she thought but didn't say. 'In the meantime, Lynne...'

'Yes?'

'In the meantime, go on to Facebook and search for Meredith Dyson. And if you can find her, see if she looks at all familiar or anything strikes you about her profile.'

This was promising; Lynne had only signed the contract twenty-four hours ago. Karen tore open the croissant package and quickly shoved two of them in the microwave. Then, she opened her laptop. As she was manager of Lynne's Ancestry account, she, too, had received this message from Meredith. Karen looked at the other woman's public information. She had a visible family tree, but a tiny one. Most information on Meredith herself was hidden, as was information about her parents; they must all still be living. Her grandfather, Frank Prior 1891-1960 was there though, as was her grandmother Hazel Wainwright Prior 1900-1980, both with tiny sepia profile pictures alongside their names. That was all. However, there was one thing that might help Karen work out what to do next. Meredith was based in Seattle, so she would surely be asleep right now.

The microwave pinged, indicating that her croissants were ready – why did she eat this rubbish? – and she stared back quizzically at the screen. No clues on the tree. But this might be straightforward; with any luck, she could find the birth, marriage and death details of these people – what they called the vital statistics – as well as their obituaries in newspapers. There were also another two shared connections between Meredith and Lynne at the fifth to sixth cousin range – including that Oliver Prior – but neither of them had logged in for ages. Time to look at them later.

She messaged Meredith straightaway.

> *My name is Karen Copperfield, and I am a genealogist managing Lynne Pendleton's Ancestry account and helping her find out more about her birth father. She lives in the UK now but was born in Vancouver, Canada, in the 1950s. I see that your shared DNA is 294 centimorgans over thirteen segments. I know that Ancestry says second to third cousins, but in fact that connection encompasses a whole range of possible relationships. Are you able to share anything at all with me about yourself, other than what is already on your public tree?*
> *Please do message us back, but check out my website first so that you know I am genuine!*

Lynne rang Karen just a few minutes later.

'Oh goodness, what do you think, I'm panicking here.'

'You'll be fine. Just breathe.'

Great advice, Karen thought wryly, something that she had so often ignored herself.

'Have you looked on Facebook yet?'

'No. I... I'm worried about my mother. I don't think she's handling this well. Maybe I was wrong to confront her. She won't talk to me and I don't want her to notice what I'm doing. I've had to walk around the corner to make this call.'

'I see. Well, if there's a café near you, why don't you go to that and we can Skype there. Do you have Skype on your phone?'

'Yes, but I've never used it.'

'It's simple. I'll email you my Skype address and you can call me then.'

Five minutes later, Lynne was there, in a deep leather armchair in a nearby Costa Coffee. Karen positioned herself against a plain white wall so that it wouldn't be apparent that her flat was so... bleak.

'I'm sorry your mother is having a hard time with this,' Karen said gently.

'I'm starting to worry about her now. I mean properly worry. Nick and Cathy told me I shouldn't do this and kept saying: she's ninety, she's ninety. Maybe I was wrong.'

'Perhaps they could come and have a chat with her?'

'They'll turn against me.' Lynne paused, and Karen could see her lips pressing together, her eyes filling. 'They already have, I suppose.'

Karen nodded sympathetically. What a mess! She had no idea what any of them should do.

'Have you had any thoughts about Meredith and whether any of what she says rings a bell?'

'No. Nothing.'

'Perhaps if you take a look on Facebook?' Karen tilted her head in what she hoped was a sympathetic manner

Lynne pulled at the ends of her hair as if to make her bob that little bit longer.

'I don't do Facebook,' she said.

'Set up an account then. I'll help you. You don't have to friend anyone.'

'I have an account,' Lynne continued. 'But I just found the whole thing... boring. Intrusive. There wasn't anyone I wanted to talk to, keep in touch with. I don't know. It just wasn't for my generation.'

Karen smiled encouragingly.

'My mother uses it and she's... much older than you.' She paused. 'You can use Facebook for all sorts of things. You don't have to post anything you don't want to. But for tracing missing relatives... it can be really helpful. Meredith may be there. Plus there are many genealogical groups that you could join and get some support.'

Lynne looked doubtful. 'Are they paying you for this?'

Karen laughed. 'Let's look now.'

She opened her own account on her laptop and put Meredith Dyson into the search bar. There she was, the right woman, and at the top of the list because Karen had emailed her.

'Yes, I recognise her from the Ancestry photo. Take a look.'

Karen watched her face during the few moments while Lynne searched for, and found, the right Meredith Dyson. Had Lynne lost weight? At any rate, her cheeks seemed more hollow, her eyes sadder, than when they met.

'Well, I don't know; maybe. I certainly don't recognise her. She seems very young.'

'What would you say? Late twenties? Early thirties? With the degree of shared DNA you have, she could be a half great-niece, half great-aunt, or second cousin. Cousins in genetic genealogy don't necessarily mean cousins as we think of them, even though the companies list them like that. There are all sorts of possibilities, so we have to consider other things like how old they are when considering potential connections. She may not have any idea about your birth father. At this stage, we're just trying to work out who she is.'

The two of them, on separate screens, looked at Meredith. Her page was mostly set to private, but its arty black and white cover picture was of a wedding. Meredith's wedding, it seemed. Her profile photo was of herself, a dark-haired woman, friendly and open, smiling, next to a man of similar age, who wore a baseball cap. Meredith was a pensions supervisor at a large company; she had studied accountancy and gained an MBA at Washington State University. A bit more scrolling showed the man with the baseball cap was her husband Michael. Also set to public were her birthday fundraising efforts: one year, for dogs; most recently, for the American Heart Association.

'What about this cover photograph? Does anyone in that photograph look familiar?'

Lynne scrutinised the dozen tiny wedding guests; a couple of them were probably older than she was, but most seemed around Meredith's age. Enlarging the photograph didn't help.

'They could be anybody.'

'Yes, well. It was just a thought. As I said, we are in the very early stages.'

Lynne nodded sadly.

'I have to get back to my mother now,' she said. 'I'm getting a very bad feeling about her.'

'Do you feel guilty?' Karen asked.

Lynne said nothing but began to sob.

'I'm sorry,' said Karen softly.

'Okay.'

Lynne wiped her eyes and visibly pulled herself together. 'I have to get in touch with Cathy or Nick.' She sighed, clicking off Skype without any words of goodbye.

Karen's phone vibrated; it might be the early hours of the morning in Seattle, but Meredith had already replied to the message. Was she an insomniac? Looking after a tiny baby? Pensions supervisors didn't work nightshifts, surely? Other people's lives and habits remained as much of a mystery to her as they had always been.

Hey Karen,
Thanks for getting in touch on behalf of your client Lynne. Goodness, these are tricky situations!! I think perhaps we are

half or second cousins but I am struggling
to see whose child she could be. Everyone
of the right generation on that side has
passed now (that I know of!!). I am trying
to get some of my male cousins to test –
with no luck so far!!!! They say they are not
interested or they just don't say anything. A
big fat blank.
So that you and Lynne can take a look, I
have attached screenshots of the sections of
my family tree that I haven't made public.
As far as I know it at this point. Lololol!!

Karen took a look at the family tree of Meredith Prior Dyson, the second child of Conrad Prior (1946-1997) and Marcia Prior, nee Josipovici (1948 and still living). Her father's brothers – Fred and Peter – had dates of birth but nothing else. Conrad's father (also Fred, for added confusion) was a more likely possibility. They couldn't be Lynne's father for reasons of age, and his father could not be her father as the DNA connection wasn't right.

Still, at least the three of them could now see that Lynne was – somehow – connected to this Prior family of Washington State. Even if they could not work out what that was, yet.

Karen quickly texted Lynne. *Does Fred Prior (1891-1960) mean anything to you? Just a query btw.*

An hour passed, then another, with no response from Lynne. The dread of yet another job going wrong settled and grew in Karen's stomach.

CHAPTER TEN

LYNNE: SWINDON, ENGLAND, FEBRUARY 2018

By ten o'clock, Barbara had still not come downstairs, although Lynne had heard the toilet flushing at both seven and nine. She gently opened the bedroom door.

'Mum. Are you ill? What's wrong?'

Her mother was in bed and awake, her head poking out from under the flowery covers, but she turned her back on Lynne as she leaned down to her. The room was in shadow; the curtains closed. Her clothes were not put away as usual; instead, she had thrown them on a chair.

'Go away. I'm staying in bed today.'

'What is it? Do you need to see the doctor?'

'Of course not! Go away!'

Lynne felt as if she had been tossed aside without warning, though in fact the warning had been clear. More than that, her mother had given an ultimatum and Lynne had ignored it.

As a result, Lynne was bereft. She remembered her mother being distant, ill, unreachable. But after she had 'got better', as everyone put it, Lynne began to rely on her mother. She thought she knew her completely, but of course, that was a lie. Then her depression cleared up, due – her family and doctors thought and hoped – to the chemistry in Barbara's brain being sorted out, settled after the menopause. For decades, everything seemed fine. And there was the yoga, the bloody yoga, which she always swore helped. Her children thought it mattered more to her than they did.

At lunchtime, and then in the afternoon, Lynne tried to get through to her mother. First, she simply got, 'Go Away, I told you.' The second, it was, 'For pity's sake, stop it.' On both occasions, she could see Barbara had her face to the wall. Literally. She seemed to be staring at the wallpaper, a spread of pale pink flowers from Laura Ashley or similar, that had been pasted up by Victor in the early 90s. Her father was good at decorating. He had been organised, measured things carefully, and his height meant he could reach much of the wall without a stepladder. How Lynne missed him; now, particularly. She went back downstairs, put her head on the kitchen table, and sobbed.

Barbara had won. No, that wasn't it exactly; *Lynne* had lost.

Lynne messaged Cathy and Nick simultaneously in the late afternoon. *Okay, I'll stop. But please come and look after Mum.*

She heard the bell and, guilt thrashing through her head, walked slowly to open the front door.

'Good heavens, Rachel!'

Cathy's daughter was a comparatively rare visitor and she had not visited her aunt since before Christmas. Lynne hugged her tightly, Rachel's woman-in-management black suit crushed between them as she buried her face in her niece's stiffly sprayed hair. They stood there for moments, without progressing further than the doorstep, until Rachel pulled back in astonishment.

'Oh my days, what's wrong? Is it Gran?'

Lynne shook her head. 'Yes. But not like that.' She opened the door and Rachel came in, dropping her bag on the floor with a thump and kicking off her shoes. It was raining hard, and although she had parked right outside she was still slightly damp. They moved into the kitchen, which seemed full of condensation. Inside was too warm, and outside was too cold, but there was nothing to be done about that. It added to the oppression Lynne was starting to feel, a sense that she was actually being suffocated and that she – not her mother – would soon die.

'Did Cathy tell you to come?'

Rachel looked surprised again.

'Well, no. I was driving through on my way to a sales conference.' She sighed; Lynne had heard about these sighs, listened to the increasingly annoying patter about the sales conferences that were an integral part of Rachel's life. It was both hard – Sales! Marketing! – and all too easy – the complaining! – to remember that she was Cathy's daughter.

'It's in Bristol and I thought, well, it would be nice to see you. And Gran of course. Where is she?'

'She's upstairs, Rachel. She won't come down. I'm afraid I've done something...' Lynne trailed off, not sure how to proceed. 'I've upset her.'

'Well, she'll want to see me, won't she?' Rachel's confidence had spread to her own children and Lynne wondered where on earth it came from. Cathy certainly didn't have it.

'Perhaps. But there's something you need to know first.'

An hour later, a shell-shocked Rachel was trying to absorb all that she had heard.

'It's my fault,' she said sadly. 'I thought those tests were nothing more than a bit of fun. And Danny had seen some family history programme on TV so he was enthusiastic too.'

'It's not your fault or Danny's. It's nobody's fault. I don't expect it's Gran's fault either. But...'

'Now we know. And we can't un-know it.'

Lynne's phone buzzed. It was a message from Cathy. *I told you not to do it. I TOLD YOU. I'm coming over now.*

Lynne held the screen between her fingers and, pinching her lips together, showed it to Rachel.

'Yikes.'

She looked at her aunt sympathetically. 'I have a hotel room booked in Bristol tonight. Why don't you take it and I'll stay here? That will give all of us time to think.'

'But not before I see Cathy. I have to do that.'

'All right. But I'm going to see Gran now. I won't say anything about this. Not unless she does first. I'll say hello and tell her I'm staying here tonight. Ask her if she wants anything, you know...' Rachel ended the conversation with a positivity that Lynne found hard to believe. After a few moments, she came back into the kitchen.

'Gran says she's tired. But I can bring her a cup of tea if I like.'

Lynne handed one over. 'Take her a biscuit too. One of these' – butter biscuits with sultanas in, Barbara's favourite – 'She hasn't eaten anything all day.'

Rachel briefly hugged Lynne. 'Don't worry. I'll make her eat something in a bit.'

While Rachel was upstairs, Cathy arrived.

'Rachel's here.' Lynne did not wait for Cathy to shut the door.

'Why? How's she going to help?'

'She didn't come to help. She came to visit, break her drive, you know.'

'Well. Huh.' Cathy's emotions played across her face. 'She didn't come to see me.'

The two of them sat down, frostily, in the too-warm kitchen.

'I told you not to. I told you,' Cathy snapped. 'So did Nick. But you had to do what you wanted, no thought for Mum.'

She opened the 80s' tan-coloured kitchen cupboard, the chipped flowers on the ceramic tiles around the worktop more than ready to be replaced. Ignoring the teapot, she marched straight to the kettle and turned it on, dropping her own teabag contemptuously in a mug.

Rachel padded downstairs, holding Barbara's cup and saucer.

'Oh, hi, all right?' She walked over to Cathy and kissed her cheek, a greeting that was not returned.

'I didn't know you were in the area.'

'Neither did I, until this afternoon. But I hadn't seen Gran or Auntie Lynne for months. I thought I'd drop round to say hello.' Her smile of apology managed to incorporate elements of sorrow, exasperation and guilt. Cathy strenuously dunked the string on the apple and ginger teabag up and down.

'Gran had that tea?' Lynne asked to break the silence, as the answer seemed obvious.

'Yes, let's leave her be for the moment. Like I said, I'll get her to eat something later.'

There was another bang at the front door, and Nick clattered in, dripping onto the carpet.

'What the fuck have you done?' he shouted. And quickly, 'Oh. Rachel. Hello.' He apologised, as though she had never heard anyone swearing before.

'She told Mum about the genealogist. Then of course Mum told her to stop, which she didn't. So Mum told her to get out. Understandably. Mum said no. We said no. But Lynne went ahead and did it anyway.' Cathy blurted this out rapidly, without pausing for breath. She gasped hard at the end and leaned against the table.

Lynne felt overwhelmed with gratitude for Rachel's presence.

'Look, you win,' she sighed. 'It's just not worth it. I'll text the genealogist to say she should stop. Okay. I'll take my DNA results off. I'll do whatever. I've upset her too much. It's her secret. Okay. Okay.'

'Stop saying okay! It's already done. The damage. She's already hurt.' Nick's handsome face appeared red in patches, his breathing fast. 'You can't do that to an old woman. You just *can't!*'

Rachel looked at her uncle sadly. 'Don't you think Lynne deserves the truth?'

'No,' he said. 'Not at this price, destroying the family and our mum's peace of mind. I really wish you and Danny had never bought those bloody kits.'

'So do I,' she retorted. 'But it's too late now. None of us were to know this would happen, were we?'

'Mum. She would have known,' said Cathy, clattering her mug on the table.

Lynne moved the mug from the table to the sink. 'That's why she "lost" our tests.'

'I didn't know that,' Rachel whispered. None of them spoke for a moment. Upstairs, they could hear the toilet flushing again. Barbara was making her presence felt, even without coming downstairs or speaking to any of them. An angry ghost.

'But she wouldn't have known when she married Dad, when she got pregnant with Lynne, would she? Nobody knew about DNA then,' said Cathy angrily.

Suddenly, opening the kitchen door, was Barbara. She leaned against the wall, her white hair spread out in a messy cloud, unbrushed; her skin pale, translucent even; her lips scarcely pink.

'You're all here then,' she said. 'I can't rest with all the arguing that I can hear from this room, every last syllable of it. I am here. I'm not about to die. This is not killing me. But I didn't want it and I'm not having it.'

She paused, glaring at Lynne.

'I thought I told you to go,' she said.

'Yes, I'm going.' Lynne turned and went upstairs. A few moments later, she came down with an overnight bag.

'I'll take you to the station,' Rachel said. 'I'll be right back,' she continued, turning towards her other relatives. 'Remember I'm making you some dinner, Gran.'

Nick put his arm around his mother and guided her into the living room, as Lynne and Rachel left. A few seconds later, they could hear Rachel starting her car.

At the station, Rachel turned to Lynne.

'Try not to worry,' she said. 'We'll talk later – yes?'

Lynne nodded.

'I just hope she doesn't start blaming you too. Or Danny.'

Rachel rubbed her fingers up and down the sides of her face.

'We bought those tests. She seems to have forgotten that.'

Lynne doubted that. As far as she was aware, Barbara never forgot anything.

CHAPTER ELEVEN

BARBARA: SWINDON, ENGLAND, 1962

She knew exactly when she got pregnant but Barbara was still astonished it had happened. For heavens' sake, she and Vic hardly ever slept together. It wasn't even a case of Christmas, their wedding anniversary and birthdays. Their lives wore them out, what with bringing up the girls (Barbara) and commuting into work (Vic), and anyway... their love wasn't like that. Neither of them was particularly interested. After she had married Victor and come to England, she felt such relief that the desperate sexual desires of the past had ebbed away. With Vic, she enjoyed warmth, affection, cosiness, domesticity, companionship. Very occasionally – once, twice, three times over the course of seven years – this turned into sex.

As for Vic himself and what magazines called 'a husband's needs', he rarely alluded to them. Perhaps he found physical expression elsewhere, but if he did, he kept it from her. He never came home late without explanation but as Barbara reflected, the physical act could be over so quickly for men. How much better life had turned out to be compared to her earlier adult years. So little striving, so much satisfaction in the everyday.

When they boarded the plane for England, Lynne was only six weeks old. Barbara was just four weeks out of hospital, and Victor had barely left his wife's side. Her terror that she would not be able to cope, that her nerves would let her down, threatened to overwhelm her. But

Victor remained kind and understanding, providing a story that satisfied his employers. They terminated his contract then and there, but they did allow him to keep the return aeroplane trip they had already paid for. Elizabeth House had, similarly, not delved too deeply into Victor's story. They might have looked askance at him, but – as well as his money for her keep – they approved of his claims to a woman they considered he must have wronged.

Barbara soon became confident in her ability to look after baby Lynne. Although she wept a little while she remained in hospital, this was considered natural by everyone and Barbara herself did not fear a mental collapse.

Relief overcame her as soon as they boarded the flight. She had escaped the past, and everything would work out fine. If only she could forget her life before, every bit of it, even the good parts, there would be a real chance to make a new start.

By the time the three of them reached England, welcomed by his parents and taken to live in their house, there was no question that everything would work out well.

And it did. They formed a family. Within months Barbara had completely reconciled herself to all the things about the country that she hated when she first arrived – no one ever saying what they meant; the thin line between politeness and coldness; damp weather that permeated the unheated, uninsulated house. Smoky coal fires, in fireplaces that had to be cleaned every morning before she laid them again. Places and events that banned women, sometimes even those accompanied by men. The all-round greyness – of the skies, clothing and buildings – that flattened everyone's spirits. After a couple of years, she and Vic moved into their own home: warmer and newer, with hot water from an immersion heater and gas fires that actually heated the rooms.

Lynne was approaching her fifth birthday when Cathy was born, and after that shaky start treated her like her own living doll, showing her off to Vic's parents as if she, Lynne, played some part in the creation of this tiny child. Possibly with justification. She had nagged both her parents about wanting a sister, just like Meg, her friend next door. Having an only child was selfish – everyone said so – and they agreed to try. Barbara fell pregnant almost immediately. Cathy had been a wanted child, a 'tried-for' baby, whereas the others were and would be... surprises. They should not have been quite that unexpected; their parents knew the workings of human biology.

In general, Barbara found the early stages of motherhood terribly hard. Why had she found it difficult with Cathy, but less so with Lynne? She relied on Victor's parents so much with both of her daughters. They – especially his mother – cosseted Barbara and never left her alone with a crying infant, unable to make herself a cup of tea or have a bath. They were kindness itself, reliable and comforting; thrilled, too, at having one grandchild, and then another. They had abandoned the idea of Victor ever marrying so they were simply delighted. They didn't ask for details or probe too deeply about whether Lynne was really Victor's child. He always acted as though she was, and nobody openly challenged that.

So when, shortly after Barbara's thirty-third birthday, she missed first one period, and then the next, she realised the true situation. She was pregnant; the signs were unmistakable. Her breasts irritated her, rubbing against her cotton summer dress that – before the weather cooled – would no longer reach around her waist. With Cathy and Lynne, Barbara had not felt particularly tired. This time, the energy drained out of her as she trudged around the house, snapping at Victor and losing patience with the girls.

Lynne had been at school for three years now, and Cathy would soon be going too. The family was plodding along nicely. Before her pregnancy, Barbara's mental state appeared to have calmed once and for all, but the anxiety had flooded back. Barbara's nerves crashed and jangled. Alongside her growing body, she became ever more tense, chewing her fingers and biting her nails until they bled. Was it going to be all right, she wondered? Probably not. Definitely not.

'Well, here's the thing, Mrs Pendleton,' the doctor said to her at around seven months. 'You need to have complete bed rest. You have very high blood pressure which could become dangerous for both you and your baby.' Barbara was already on his list of high-risk pregnancies, and this pushed her towards the top of it.

'I cannot overemphasise the seriousness of this situation,' he continued, in a voice to convince her that she had to believe him or die. 'I'm admitting you to hospital where you can be monitored. Your husband, or perhaps your mother-in-law, will have to look after your other children.'

He also looked at her sternly. 'I remain concerned about your state of mind,' he said. 'I remember only too clearly what happened with the last baby. I hoped you would have had the... foresight... not to get into this condition again. Or perhaps I should blame Mr Pendleton.'

'He's a wonderful husband,' she whispered, tears dripping onto her stomach.

'No doubt,' the doctor replied archly. 'And over the next few months, he'll need to show just how wonderful he is.'

At thirty weeks – in the gloomiest days of the new year – Barbara went to a maternity home to be observed at every hour of the day and night, stuck in bed with her feet on pillows, unable to walk from one side of the ward to the other. Lynne and Cathy were not allowed to visit, children being likely to carry infections to patients, and Barbara swam in guilt. What would happen to those little girls without her? It might not be bad, perhaps they would manage well. That prospect made her feel no better.

There was too much time to think, to remember the past, the people she would never see again. All those years, and every one of them haunting her.

The emergency caesarean to save her life, the hysterectomy following straight after; neither was a surprise. Nor were the depths of misery into which she plunged. At times, she could not bear one single instant more; the torture of being alive. And yet, she bore it. There was a baby.

When the nurses brought the tiny creature to her, calling it Baby – not the baby, or Nicholas – her brain swirled in confusion.

Was this a little boy baby or a little girl? She remembered both, but not their names. Tiny phantoms floated around her consciousness, sometimes visible in the ward, sometimes not. Where were they, why didn't she know them? Perhaps they had been taken from her. Or maybe – worse – she had given them away, let them slip out of her hands. She was not up to this: having babies, the process of giving birth and the demands of new motherhood. She was set apart from other women by this perceived failure. What was wrong with her?

This time, they gave her no electric shocks, instead, she was prescribed a range of drugs. After a while, the torture was replaced by numbness. She was sedated, and when the drugs wore off she would shout, 'Where is he? Where is he? They took him, didn't they.'

And so, she was drugged once more.

Separating babies from their mothers was not the goal of this, so caring, hospital. Barbara had not been able to breastfeed – the drugs she needed for herself would affect Baby – and Marjorie had stepped into the breach with formula, while Victor looked after Lynne and Cathy. It would all work out, the adults reassured each other. Barbara would get better eventually. But they did not discuss this. They each hoped that this situation would simply go away because, after all, what could any of them do? Talking about it would not change matters.

After six months, Barbara left hospital. She took other drugs now – smaller doses of less terrible drugs, and remained groggy but able to carry out her domestic duties – and she could take them at home. She did what they said she must and carried on with her life. She functioned and, in time, things did indeed get better. Eventually, they got much, much better.

There would be no more babies.

CHAPTER TWELVE

KAREN: LONDON, ENGLAND, FEBRUARY 2018

She looked at her phone, willing something to happen. Three hours since Karen had texted Lynne and there had been no response so far. She tried, unsuccessfully, not to think this was a very bad omen indeed. In the meantime, it was easiest just to keep investigating. She looked at Meredith's tree, wondering where Lynne could fit in.

Meredith might not be able to work out the identities of all of her relatives, but she did not seem to have done all the things she could. For instance, she had not looked for her grandparents in any of the available censuses or found any obituaries for them in newspapers. Some of those could be hard to locate if you didn't know how to find your way around them or use the right sort of paid-for accounts. The main issue was: where were Meredith's paternal grandparents living for the 1930 and 1940 US censuses? That would help. Then there were her great-grandparents, during the 1890s and 1900s. Where did they live? She needed to see if there were any brothers and sisters.

A mere half hour into this – and having found nothing – her phone pinged with a text from Lynne. *Sorry about this. See email.*

The email was short and to the point.

Dear Karen,
I'm sorry to say that I have bowed to
family pressure and will no longer pursue
the identity of my unknown birth father
– at least at the present time. My mother
has reacted very badly indeed, to the extent
that we are all worried about her health. I
am currently staying in a hotel as she has
demanded I leave her house.
I am closing my Ancestry account, which
I have not paid for, so you won't be
managing it anymore. I hadn't signed our
contract yet, but I have transferred £1,000
into your account which I hope will prove
satisfactory.
With best wishes and apologies,
Lynne Pendleton

Karen put her head in her hands. So that was that then. The money was a temporary relief, of course, but she'd had such high hopes of this. That genetic genealogy could be the beginning of a whole new strand of work that – given the way so many people were starting to buy the tests – would inevitably lead to... what? Income? Security? A career path? Some new purpose that suited her psychologically? Possibly all of the above.

Oh, get a grip, she thought. 'At the present time' probably meant that she wasn't going to do anything while her mother was still alive. Karen bought herself up short; no, she refused to wish an elderly woman dead.

Dear Lynne,
I'm sorry to hear this. Family secrets often
bring up conflicts and sometimes there is no
way to get over that in the short term. I hope
that, by stopping this search, your family
can come together again.

Thanks for the money; I appreciate your
speedy payment.
Yours,
Karen Copperfield

Perhaps she should have checked that she had actually *been* paid first, she thought. What a useless small business owner she'd turned out to be. But yes, the money was in her account so there was at least that.

'Anna.'

Karen had hoped not to go straight to her ex-lover when she needed help, especially since she had (caringly) told her that she was really stressed at work right now. Nevertheless, she wanted someone's kindness. Not Ben's – it was only yesterday that he had told her to be careful – not her sister Lisa, who thought she should get a proper job without explicitly saying so. But Anna was someone good and reliable. Loving.

'Sweetie.'

'Sorry to bother you.'

'Come on, don't be silly. What's up? I know it's something.'

'Work offered. Work dangled in front of me. Work taken up, then taken away again.'

'Oh shit.'

'Yes, really.'

Anna lived mainly in Switzerland, her success as an international health consultant always a contrast to Karen's failure. In Karen's eyes, anyway. Anna thought of the situation somewhat differently, feeling trapped and exhausted by the job for which she seemed so suited. Anna admired Karen's intellect and persistence but did not admire the impulsivity, disorganisation and untidiness that had made her impossible to live with. Eventually, the sheer emotional exhaustion of their relationship ensured she was happy to be in Geneva most of the time.

'When will I get to do something that works for me?'

'Well, you don't know this won't work. What happened?'

In a burst of energy, Karen told her about the events of the past few days.

'I think this woman came to you prematurely,' Anna reflected. 'She should have made sure that all her family were on board with it before she paid for a genealogist. I mean really!'

'She was desperate!'

'That was too soon to be desperate. Maybe her mother would have told her, given a bit of time to come to terms with it. If you've had a secret for over sixty years, of course you'll be shocked when it's not a secret anymore. She had no control over what happened. But maybe, given time, it would all have been all right again.'

'Hmm.'

'She may come back to you, later. Just don't freak out about it.'

'The money, though. I mean I'm not in any immediate crisis now, and she may not have given me more than a grand anyway, but still...'

'Yes, yes, don't worry about that. I'll give you some work. There's reports you can write. Okay?'

'Thanks, babes.'

Karen hated being helped out by anyone she loved; it was intolerable, but she couldn't see any options. It was a lot harder to get minimum wage jobs than people thought. Heaven knows she'd tried.

Straight after putting down the phone, it pinged again. To her surprise, it was her work email, with a message from Meredith Dyson.

Hi Karen,
I just noticed that Lynne is no longer on Ancestry. Has she deleted her account?
Kind regards,
M

Hi Meredith,
Yes, she has decided against it and so I am
no longer managing her tree or involved
with her case.
K

Hi Karen,
This is so sad because it's clear I am
related to Lynne somehow. I had already
taken a screenshot of her information and
connections just in case this happened. It
happened once to me before, but I hadn't
screenshotted and now I am not 100% sure
if I have the right details about that person.
They are lost now.
According to your website, you've done so
many interesting things!!! If I have money
later, perhaps you can help me make sense
of my unknown family!!
Kind regards,
M

• • • ● ● • ● ● • • •

Once again, Karen was woken far too early – especially as she had experienced a mainly sleepless night, worrying about her future. The video intercom buzzed, displaying a motorcycle courier with an envelope marked 'By Hand' with Dr Karen Copperfield, and her address typed neatly in the centre. As she signed for it, she wondered whether there was some debt she had forgotten to pay or some urgent matter she had somehow neglected.

Instead, it was a letter from a firm of lawyers in Sausalito, California. Her shock was replaced immediately by disbelief. What on earth was this? And then, but surely this has no legal standing? But there was the implied threat and that did piss her off.

Dear Miss Copperfield,
This letter serves as a notification that you must cease and desist from any further investigation into the genealogical background and descendants of William Prior, born in Glasgow, Scotland, on 15th July 1850.

In addition, all family trees available online that include this gentleman, whether through individual blogs or websites or public or private family trees on genealogy sites, must be withdrawn immediately as they constitute a violation of our client's right to privacy.

Your actions, and the actions of your client, infringe upon our client's right to remain free from harassment, and emotional and financial distress.

We demand that you cease and desist from this activity immediately. If you fail to do so, we will be forced to take appropriate legal remedies against you, your business, and any relevant clients.

Sincerely,
Anthony Rollason
Attorney at Law

No doctorate then; were they putting her in her place by using 'Miss' rather than the 'Dr' someone had written on the envelope? This letter looked threatening but Karen simply didn't believe it. Her knowledge of the law – whatever country it was – indicated that their legal threats were completely unenforceable. How could individuals possibly have a case against other individuals putting already public information into the public domain? It wasn't even as though people had a 'right to be forgotten' on the internet, as was sometimes the case in European law. Existence could not be forgotten because it was there in official records. This threat amounted to nothing more than horseshit. No doubt it would freak out Lynne, though, and perhaps Meredith if she had received the same letter. What did these lawyers think their clients would gain by this?

The answer came immediately: frighten them. Lynne and Meredith, and their families, were private people who had not been the subjects of even the smallest twitter storm. She, of course, had weathered far worse, both as a journalist and when she had been forced out of her academic job. What's more, she hated – *really* hated – bullies.

Her phone rang immediately.

'Hi, Karen. It's Lynne. I just had a rather strange letter hand-delivered to me and I wonder if you had one too.'

Karen was taken aback by Lynne's calm voice. She had expected a different reaction.

'I did, yes.' She paused. 'What did you make of it?'

'It makes me regret giving up on the search. I can't imagine who this William Prior person is to me or why these legal idiots think you and I are harming someone they haven't named. But there it is. I have given my word to my family.'

'Well, the legal idiots will go away, presumably, as you aren't on Ancestry anymore.'

'Yes. Oh, Karen. What secrets there must be in my family! I suppose I realise that now. And they will stay secrets for at least as long as... my mother is around.'

Karen could hear the guilt in Lynne's voice.

'Try not to worry about any of it,' she said reassuringly.

'Karen – thanks. For everything. I hope... well, anyway. Thanks.'

A few hours later, Meredith emailed.

Can we talk? she wrote. *I got a letter today and I'm very disturbed by it.*

Karen Skyped her straightaway. Meredith looked so much like her Facebook photograph – friendly, endearing, her face still unlined. Karen recognised that look: hope.

'I expect you got the same letter as both Lynne and I,' sighed Karen.

Meredith shuddered.

'Yeah. But I don't understand – why would anyone do this?'

'Legally, you mean?'

'Right. What do they think we're doing?'

'I'm sure they want to scare us off. And they have scared you, haven't they?'

'Kind of. I've never gotten anything like this before.'

'That's what they're banking on. That you see a threat and you act on it by doing what they say. But legally, there is nothing they can do. You aren't harassing them. Do you know who this William Prior is?'

'He's my two times great-grandfather.'

'Do you know anything about him?'

'Nothing at all. Just his name, and that he died in 1920. My research hasn't gone any further than that.'

'My advice – for what it's worth – is to do nothing about this for the moment. But if you want to take down your tree or delete your account, I wouldn't blame you, because they are trying to scare you.'

'Trying to! They have!'

'I know.'

'How do they know who I am? That I'm trying to find out about my family history? And where I live?'

'Probably, you have come up as a new cousin and they found both you and Lynne that way. Then if they have worked up a full family tree – I mean much more than you or Lynne, or indeed I have done so far – then they would be able to work out who you were. And if they were experienced researchers... well, it would be possible.'

'Whoa! That sucks big time.' Karen could see the alarm all over Meredith's face as she wondered what else these unknown aggressors might do.

'As I say, if you want to delete your account, then you could always do that. Personally, I wouldn't because you have done absolutely nothing illegal. But then this isn't my family.'

The call ended with Meredith considering her options. It was only 3 pm, UK time. The letter must have been delivered to Meredith very early that morning. Karen was fizzing with anger, and also confused. Who were these people and what did they think a couple of entirely ordinary people could find out that would cause them 'distress'? What counted as 'distress' anyway? There certainly had been no harassment.

She sighed. Not my problem, she thought, although the puzzle nagged at her. She could always do some kind of paper family tree and see where it got her. Was that ethical? It wasn't as if she was going to actually *do* anything with it. It was that old research problem, the reason that she lurked on Websleuths and used to spend hours in the archives looking through one more folder of barely legible scrawl. It was also the reason – at least partly – why she had got into such trouble as a journalist. Once there was a mystery, potential leads, things that could be slotted together to make a coherent whole – she couldn't bring herself to stop. Something made her carry on until every part of it came together.

By mid-afternoon, Karen was sitting in her usual café, in her usual seat next to the window, staring at the rain falling in sheets. Water was rushing down the slope of the pavement towards the gutter where it was starting to pool. Too much for the drains, she thought, watching as it slid ever faster, lit by the streetlights in the growing gloom. Were the sales still on, she wondered? Now that she had a tiny bit of money, she really should buy a casual jacket that kept out the rain. She looked sadly at her attractive, but no longer waterproof jacket. It had been around too long, a feeling she sometimes shared. 'February,' she thought. 'Horrible month'. And here it came again, the sinking feeling that spelt doom. She longed for a cigarette, but no. Another coffee it had to be, and stronger this time.

'Double espresso, please.'

At least the café was bright, glaring electric lights on the ceiling and walls, illuminating the dried-up flaky pastries and the luridly coloured creamy cakes. An extra spotlight dangled above her for luck. It was better than it could be, this café, stuck in the arse end of nowhere. The coffee was good and no one minded if she – like several others here – spent hours on their laptops pretending to, or trying to, work. These attempts or pretences also meant that no one struck up a conversation. They were just there, as she was.

Water was now dripping regularly from a spot in the ceiling perilously near a light fitting. This was clearly expected, as the owner had put a metal cutlery trough underneath, to prevent water spreading all over the floor. It would soon overflow. She sighed.

So many secrets in the world, she reflected, staring at her laptop screen. She was looking at Lynne's family tree – all the information Karen had been given, and all the gaps that were so evidently there with the most casual research into public records. How had the Pendleton family closed their eyes quite so tightly?

People were lying and, as life had already taught her, everyone lied. She lied, he lied, I lie and you lie. We lie. We all lie. For the whole of our lives sometimes, and that is just the fact of the matter.

Family Tree: Pendleton/Thompson 2018

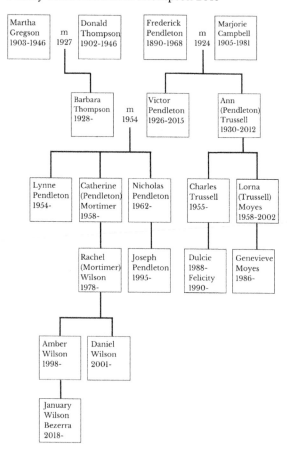

PART TWO

CHAPTER THIRTEEN

JEAN: NEW LAKE CITY, CALIFORNIA, JUNE 1946

Jean Woods ran, leapt and jumped down the polished wooden staircase, almost colliding with her little brother, Larry. He, and a whole automobile factory's worth of toy cars, were spread out all over the floor.

'Out of my way,' the seventeen-year-old yelled. 'I'm late for the race, and if I miss it Joe will kill me.'

Her chestnut curls flew around her face when she ran, so Jean smoothed down her hair as she stood in front of the mirror. Her bangs were styled up and back into the highly fashionable pompadour. The set was a messy disappointment, but it would have to do.

Larry shook his head, deadly serious with the wisdom of a sports-mad boy of eight. 'He's not thinking about you at the moment. He's thinking about all the things he has to do to beat Fred.'

Jean ran out of the house and turned left along the sidewalk under the cooling shade of the trees, crossing several roads before she reached the entrance to New Lake High School. She ran so fast; perhaps she should have tried out for the girls' team herself. Oh but her hair! It flew all over the place, bothering her.

She had not watched the many other sports events that day – bad for someone on the booster committee – but other girls would have been there to give the boys their support. Jean had so many things to do during this last week of school. So many small tasks that no one else seemed to have done when they *promised* they would.

Everyone would be watching their boyfriends or the men they had their eyes on.

Jean took her seat on the bleachers, near enough the track to catch Joe's eye. He winked, and she winked back, as he and the six other men bent and stretched their long limbs. There were hundreds of people there – parents, friends from other high schools, brothers and sisters – and the noise was overwhelming. How did he feel, she wondered? Joe had always been good at the 220-yard dash, but he had been distracted recently. There was a lot to consider before graduation and, while she would be helping children with their art at summer camp, and then taking her own courses at junior college, he was unsure. Should he start work as an engineer – as he wanted – or should he enlist in the navy like his brother? His mother would not mind that so much now with the war being over, and neither would Jean. But people were saying this was a bad time to join the service as there were already so many men enlisted.

They were off. Round and round the cinder track, would it be, would it be, would it be Joe? Oh, it took no time! Fred, his friend and rival, ran a hair ahead, raising his arms in the air as, elated, he passed the finish line. Ah well. Joe shook Fred's hand, before looking down briefly at the track and shaking his head. He pressed his lips together and glanced up ruefully at Jean. She pressed her lips together in turn, giving a quick shrug of sympathy. The last race of his high school career, and he had not won. No going out in glory, then; that was for Fred. The six boys huddled together, laughing and slapping each other. They were all good-looking boys, no doubt about it, but she was glad she was going with Joe. He was tall and finely muscled but still on the skinny side. She felt another wave of sadness for Joe, who was showing no signs of the dejection she knew he must feel, before getting up and going to the students' office.

There was so much to do before they graduated in a few days' time. Jean's concentration was focused on the leaving dance organising committee; the Farewell Seniors banner – which would be draped across the sports hall – was causing no end of problems. Jean wanted to make a bigger and better one than before; the old version seemed to have been nibbled at by some bug or other. Did last year's committee have no eye at all for detail? Or perhaps the creatures had been feasting between last year and this. Despite her efforts, she just couldn't get it right. The felt letters wouldn't lie flat on the calico backing either. She threw it on the ground in frustration.

'Need any help?' A friendly head with strawberry blonde curls poked around the door.

Thank heavens, it was Audrey. 'Yes, this blasted thing, I can't get it to go right.' Jean grimaced, thrusting one end of the banner in her direction.

Audrey set to work; she was a talented seamstress. Her clothes reflected that; her family didn't have money but she could make the least expensive frock look double the price with some added fripperies. And as for her own creations, well! 'Look, we just need to hem these edges, and then we can iron down the letters.'

She thrust the other end of the banner back towards Jean and the pair sewed and chatted excitedly.

Audrey looked up at Jean.

'I've had exciting news! I'm going to be a student fashion adviser at Goodman Maddox starting in August. I'll be working in the teen section, 'hip to all the new styles' so they tell me. And not only will that be the greatest fun but I can save money too.'

Jean loved Audrey. She didn't take herself too seriously. She said 'hip to all the new styles' as if she were a comedienne in the movies, yet Jean realised that Audrey would be very happy working in a large department store. The position would suit her down to the ground, not just using her talents but to help prepare for her future ambitions. Because what Audrey wanted most of all was what she was going to get – marriage and children – and she wasn't wasting any time about it. Jean had seen her entry in the yearbook: while Audrey liked chocolate and playing the piano, and disliked feeling cold, her one and only ambition was to be a good wife to Ed. Her entry in the yearbook said so, and Jean had often heard her friend speaking those words herself: 'my one and only ambition is to be a good wife to Ed'. Jean shook her head affectionately and smiled. How grown up to be so certain about the rest of your life.

Jean had no desire to be engaged to be married, a state in which Audrey already gloried. At any rate, she would be going to college which Mother and Dad thought was a great, if expensive, achievement. Then she had to consider whether she would be an illustrator, or an art teacher, or who knew what else. After college, it would be fun to earn some money, wouldn't it? Audrey was only likely to stay as a student fashion adviser for a year or two at most. Then some other, younger girl would replace her, she would walk down the aisle, and nine months later the first little Ed and Audrey would come along.

'Hey, dreamer.' Audrey barged into her thoughts. 'What ya thinking?'

'About the children you are going to have!' Jean laughed, returning to her sewing.

Jean always found it easy to drift off into her thoughts, and Audrey teased her about that. It was what *Jean* was mentioned for in the yearbook. That, and her dislike of too-hot summers. She experienced no overwhelming passions and had no ambitions, or at least, nothing she felt strongly enough about to have it written down for all time alongside her photograph where she wore a white peasant blouse and the necklace that once belonged to her grandmother.

There was so much still to do. They needed to make sure all the tickets for the hop had been sold. That the refreshments had not only been ordered but would be delivered. And that their gowns were ready. Oh so many things!

The table was laid for dinner when Jean reached home at half past five. Shortly afterwards, with her father back from the office and Larry washed clean of the day's dirt, the family sat down at the table and said a simple grace.

'Did Joe win the race then, or was it Fred?' Jean's father Walter asked, his mouth full of meatloaf, his blue eyes sympathetic.

'Fred,' Jean sighed. 'But never mind. They both did well.'

'So that was his last high school run,' her mother Dorothy continued sadly. 'You're all growing up so fast.'

'I was very busy today,' Jean said. 'We still haven't quite finished our preparations for the dance or for graduation.'

'You're always so busy,' Walter smiled. 'You'll need a rest when it's all over.'

'No, she won't, dear,' Dorothy continued. 'She's got enough energy for ten girls.'

Jean smiled.

'Audrey told me today she has a job starting in August, student fashion adviser at Goodman Marcus. I saw the advertisement. It said we students can be 'swell-elegant' if we shop there.'

'Oh, such silly words,' her mother chided gently. 'We should, you should, be worshipping God by dressing simply and gracefully, not trying to make yourself into something you are not.'

Jean sighed to herself. Shouldn't her mother's religious beliefs give her the compassion to realise Audrey's family needed the money? The Woods family wasn't rich, but owning a canning factory meant they had some kind of standing in the community. Jean wouldn't be compelled to work if she didn't want to.

'Well, I think it is grand that she is working. Audrey always looks 'swell-elegant' anyway.'

'I don't know what that means, though Audrey looks splendid,' her mother agreed. 'She is a lovely girl, so sweet and charming. She will do very well at that job.'

Jean waited for the 'but' that lurked behind the words; it never came.

'I like Ed,' said Larry. 'He says he'll teach me how to swim this summer.'

'You like anyone who'll play sports with you,' Jean teased.

'No.' Larry screwed up his face in confusion. 'Well yes, maybe.'

'Now, Jean,' her father said slowly. 'When are you coming to help me in the office? I'll increase your allowance if you do.'

'Thank you, Dad. I will.'

'I need her too, you know,' her mother continued. 'There are lots of things she could do round here.'

'And I already said I would help on summer camp art projects,' Jean added anxiously.

'It will all work out, dear, don't you worry,' said her father.

Jean nodded. Before any of that could happen, she had high school graduation and, even before that, a dance to attend. It was going to be the dance to end all dances, she was sure – far better than the usual hops – and she couldn't wait to see her friends in their lovely gowns. It would be her birthday soon and she would be eighteen! Once that had happened, well, then it would be time to plan a summer spent looking after her brother, teaching little children how to paint, and, in only a few weeks, her first-ever vacation without her parents.

The journey had taken hours but eventually, there they all were, right outside Tony and Maureen's home in the Sunset district. What strange weather. It was like spring or fall in Lake View. Jean put her arm through Joe's and pulled him closer for warmth.

Compared to the houses in Lake View, this one seemed hemmed in. There was no yard to speak of, just a short driveway out front for the car, with some bushes around to screen the house from the road and separate it from the one next door. There was no porch, nowhere for roses, or any place to sit in the shade when it was hot. Still, she thought, perhaps you were meant to go to the beach for that. You could walk all right, but why walk when you could drive? The thought of having an automobile excited her. She knew few girls of her age with cars; it seemed like the very marker of growing up, of turning into the sort of sophisticated woman she had never considered becoming until just that moment.

Tony had driven them all the way from Lake View. He was Audrey's cousin; he and his wife Maureen were the first in both their families to own their own home. Up and down the street, there were lots of ex-servicemen like Tony moving into their bright new houses, taking up jobs as salesmen and engineers, high school teachers and police officers. Small children played on the sidewalk and everything seemed so bright and optimistic – except for the weather.

'So, what are you kids going to do while you're here?' Tony queried, as they sat around the dinner table with their potato and hot dog salad.

'Are there any games on?' asked Ed.

'Sure there are. But you'll want to go to Playland. Even we like that!' Maureen and Tony smiled at each other.

'Then there are all the stores you don't have in Lake View,' Maureen continued. 'I know you're going to work in a grand store, Audrey, but Lake View has nothing like the City of Paris, which is a work of art in itself. And everyone dresses up. People even wear fur coats!' Maureen looked at Jean and Audrey in anticipation. 'You really must let me take you.'

'And church?' Audrey wondered quietly. 'Which church do you go to?'

Maureen and Tony glanced at each other.

'There's a United Methodist church a few blocks away,' Tony said. 'I'm sure you'd be made welcome if you wanted to go.'

Tony hadn't wanted to have anything to do with church after his experiences of combat, and Audrey knew this. Now they all knew it too and felt embarrassed. Why had she said that?

The girls stood up to help Maureen clear the table. Jean was particularly struck by the decoration in the house. Even the furniture was brighter and shinier than that of her parents'. The kitchen cupboards were pale pink, for goodness sake, and the floor an elegant shade of grey.

'Your kitchen is beautiful!' Jean blurted out.

Maureen smiled. 'It makes the chores easier.'

Tony pulled out the Monopoly board and they played until Joe – the Scottie dog – won, with hotels across the board's best addresses. At 10 pm Tony and Maureen went up to bed and Joe and Ed went off to sleep at a neighbour's house.

Audrey and Jean had twin beds, one of which was usually Jilly's, Maureen and Tony's three-year-old daughter, who was staying in her parents' room. 'If Ed and I had a house like this, why I'd never want for anything else.' Audrey gently tapped cream into her face, grimacing this way and that in front of the mirror.

'But you would, Audrey. Of course you would! What about the kiddies?' Jean teased.

'All right. But there is a lovely bedroom for them here.' Audrey began to roll up her hair in metal curlers, guided with her fingers alone as Jean took her place at the vanity. Her skin tapping and hair rolling was more casual; she cared less than Audrey.

'You know, If Tony has lost his faith, you need to leave him be,' Jean whispered. 'Let him decide for himself what he wants to do.'

Audrey turned her face towards Jean, upset. 'How can I do that?' she said. 'It's too important. My faith has been the one sustaining thing in my life. Why can't it be the same for him?'

Oh, Audrey, Jean thought, stop going on about it! Nevertheless, she took her friend's hand tenderly. 'Let him come to it in his own time, if he is going to. You can't push him. Besides, we don't know what happened to him overseas, do we?'

Audrey sighed. 'That's just what mother says.' She kissed Jean on the cheek. 'I'll pray for him.'

There was a street light just under the window and Jean could see and hear people laughing and shouting, happy activity all around her even though it was time for bed. She had rarely spent nights away from home – sometimes she had stayed with Audrey or another school friend, and a couple of times she had stayed in a tent at summer camp. But staying in someone else's house, in the city, that was different.

Tony and Maureen were seven years older than Jean and her friends, and their experiences of everything were so different. What would she be like in another seven years? She couldn't imagine a world as far into the future as 1953.

· · · ● ●● · ● ● · · ·

They were on vacation in San Francisco for a week, and they spent their first full day at Playland at the Beach, a huge amusement park the like of which, Tony assured them, they had never seen. Jean would have rather gone to the old historic areas or visited an art gallery; Audrey was keen on the big stores promised by Maureen. The boys most wanted to watch and play sport, but to please the girls they agreed that there'd be time for everything. They all wanted to take the cable cars and maybe a photograph of the Golden Gate Bridge. Still, as they woke in the morning the weather was glorious and so they had to, they really must, Tony insisted, visit Playland at the Beach. There might be bad weather on other days and they had to make the most of the sun. It was only a short trolley ride away – they could not get lost, and they would have such a grand time. Besides, it opened at noon and once they had paid, they could go on rides all day.

'Oh, Audrey,' Jean nudged her as they waited to go in. 'Doesn't everyone look fine!'

There were so many people around their own age, some of them dressed very informally in comparison to their little group. Jean and Audrey had both dressed up to the nines, in a pretty dress and a smart suit and hat respectively, while the others – even the girls – sported denim or brightly coloured shirts.

'Not what I'd go for,' Audrey said. 'But they have certainly made an effort.'

Everyone was staring at each other – sometimes giggling too. The crowd here seemed so much louder than the people they were used to. They took up more space and Jean just knew they would be less polite and respectful.

Then, suddenly, they were inside, swept away by a great wave of smiling, shouting people. The first thing they saw was a strange red-headed figure, a huge plaster woman cackling loudly at them. Everyone else acted untroubled by this, but the four of them gaped at the creature, bewildered.

'What do you think of Laffing Sal?' a smartly dressed young man said to Audrey as she stared. 'Whoever dreamt that up, eh?'

She looked around for Ed, whose attention was taken by a big group of girls. She tutted at the man, and sidled over to Ed, hooking her arm through his.

'Let's go on a ride,' said Joe happily. 'This is sure going to be fun!'

The first they chose was the huge and looming Big Dipper, which Tony had told them was designed to scare the living daylights out of anyone who went on it. People who'd rushed to be at the gate before it opened were already being flung around and about, looping the loop, and screaming with all their might. It stopped and the friends clambered in, Jean with Joe in the back seat, and Audrey with Ed just in front of them.

'You know,' Joe whispered confidentially. 'A soldier from Chicago sitting right here was on a date. He stood up and he knocked his head on one of these beams' – he gestured at a support – 'and died instantly. His date was left just staring.' He turned towards Jean, and they both opened their eyes very wide. 'That was only last year. Really. I read it in the newspaper.'

Joe pulled her arm through his, and the two huddled together. She knew he was trying to scare her.

'It doesn't appear to be very safe,' she said to him – and indeed, the light wood barriers holding them seemed thin and rickety.

'Just stick close to me, and you'll be fine.'

There would be no problem as long as neither of them stood up, she thought, and signs everywhere strictly prohibited this. The ride started and gathered speed before she had chance to think any further, and suddenly they all seemed to be flying into the air. Passengers were pulled up and then dropped down, the cars moving faster and faster until Jean wasn't sure whether or not she was still in her seat. The screams echoed loudly across the sky, and Jean and Joe, Audrey and Ed, yelled along with everyone else. Jean was genuinely frightened. But there was an exhilaration too. She wanted another turn.

'No, I'm not doing that ever again,' said Audrey as they got off the ride. 'I wish I hadn't bothered.' She wobbled on her elegant white shoes with their too-high heels, something that had never been a problem before. Her face was also strangely pale, and Jean started to worry that her friend was going to vomit on her expensive and showy new outfit. Instead, Audrey took off her jacket and sat down on a bench.

'Shall we have a soda, Ed?' she said, dolefully. 'I need to settle my stomach.' He put his arm around her, kissing her cheek. 'Of course.'

'Well I loved it and now I want to go on Shoot the Chutes,' said Jean, pursing her lips. 'What about you, Joe?'

'If you like,' he said, so slowly that Jean felt mean that she had suggested it.

They joined the line of jostling, giggling people of their own age, along with a few children and their parents.

'Let's go,' shouted Joe as they climbed into the boat, although he obviously already regretted it.

Their small boat snaked around some small channels of water and through a tunnel until a hoist pulled their boat to a ramp. It then slid down the chute really fast so that the water sprayed out and around so that they – and anyone nearby – got soaked. Joe and Jean were both laughing but drenched. They hoped the sun was strong enough to dry them off.

Audrey and Ed, warm and full of soda, looked at them askance.

'You're wet,' said Audrey half amused, half disapproving.

'You don't say,' Joe replied sarcastically.

But Jean was less disturbed by her sodden outfit than Joe was about his. Denim took a long time to dry, probably longer than the sun would shine that day.

'I know,' Jean said, 'let's get our picture taken right now.'

In the Funny Foto studio, they positioned their heads carefully through the wooden holes – their bodies now cowboys with plaid shirts or cowgirls with whips. This seemed the most suitable because some of the painted bodies were embarrassingly risqué; they wouldn't have wanted to show their parents anything like that. They would collect the photographs later.

For now, after the mixed pleasure of the big rides, they strolled up and down the Midway, where the boys tried and failed to shoot any targets, or throw any hoops over prizes. They ate tacos – which none of them had ever tasted before – and listened to the music which floated in from the ocean. 'Don't fence me in' a man crooned in the distance, and they moved back and forth along with it. There were plenty of other rides, but they rested, happy just sitting there. Perhaps later in the week, they would lie on the beach itself.

Jean wanted to go in the diving bell, but she was alone in that so she left the others listening to the music and waited for the opportunity to climb into a strange metal ball, sinking under the water where she could make out sharks, an octopus, and other fish that she did not recognise. The rotting odour stuck in the back of her throat and the sides of the diving bell pressed in on her. That wasn't something she cared to repeat.

But the day as a whole, that was grand, and they collected their photographs to take home. What a bunch of dopes they looked! Around eight thirty, when the daylight started to dim, the fog out at sea crept towards them and Jean could see why this was called 'rolling'. Suddenly, her frock felt damp once again.

'Let's not go back just yet,' said Jean. 'Let's take a bus, a trolley, a tram, somewhere, anywhere.'

They weren't sure which bus it was that they got on, or in which direction, but they ended up at a large and busy intersection, crowded with people and automobiles.

'This is crazy,' said Audrey, with panic in her voice. 'What are we doing? We need to get back now. What if we run out of money?' All her sentences came out in a rush.

'Audrey's right,' said Joe firmly. 'We have no idea where we are.'

'It's not so hard.' Jean pointed to a street sign. 'Look, this is Geary Street, and there – that's Fillmore Street. What's more, it's only nine o'clock. Maureen and Tony won't be worrying about us for a few hours yet.'

Ed had his arm around a nervous-looking Audrey. 'I think I've heard about this neighbourhood,' he said, glancing about. Ed played clarinet in the high school dance band and occasionally read the music papers. 'It's the jazz area.'

Sure enough, in the neon lights of the mid-evening, people gathered on the sidewalks outside open doors through which the sound of saxophones drifted on the air.

To the surprise of all of four of them, there were people of many races – women with elegant gowns and furs, men with sharp suits and ties – talking and laughing and going downstairs to places Jean yearned to discover.

'Hey, kids. Wanna have a little fun?' A man, not at all elegant and looking a lot like Tony in his shirt sleeves, tilted his chin. Several men around him stood smoking, and Jean was confused by the smell. The four walked quickly past him, shaking their heads.

'No? You sure?' he mocked, as the people around him laughed at them too. Jean stared. What sort of fun was he offering? She reckoned he was thinking that they were hick kids who had somehow wandered into this area by mistake; sometime soon, she would not be a hick kid.

As they walked north, mostly ignored, Audrey began to lose her nervousness.

'Maybe we could eat Chinese food,' said Audrey. 'I'm getting hungry.'

Lake View had a Chinese restaurant but because their parents very rarely patronised restaurants neither did they – just drug store counters for sodas and milkshakes. If they ate here, then they would have tried – in one day – two new cuisines.

'I know,' said Joe, pointing at a line of people boarding a bus, 'let's get on that. It says North Beach, so maybe that will be nearer to Tony's. Their place is near the beach.'

Anxiously, they climbed aboard and the bus lurched off at a faster pace than the trolley. The other passengers

– seeming poorer than the glamorous club patrons – looked them up and down wearily, registering their youth, Audrey's self-conscious dressed-upness, and Jean's bedraggled frock which flapped around her in rumpled creases.

'Those are Chinese restaurants, look!' Ed pointed out of the window at a wide lantern-strung street decorated with bright neon dragons and pagoda-style roofs. One huge vertical sign offered Chop Suey.

'Shall we get off then?' he asked no one in particular, turning his head around quickly for someone or something who could stop the bus. But he was too late; the bus had already passed through Chinatown and having just stood up, they had to sit down again.

The passengers raised their eyebrows and sucked their teeth. In ones and twos, they were leaving the bus and soon it shuddered to a halt. Now, at the terminus, they could see a completely different sort of city, a much scruffier and darker place. They trudged up a hill, hoping that they would be able to get a clearer sense of their location. There was a looming tower, closed at that time, though the view was stunning, lights sparkling everywhere. They had no idea where they had ended up. Dispirited and tired, they walked back again.

Suddenly, they were right by a huge mural painted on the side of an old building, a scene of the city with bridges, industry, men in naval uniform, women operating machinery. The colours were rich and luscious, reds, blues, greens, and yellows all picked out. It was beautiful.

'Oh!' Jean's mouth fell open at the scene. She only knew art as being in set spaces – small and refined – not robust and literally larger than life. She stood transfixed.

'What are you doing?' she asked a small woman, wearing dungarees and tennis shoes, her long hair in braids. She was one of several people filling in small sections of grey on a very large train. A bright light, powered by a noisy generator, allowed them to see what they painted.

'No one wants murals anymore. The city is destroying them. But we are putting them back, covering the walls with what they have destroyed in the high-hatters' clubs. And if they don't want them, they'll have to tear the buildings down too. This will be too difficult for them to clean. And if they want to send us to jail, well, let them.'

Ed and Audrey seemed to have lost all interest in the city and simply wanted to go. Joe bit at his lip with annoyance.

'Come on, will you?' said Joe. 'We need to get back. We're lost. This could be anywhere.'

Jean disagreed on both counts. This was somewhere, and she wanted to know exactly where that was. But he took her arm and pulled her along with the rest of them.

'Montgomery Street. There,' he said irritably. 'That's where we are. Montgomery Street. Could be anywhere.'

They walked further down the street, soon finding the Black Cat Café where light filtered through the blinds and noisy conversation spilt out of the door. While they wondered what to do next, a couple of men came out to stare. Others came to see what the fuss was about, and one of them whistled.

'Don't look, don't look,' said Ed. He was a very attractive boy and blushed as a man in the doorway let his eyes linger on his body. They all looked though, even Ed himself, though he clutched at Audrey for safety.

A woman of around their mothers' age, sharply dressed in a man's suit and tie and with very short brown hair, came to the door.

'You kids are lost, aren't you? Where d'you wanna go?'

'Uh, the Sunset district,' said Ed.

'Sunset,' she put her hands on her thighs, bending down and laughing raucously in a way that reminded Jean of Laffing Sal. 'Oh good Lord above, the Sunset! That's sure a long way from here.'

Joe, Ed and Audrey all shrank away, but Jean didn't see anything to scare her.

'There's no need to be so mean. How do we get back there?' asked Jean firmly.

'Okay, kid. You don't want Shirley Temple' – she pointed at Audrey – 'left to her own devices in these parts.' She laughed lasciviously, a reaction so unexpected that all of them stayed rooted to the spot.

'All right,' she continued, stroking her hair down by both temples. 'I am a gentleman and so I am going to be of some assistance. Do you see that tram stop there?' she waved her hand in its general direction. 'It will take you to Market Street. Then you need to ask the conductor the method of transportation you need to take from there. Which part of the Sunset is it, honey?'

'I'm not telling you,' said Jean firmly. The woman burst out laughing again.

'What's so funny?' Jean retorted.

'Why, nothing at all.' The woman turned her laughter into a wry smile. 'You're a game girl. Now get over to that tram stop because it's already past your curfew and it takes a while to get where you're going.'

They all stayed silent on the way back, staring out of the window distracted by their thoughts. Even when they had to change onto the trolley, they said nothing, Audrey's quest for Chinese food forgotten by them all. Ed and Audrey sat close together, her head on his shoulder; Jean and Joe were on the same seat, but far apart. He had not protected her. If anyone had been a protector, it had been Jean and all of them knew it.

Jean lay wide awake, staring at the ceiling and wondering how her life would go from this point on. She felt... free. She wasn't free, of course, she knew that. But the future was spread out in front of her, so exciting that she thought she would choke.

All the things she had seen! All the people! Everyone so different to what she was used to in Lake View. Jean sat up and pulled her bare knees towards her. If only she could turn back time so that the young journalists' society could ask what her ambition was. Well! Her entry in the yearbook would have been so very different.

She would come here, to San Francisco. Where else?

This was her future. No more sock hops, no more coaxing little kids to depict their tiny houses in poster paint, no more sitting in church being told how to live her life. No. And if this couldn't happen now, this month, this year, then it would be next year and the year after and the year after that. This trip marked the end of her beginning. She had become an adult – if not yet legally, then in her heart, her soul, her mind.

She turned on the bedside lamp as Audrey shifted slightly in the next bed. Jean leaned down to the other side of her bed and grabbed her sketchbook and pencil. She would draw some of those scenes from memory. Sketch after sketch flowed out of her and by seven the next morning, when Audrey opened her eyes and smiled sleepily before turning over to doze some more, she had filled her book with drawings. Of her friends, of jazz musicians, the Chinese restaurant, trees on the far side of the beach, people raising their hands on the top of the Big Dipper. Her pencil had almost worn down to nothing. She did not even care whether or not they were any 'good'. They represented 'her' in some indefinable way.

Still, she did not feel tired. The sun had completely risen and the room was bright. But oh the sheer thrill of it. The combination of doing something she wanted to do while at the same time being somewhere that seemed like the most exciting place in the world. Jean had drawn so many times before, of course she had. But this would be absolutely and entirely different. A switch had been turned on not just in her brain but in every part of her. She was becoming herself.

CHAPTER FOURTEEN

LYNNE: SWINDON, ENGLAND, JUNE 2018

The air in the garden was still and fragrant, giving every sign of an unexpectedly peaceful summer morning. Lynne looked over at her mother, relaxing on a picnic chair as she read the *Daily Telegraph*. Barbara's newspaper of choice was not her children's, who preferred something more liberal in its politics. Victor and his parents had both taken the paper; she continued the tradition without thinking about it.

'It's hot today, isn't it?'

Barbara looked like a sweet old lady, white-haired, overall a little smaller than she used to be. But nothing sweet about her remained; she now seemed sharp, prickly, difficult. Lynne had only been allowed to return to the house on the condition that she 'stop this nonsense'. She felt manipulated by her mother and there had been forgiveness on neither side.

'Make sure you drink that fruit juice,' Lynne continued, pointing at the ice-filled glass on the table. 'It's easy to get dehydrated in this weather.' The unusual warmth meant that they were both sitting outside in the garden, shaded by next door's overhanging tree. Lynne knew of cases across Europe of old people dying due to the heatwave, and this increasing anxiety around her mother made her nag and hover. She realised Barbara found that irritating.

Her mother looked over the top of her reading glasses. 'You aren't my carer,' she said. 'So stop nagging me. I will drink when I am thirsty.'

'But you might need a drink whether you feel thirsty or not.'

Sighing, she drank half the juice, and banged the glass on the table.

'Too much sugar,' she said, taking up her newspaper again.

Had her mother ever been like this before, Lynne wondered? She only remembered an easy-going, warm-hearted, energetic person. The ethereal and depressed version of Barbara – a wraith she remembered from her earlier childhood – had long been superseded by the bright and vibrant one. It was as though the earliest memories of her mother were imaginary. Not even ghostly; it seemed unlikely they had ever existed. But this Barbara, she shuddered with fury and more presence than seemed possible at her age.

'You'll be sorry when I'm gone,' she said quietly, looking up and glaring. Lynne gasped and turned from the pleasant warmth of the garden into the airlessness of the house. How could she? Lynne's guilt and fury twisted, and kept on twisting, back and forth, into a wave of cold anger. Not that the guilt had entirely disappeared, of course, or the feeling that she was lucky to still have her mother when so many didn't.

The doorbell rang, revealing a courier with a small package to sign for. Had she ordered anything, she wondered briefly. Had Barbara? It was a large cardboard envelope for her mother, which she presumed must be some kind of publication. Barbara never stopped wanting to learn. Her interest in the theory and practice of yoga, in all its various manifestations, never ceased to amaze Lynne. She went back into the garden and handed her mother the envelope.

'For you,' she said, turning back towards the house. Her mother tugged the tear-off strip on the packet;

Lynne heard her swearing as she did it. Then, all was quiet. After a few moments, Lynne looked out of the kitchen window to see her mother sitting back in her chair, so pale as to be almost blue. Her chest rose up and down rapidly, as she took short breaths, panting.

'Mum,' she rushed out. 'What's happened? Mum.'

Barbara held on tight to the packet, to the side of which, with eyes closed, she clutched three photographs and a piece of paper that Lynne assumed was a letter.

'Oh my God.'

Lynne grabbed her phone and called for an ambulance.

The paramedics, very kind and very young, took Barbara to hospital for observation. She was too old for anyone to take any chances despite extraordinarily good health for her age. Normally, people aged ninety-in-a-couple-of-weeks would be on any number of medications and spend much of their waking hours being treated for this and that. Mrs Pendleton had won the genetic lottery. Of course, there was the yoga too. If only everyone could be so sensible.

This was not a stroke or heart attack. Her blood pressure was not worryingly high, or low. Instead, she had had a shock. Barbara was kept on a trolley, in a curtained-off cubicle, while Lynne held one of her hands. Her mother seemed half asleep, more than half, but she still seemed to be pulling away from her grasp. Lynne, in turn, did not see how she could prevent herself from speaking about these events, not when it was so blatantly clear that the pictures had caused this collapse.

'Why won't you tell me about it, Mum? Who are they?' Barbara had been unable to stop Lynne from taking the photographs. The first, she thought must be a picture of her parents at their wedding, but, no – they were too old. The next showed a picture of two little girls who were not Cathy or herself, and the third photograph was of a man, wearing a loud checked suit and 1970s moustache, who was definitely not her father. They meant nothing to her.

'I don't know,' she lied. Barbara had held on firmly to the envelope with the letter in it and tucked it firmly under her leg where no one could get at it.

'Mum, please! What happened? Who are they?'

Barbara turned her face to the wall.

'I can't do it anymore,' she said. And with that, her eyes flickered shut.

Barbara's children felt fortunate that they had decided to live within a reasonable distance of Swindon. As adults, none of them wanted to make their homes there – it was handy for the motorway, and a good commuter town – but why live there rather than Oxford, like Nick, or a picturesque village with 'on' or 'under' as part of its name, like Cathy? Lynne had lived in several parts of England during her career as a social worker – Wolverhampton, Bury, Great Yarmouth – but without any strong bonds to any of them, was happy enough retiring back home.

When 'observation' for Barbara extended into an overnight stay, Cathy and Nick rushed straight to the hospital. By the evening, she had been there for eight hours, and patient, loved ones and hospital staff were hot and irritated.

'What happened?' asked Nick, distracted by the aftermath of endless meetings. Lynne stressed to both her siblings that their mother had experienced no more than a shock, and she was recovering. Nothing more. The three of them crowded around the bed, elbowing their way through the unwieldy curtains that constituted a flimsy separation from the next cubicle. Barbara was going nowhere, not to a bed in a ward, because there weren't any available and not back home yet, on the off-chance that she got worse. In fact, she was calmer and dozing, something Barbara was glad to do as it meant she did not need to speak.

Lynne looked at Nick and shook her head. 'She's going to be fine. Something came in the post that she wasn't expecting.' She mouthed 'no' at Nick, as she shook it again. He glared back.

'Right,' he said tersely.

Lynne had grabbed Cathy earlier. She'd been in her shop that day and came as soon as she heard. 'Do you recognise any of these people?' Lynne asked her sister. 'Something about them, or about the letter she won't show me, shocked her so much that I called an ambulance.'

Cathy glanced at the photographs for two seconds, before thrusting them back. 'No. Who are they?'

Lynne shrugged. 'No idea. I wondered if you... But then, why would you?'

'Leave it, Lynne.'

'Don't worry, I intend to.'

A couple of hours later, Lynne and Cathy returned to their separate homes, while Nick stayed with his mother for a while longer. Barbara was warm with him, smiling, while he went to fetch her tea and watched over her carefully as she ate a yoghurt he'd bought in the hospital shop. He had also found a fan from somewhere, and it was whirring steadily in the corner. She was, as they say, comfortable. Nick could be trusted not to talk about anything difficult.

Rachel texted Lynne soon after.

I've talked to Mum. Call me when you can. R x

Lynne was so relieved. When and how had her niece become her ally?

'Rachel, hi. Gran's fine. It was just a scare, a shock.'

'I'm going to visit when she gets home. But wasn't it an awful shock for *you*?'

Lynne started to cry, panting in a similar way to her mother.

'It was awful. I thought she'd had a heart attack, a stroke, a fit, something terrible.'

'What exactly was it? Mum was a bit vague.'

'There was a letter, which I haven't seen. And some photographs. Why don't you go on Skype and I can show you.'

The two women looked at them closely. The first one showed a couple, a man and a woman, with a small child on the woman's lap. The photograph was in black and white, a carefully posed family grouping, with the man turned slightly towards the woman and child. He smiled warmly; the other two looked towards the photographer. The adults appeared to be in their thirties.

Lynne and Rachel shared an expression of confusion.

'Is there anything on the back?' Rachel asked.

'It's a scan,' Lynne replied. 'So, no.'

'But these two,' she continued, 'are the originals.'

The first was of two young girls, perhaps six and ten, laughing as they ran out of the sea towards the camera. Their one-piece red and blue bathing suits were functional rather than cute, and sand clung to their wet skin. The sun sparkled on the sea and children played in the background. A family day out, then, and perhaps it had been kept on display because the whole photograph was slightly pink.

'Do you know who they are?' Rachel asked.

'No idea.' Lynne brought out the other picture. It showed a man aged around forty, his shoulder-length hair brown, with sideburns and a moustache to match. His suit – brown, and lighter brown checks on a whitish background – looked very garish to Lynne's eyes.

'What about this one?' she asked her niece.

'I think my dad owned a suit like that.'

'Yes, I remember. But it isn't him.'

'No, they don't resemble each other in any way.'

'So what are you going to do?'

'Nothing. I can't do anything. Gran won't let me. And I'm not going to risk a repeat of what happened today.'

Lynne observed Rachel's disagreement written across her face, along with her attempts to work out what to say next.

'We can't even really work out when they were taken. I mean the black and white one is more recent than Victorian, but I wouldn't know if it was 1920 or years later. When did women wear skirts just below the knee? And the others. Sixties? Seventies?'

Lynne thought for a while.

'We both remember your dad wearing those clothes, so seventies, but I don't recognise the girls. My swimsuits had frills until I started secondary school, so perhaps they are younger than me.'

'Take them to a local history museum,' Rachel said firmly. 'See what they say.'

'But what about Gran?'

'Don't tell her. Copy the photos yourself and take them to the museum.'

Lynne sighed. 'It seems... underhand.'

'But what if they are threatening her, I mean actually, not just in her head. And even if it is just in her head...' Rachel paused. 'I've got a friend with experience in this sort of thing. Not an expert, exactly, but who has more knowledge about old photographs than we do. Scan them in and send them to me.'

'Good plan, Rachel.'

'You know what else I am going to do?'

'What?'

'I'm going to do our family tree. Not with DNA, I mean, but I am going to take a good look at who might be in Gran's family in case there are any clues. She clearly recognises them. Do you think any of those people look like her?'

Lynne scrutinised them for a few moments.

'Could be. Perhaps I have been staring at them for too long. I'll scan them and you look.'

Another text. *I think they do look a bit like Gran. But let's see what my friend says.*

The next morning, Lynne drove to the hospital to collect Barbara. She stared at her daughter.

'Don't, just don't,' she said sternly. Lynne pressed her lips together and nodded.

'Shall I get you an ice cream?'

'Yes. And if you don't stop fussing, I'll die just to spite you.'

CHAPTER FIFTEEN

The screen turned black as Karen stared and stared at her laptop, lost in thought.

After Lynne dropped her – she really needed to stop taking things so personally – Karen felt crushed. The problem was that work made her feel good, like she exerted at least some control over her life. Not to mention the absolute and constant need for some, *any*, regular income. But she didn't have superhuman levels of motivation. So that was why when, after she had finished writing reports for Anna, she was relieved to be offered more work as a freelance probate researcher.

This amounted to an in-depth genealogical investigation into people who had died without a will and whose nearest blood or legal relatives, aka 'rightful heirs', needed to be found. If they weren't, the estates (often fairly small amounts of money) would go to the government. What, in this parlance, was called 'The Crown'. These days, big companies competed for the largest and easiest estates, so she only took on the smaller and more difficult cases.

Who would be the rightful heirs to her estate, she reflected? If she had an estate, of course. Well, she *did* have an estate. But only a tiny one, far too small to interest probate researchers. Her possessions amounted to some furniture (from Ikea); a lot of books – none valuable; a Student Journalist of the Year Award from decades ago; a pretty good bike which Ben had given her; and some once-expensive work suits. No property; no money left in the bank despite decades of so-called careers.

Lisa would be the rightful heir to her estate and that was all right. Anna and Ben could have some of the books if they wanted. Then... she suddenly realised. Her closest relative, her next of kin, would be her mother. Hmm: less satisfactory. Marian would probably dump the lot, sending someone else to clean out the flat. Her mother approved of nothing about Karen and whenever they met, Marian found something new to criticise. In particular, she hated Karen's bisexuality. It had been surprisingly easy for both of them to break off contact.

Still, spending money she barely had on getting a will was no more than a waste. Karen didn't care enough about the fate of her not-yet-vintage clothes. Or the Perspex award in the shape of a globe that once took pride of place on her mantlepiece. Now, it sat in a box on the top of the wardrobe.

But this should be a good day, one to prepare for another big tranche of work: a week teaching on a genealogy course, involving lectures on historical context, visits to archives, expeditions to graveyards and a probably endless round of individual consultancy and mentoring. Her brain needed to be clear and uncluttered, and she willed the prospect of work to energise her as it usually did.

The phone rang, shaking Karen out of her ruminations. It showed a number she didn't recognise. After a nano-second wondering if someone was going to scam her, she answered.

'Dr Copperfield?'

'Yes?'

'My name is Rachel Wilson and I am the niece of Lynne Pendleton, who was your client earlier this year.'

'Right?'

'I know that she stopped looking for her birth father after pressure from her mother, my grandmother. But other things have happened now, and I wonder if you would take me on as a client instead?'

Rachel paused.

'Please say yes. I can tell you why.'

'All right then!' Karen smiled. 'Tell me why.'

Rachel took a deep breath.

'Last week, someone sent my grandmother a few photographs and she reacted so badly that she ended up in hospital. We – that is Auntie Lynne and I – don't recognise the people in them and we can't tell where they were taken. Everyone has agreed that we won't talk to my grandmother about it. But of course, we are really worried. We don't know who the people are. And then there's the letter. She hasn't let anyone see that.'

'I see.'

'We agreed, me and Lynne, that I would take up the investigation, not her. After all, I was the reason everyone took these bloody tests in the first place and it isn't fair that all the flak from the family is directed at her.

'Plus, we are concerned about my grandmother. She's gone downhill since January. She's dropped her yoga teaching and stopped going out. The doctor has prescribed her antidepressants but she refuses to take them. Something really bad happened but she won't tell us what.'

'What do the rest of your family think?'

'Honestly? We haven't told them.'

Karen rubbed her right index finger across her mouth, her habit when she needed a few seconds to think.

'Look. I'm about to spend a week away. Let's talk again when I get back. From my point of view, I am a bit concerned about your grandmother and the conflict within your family. I don't want to add to it.'

But the money, she thought to herself. Stop being so *ethical*. You can't afford it. Anyway, what did ethics mean in this situation? Whose secret was this? Who had the right to know?

'There was something else. I have spent the past few days trying to teach myself genealogy and I made a family tree for most of my close relatives. That was easy. I found everyone with no problem. But not my grandmother. As far as I can tell, that's because you can't get much information online from the British Columbia Vital Statistics Agency. You have to write to an office address. Unbelievable.'

Karen smiled to herself at Rachel's expectation that every single thing could and should be done online.

'Anyway, Lynne has the original birth and marriage certificates and sent me the scans, but I can't find my grandmother's parents. She always said they died in a fire, but I can't find anything that matches up.'

'Don't worry about that too much. There are various reasons why that might be, some of them very mundane.'

'Should I take a DNA test?'

'How would your mother feel about that?'

'She would object, no question.' Rachel sighed. 'I don't see eye to eye with her on many things. She has never logged into her Ancestry account, though, not since she got the results. If she does, I'll cross that bridge then.'

'But also, there's probably not much point. You are one further generation away from your grandmother and so the DNA overlap between you and her will be only half of what your mother's is.'

'Oh,' said Rachel, disappointment colouring her voice.

'And you aren't so worried about the identity of Lynne's biological father?'

'Surely the two things are connected? My grandmother has never told us much about her life before Lynne was born. But what was easy to cover up sixty or seventy years ago... Now it's just as easy to uncover it.'

'Not *always* easy. But sometimes. Often.'

Karen cast her mind back to what she had found in the few days when Lynne had hired her. She knew any family tree researcher (whether related to Barbara or not) would discover what she had and suspect what she had suspected, but could not prove without more work. This family would do it with or without her. But with Karen's involvement, it would all happen much more quickly and perhaps she could make it a bit less painful.

Fair enough. She would say yes.

CHAPTER SIXTEEN

JEAN: NEW LAKE CITY/SAN FRANCISCO, AUGUST 1947

It was a little too warm for her new cornflower-blue linen suit. Still, Jean knew that wearing it gave the right sort of impression – to her parents, to anyone looking at a young woman off to make her way in the big city, to any disrespectful men whose first thoughts might have been... off-colour. In it, she appeared a serious person, someone to be reckoned with, not a silly little co-ed.

'All aboard,' said the bus driver. Jean smiled to herself: they really did say that. She waved enthusiastically at her parents and brother, posed beside the door. They were the very picture of a family grouping, a staged photograph. But a sad one, because things would never be the same again and nothing could be done about that.

Joe had stormed off in a huff earlier in the summer, unable to dissuade her from moving away from home to pursue what he described as 'a pointless and expensive waste of time, designed to force my hand'.

The way Joe had made her need for experience and adventure to be about him, rather than her desire to be an artist, had ended it once and for all. Their friendship, their romance, which he had presumably thought she wanted to end in an engagement; all that was over. But she missed him. They'd had many good times together but once he had decided it was over between them, he had soon taken up with Noreen Glass.

Jean took off her cornflower blue hat, placing it carefully in the luggage rack above. It was too heavy for comfort, its brim extending a full nine inches around her face, as though she was balancing a huge plate on the crown of her head. Nevertheless, she was proud of it.

'Off to school?' said a much older man from across the gangway. 'That's right,' said Jean curtly, not wanting to encourage conversation.

'Well, don't get too fancy,' he said.

Jean dug her fingernails into her palms.

'Oh, I won't.' She slid a magazine out of the dressing case she'd placed in the centre of the seat beside her.

'I know all the joints in town,' he continued. 'We could take in a show.'

'Thank you, but I will be staying with my aunt.' This was a lie, but how else would she shut him up? They had several hours to go if he was also travelling into the city, and she particularly wanted to be alone with her thoughts. Perhaps the suit was attractive in ways she had not considered.

She turned her face towards the window and closed her eyes, trying hard to block any awareness of the man staring at her.

On one hand, Jean was so stupidly, ridiculously excited about this new step in her life; spending the last year at the local college, learning how to draw and draw and draw some more, she'd felt like a car with its brakes on. She wanted to speed away, roar off into her future.

That meant hurting the people she loved: in particular, Mother and Dad, who didn't want her to go anywhere and couldn't understand why she needed to leave the area. There were ways of being an artist without leaving home, they thought, and in any case, she had done so well in her part-time job teaching art to the younger ones. And Joe. He was not someone she had wanted out of her life, but he didn't understand her and wasn't interested in understanding her either. He had been a good pal as well as her high school sweetheart. That was his role and that was where he would stay: in her past.

But her mother, who had wanted to go to college and whose parents had not allowed her to, understood – at least a little. That was why she had bought her such an elegant suit. It was a sign of Jean reaching maturity, and she loved her mother for recognising that. Jean herself had bought a suitcase which she had filled with Levis, peasant blouses and saddle shoes, but a girl could always use something genuinely chic.

Oh, but she did love drawing, and she wanted to do it night and day. Other than that, she had tried oil painting, watercolours, clay sculpture, fashion design and jewellery making, and she would be trying them all some more. She was good and she was going to get much better.

When the bus reached the terminus, Jean grabbed her bag and got off as quickly as she could. She could feel the man's eyes looking at her hungrily and she didn't like it. Men had looked at her before but travelling alone she was unprotected in a way she did not recognise. The man knew this, of course. But soon she was in a taxi off to the women's dorm and the level of protection her parents considered appropriate. Men were only allowed in the building before dinner, they could not visit the girls in their rooms and the girls had to sign out if they were asked out to dinner elsewhere. Jean didn't care a bit; she wanted to meet serious girls and the boys would have an appropriate place in her life when the time came.

The house mother took Jean up to her dorm room, which she would be sharing with Betty, a thin, dark-haired girl with glasses. Betty sat in a hardback chair plucking at the strings of a guitar, her clothes – a white blouse embroidered with tiny roses and grey pleated skirt – underlining her innocence. Betty sprang up out of her seat to shake Jean's hand, a smile suddenly popping onto her face.

'I'm so glad to meet you,' she said. 'I've been wondering who I'd be sharing with.'

Their two beds stood on either side of an already narrow room, with around four feet of space between them. At the end of the beds were matching desks, chairs, and reading lamps. At the other end, near the door, twin wardrobes and matching bookshelves were jammed in as well but at least, if they slept facing the window, they could see the trees whose branches seemed to be making their way into the room. Despite the lack of space, most of their belongings were still in transit.

Jean had a moment of panic. Immediately, she could see that Betty was also panicking, and probably for the same reasons.

'We need some flowers, or some pillows, or a calendar. Anything to decorate this room. It looks like we are in an institution,' said Jean.

'Yes I know,' said Betty. She giggled nervously. 'Of course, we are though. In an institution I mean.'

'So how shall we make it feel like home?' Jean turned towards Betty who looked at her intently.

'Sports pennants, photographs, toys?' Betty said nervously.

'Tapestries, postcards, our own paintings.'

'Life-size sculptures of us by our lovers!'

'All of that,' Jean replied. 'Yes, all of that and more!'

The two of them laughed until tears came to their eyes. Everything would be fine after all.

A few days later, classes began. The lessons were not so different from what she had been taught back home. This first semester, they would be drawing a vast range of subjects and items, including landscapes. They would also be studying the history of art. Jean was looking forward to all of it. She was so aware of all the things she didn't know and couldn't yet do. Betty – who was taking technical drawing – would be taking other classes so they would only meet in the evenings.

It was on the first Thursday that she came across Johnny Costello, the school's star tutor, whose reputation had gone before him. This reputation was mixed. Of course, there was his work, which was the reason the school had gone out of its way to hire him. Jean had seen photographs of it – huge murals of people working: picking fruit, driving trucks, operating machinery. Her parents had seen his canning factory mural – not of their factory, or their town, but a fruit-canning place further south. Jean herself was too young to know what they had thought about it then, but when they saw the mural's photograph in the school brochure, they remembered it and told her it was probably in a courthouse somewhere. Jean herself supposed the colours were what made it and she was unable to appreciate them through the black and white of the brochure.

Costello's work had been very popular before the War, but he had painted nothing since. The social realism of the 1930s' murals had gone completely out of fashion. The Great Depression was over and no one wanted to see miserable depictions of the suffering poor, the like of which had been popular when he started painting. Now, there was peace and thank God for it. Everyone was happy these days, you bet they were, and looking to the future with unprecedented levels of hope. But he wasn't sure he wanted to look forwards, not to that future or any other.

Suffering was not the subject of Costello's murals; instead, he had painted strong and noble workers, proud of their jobs and happy to do them. He had been a New Deal painter, given money straight out of art school by the government, paid to cover public buildings with bright depictions of American prosperity. But that was another time, another era altogether. Ten years later, many people thought them Communist, something that made him laugh bitterly.

His murals were not what students knew best about him though. What was at the forefront of their collective minds was that he was 'troubled'. Costello drank. Of course, many artists did – that almost went without saying – but he was not a good drunk. Sometimes, he would throw things – pencils, brushes, screwed up bits of paper – at students whose art he did not consider up to standard. His standard. He contemptuously shouted things that were not suitable for young people to hear, and one boy's parents complained. Once, he had a fist fight with a homeless man, and there were all kinds of rumours as to what had happened and why. Who was the other guy? No one knew. At any rate, the event was hushed up by the school authorities and the police. The truth of the matter remained hidden.

Because he had served his country, been blown across a beach, and then spent weeks – he never knew how many – expected to die. A year later, after he had left the hospital, his broken bones more or less healed, the head injuries that had caused headaches, vertigo, and lapses in memory, under some kind of control, everyone thought that he would soon start painting again. But he had shown no signs of doing so. He had not even picked up a brush, or used so much as a pencil to draw preliminary sketches: even when eating, or tying his shoelaces, his hands would be steady, then they would start to shake. So for the moment, he had to do something and he preferred teaching freshmen with their unformed taste to seniors who might have opinions. He had an ex-wife and a young daughter to support and anyway, he couldn't bear to sit around doing nothing. His demons needed fighting and drinking just made them fight dirty.

So when Johnny Costello swept into the studio on the fourth day of Jean's life as an art student, his blue sailor's sweater tight over his muscular arms, she was not sure what she was seeing

'Good morning, ladies and gentlemen. This class is for drawing technique and I hope I will be able to cleanse you of any bad habits you may have fallen into. To become artists, muscular artists who will make a mark for their generation, you need to abandon what those spinster art teachers taught you at high school about delicacy and fine lines. No, you must be bold with your pencils and, later, even bolder with your brushes.'

He paused, narrowing his eyes, and moved his head slowly so that he could see all eighteen students looking at him.

'And, ladies, I know that most of you are here to find husbands. So be it. There are some fine fellows here. Others of you want to become teachers. Again, do so if you must. But I will not stand for any of your...' he screwed up his face with distaste '...your flimflam. You had better be muscular as well, doubly muscular if you truly want to be artists. Flimflam means failure, in this studio at any rate. Got it?' The few female heads nodded, not sure what else to do, whether they believed him or not, or were repelled or attracted by this arrogance.

Jean had never seen anyone like him before. Oh, but what a spectacularly handsome man he was He had blond hair – cut short for an artist – and eyes that almost seemed to be shutting on their own, screwing up as if the too-bright sun were shining right into them. He was very tanned, the wrinkles around his eyes deep and white, as though once he had smiled a great deal. Tall, broad like a football player, and almost fifteen years older than his students, Jean already knew that he had spent many months in hospital after the Omaha Landings. Back in '44, he was thought a war hero. To her, three years ago seemed like decades. It wouldn't to him, though, and she was perceptive enough to realise that.

'So, Miss Woods, what are your thoughts?' he asked

'What do you mean?' She spoke clearly, with no sense of intimidation.

'Do you draw flimflam? Or sturdy subjects in a way that encourages flimflammery?'

'I most certainly do not,' she said as staunchly as she could.

'I'm pleased to hear it.'

Jean could only imagine what he was talking about, and although she could see he looked very fine indeed, his character seemed pretty objectionable. Unpleasant, even. He turned his attention to another girl, whose reply was very similar to her own. What were they supposed to say? There were only four co-eds after all and he was in charge.

Costello pulled a sheet off a strangely shaped sculpture, which Jean thought seemed to be formed of jello that had not set properly.

'Today we are going to look at edges because looking comes before drawing. You need to learn how to see. So where are the edges in this... monstrosity?'

They looked and talked and then, later, began to take up their pencils to draw.

That day, it was Richard, the quiet boy sitting next to her in the studio, who started to grab her attention. It was his concentration that did it. He did not look at anyone or anything, seemingly unaware of them, then all of a sudden – when the studio time was up – he became someone else. Gathering up his sketches, a switch seemed to have been turned on and he smiled at Jean.

'That was good,' he said, pressing his elbows back towards his shoulders. 'Did you enjoy it too?'

'Yes, I think so, I needed to do more.'

'That's a grand feeling to end with.'

They walked over to the lunch stop, sitting on stools as they grabbed sandwiches and sodas, talking about their art, which of their fellows could be potential stars, and what they thought of their tutors so far.

In the afternoon, they went back into the studio and carried on drawing. The jello shape seemed stranger than ever, its edges more blurry. What was going on? Jean walked around it, trying to get an idea as to what she was seeing.

Then, sitting down next to Richard, she started drawing again. She was so wrapped up in this that she was entirely unaware of her surroundings. The paper, the shape and the edges; they were all she was, or wanted to see.

Hours later, when the caretaker wanted to close the studio, she and Richard were the only ones left in front of the shape. Suddenly, she looked at the clock. It was nearly time for dinner and she would be fined if she missed it.

She stood up abruptly, gathering all her art supplies to her.

'That was a productive day,' she smiled at him, as he too collected his things.

'Yes, it was,' he agreed, smiling back. 'And I am very pleased to make your acquaintance too. Perhaps we could meet for a proper lunch sometime soon? Tomorrow? My treat.'

'Well, all right, thank you.' Jean felt so full of energy, that she was not sure if she could stay still. She had to act, to rush. Richard looked at her retreating back and smiled.

Although it was not even four months since she had left for the city, Jean felt as if she had been away from home for a long, long time. She climbed aboard the railroad car and, until the air became too cold, she stood by the open window, watching the landscape of rural California chug slowly by. As soon as the train pulled into Lake View, she knew that this was no longer her home. She'd avoided coming back for Thanksgiving, making excuses about there not being enough time and having papers to hand in. On the day itself, lonely, she wished she had not lied.

Her father stood smoking as he waited for Jean outside the station; too old, she thought, for leaning against the car with a cigarette in his hand but doing it anyway.

'Jeannie, Jeannie,' he said, his arms around her, hugging her tight. Her heart swelled as she fought back tears.

'We have all been looking forward so much to seeing you!'

'It's grand to be here, Dad,' she said, hoping her doubts remained hidden.

He patted the bonnet of a light brown Chevrolet for which he had been waiting a year.

'The car finally arrived,' he said proudly. 'I reached the top of the list. Isn't she grand?'

'Sure is, Dad.' She smiled, inhaling the luscious new-car smell.

The house looked the same, of course; the pillars by the front door, the porch the width of the house, the trellis alongside, which, at the right time of year, would be covered in sweet-smelling vines. This was not the right time of year, but as she went into the house she could see the Christmas tree sparkling brightly in the small hall. Her suburban background saddened her, but then her spirits were immediately lifted by the candles on the tree.

'Hello, dear.' Her mother kissed her cheek and smiled. Larry punched her arm and she rubbed his shoulder.

'You look funny,' he said quizzically. 'It's your hair.' He thought for a moment. 'It's messy.'

'Well thanks a lot,' she laughed. 'I've changed the style,' she continued, twisting the ends with her fingers. 'This is how artists wear their hair, I don't put it in rollers anymore.'

Jean knew her mother disapproved of this change but she didn't make any comment, and Jean went up to her bedroom to start unpacking. The room's comforting femininity – the wallpaper with flowers, the soft quilt she'd finished herself, the pale, warm wood – all seemed so familiar and welcoming.

Shortly afterwards, they all sat down to dinner.

'Thank you, Lord, for the food you gave us, and for the gift of having Jeannie back with us again,' her mother intoned softly, her eyes shut.

Jean did not close her eyes; she looked at the familiar people and remembered that she had not said grace once since she arrived in the city. Why hadn't she? They didn't in the dorm, and, of course, they didn't at the diners, drug stores and lunch counters she visited with Richard, Betty, and all the other students whose acquaintance she was making. It simply had not occurred to her. She was sad, knowing this would be such a disappointment to her mother. Suddenly, she saw her father's eyes were open too, looking at her. She glanced away, embarrassed.

The conversation over dinner focused on the factory, Larry's progress at school, and how Dorothy was setting up a welfare clinic for the workers. When would they ask her about her own life? Perhaps the scant information she provided in her letters was enough.

'Are you enjoying school,' her father asked eventually, as he put down his cutlery at the end of the meal. 'Learning a lot?'

Jean nodded. Yes, she was enjoying it and learning a lot. What else could she say about it?

'Have you met any nice boys at school?' her mother continued casually. Jean knew this was what she really wanted to hear about, not her class assignments. She composed her features into what she hoped was the right sort of expression.

'No one special.' She paused. 'I have been on a few dates with a boy called Richard.'

'Urgh, that's horrible,' said Larry. 'You should have stayed with Joe.'

Jean sighed with irritation.

'When will you be seeing Audrey?' her mother asked. 'She asked me when you'd be back.'

'Soon, I think. But I expect she will be at work much of the time.'

'Do visit her there and buy an outfit,' Dorothy continued. 'She is selling some lovely party gowns.'

'I thought you disapproved,' Jean responded, twisting her lips.

'Not really.'

Surely Dorothy was not annoyed? Her rather testy response implied that she was.

'I always thought it was a good job for Audrey. That she'd enjoy it.' What did her mother want her to say?

Dorothy smiled apologetically.

'She does enjoy it. It was the advertisement, the one to which she originally responded, that irritated me. But I have seen her at work, and in church, and I know that she is doing exactly what she should be doing at this stage of her life. And besides, Goodman Maddox really does have some beautiful gowns that would suit you very well indeed.'

That night, Jean slept fitfully in her too-warm bedroom, used to her dorm room with its cold draughts. More than that, she missed Betty, her sleeping body just a few feet away, the other girl's steady breathing underlining that she was not alone but part of a community of artists. Jean valued Betty's gentle friendship. Now, just a few days before Christmas, she felt both alone and suffocated by her family's loving solicitude.

Goodman Maddox – the most substantial department store in the area – took up an imposing, 1900s-era building on Hall Street, the widest and busiest street in town. Its teen section was on the third floor, way up past ladies' fashions and cosmetics, and Jean took the softly carpeted stairs up to meet Audrey for lunch, apprehension pressing down with every step.

They only had forty-five minutes in which to leave the store – staff could not patronise the café or restaurant, and Jean could not eat in the staff canteen – find a lunch counter and eat. As always, Audrey's ability to walk very quickly and steadily on high-heeled shoes made Jean shake her head in wonder. Her own saddle shoes meant that she was shorter than Audrey; they had swapped heights and now Audrey towered over her. It was only when they reached the diner and were sitting on stools, that they were back on their usual level – Audrey a little slighter and shorter than Jean.

'So how are you, Jean? How are you really?'

'Enjoying life, painting, dating Richard.'

'Richard, eh? You haven't told me anything about him.'

'But there's nothing much to tell. He's just a boy, a classmate. I want to hear about you.'

'Do you, Jean? Because you don't write and I wonder what I have done wrong.'

'Nothing, dear Audrey. You haven't done anything wrong.'

There was the trouble. Audrey hadn't done anything wrong, but nor had she done anything particularly right either. She was in the same place and the same state of mind, as she had been twelve or eighteen months before, with identical interests, experiences and overriding ambition. That same one: Audrey wanted to be a good wife to Ed.

'So tell me, dear, how is your beloved?' Jean took a bite of her sandwich.

'Ed is grand, as you will remember if you have been reading my letters. He is working hard, enjoying his job, and we have both saved enough money to be married this summer.'

Tears came to Jean's eyes.

'I'm so happy for you. Really I am.' That was the trouble, or part of it. Jean was happy for Audrey and Ed, two people getting exactly what they wanted. Nothing grand or unusual, just a good life.

'I've told the manager that I will be married at the end of June. That's just before I stop being a teenager, so a good time for them to hire a younger girl.'

'Very organised!' Jean said tersely. Audrey stared hard at her friend.

'I wanted you to be my maid of honour! Should I ask someone else instead?'

'Oh, Audrey!'

Jean felt shaken, her emotions stronger than she had anticipated. She loved her friend and wanted to see her onto the next phase of her life.

'I would love to be your maid of honour! I'd be so proud to do that.'

She was surprised to realise how much she had missed Audrey. 'I'm sorry,' Jean whispered. Why had she turned away from her friend? She shook her head again.

'I suppose I have been wrapped up in my new life. It's what I want and I'm finding out lots about myself. Perhaps that has meant I have neglected the people that I love here. That includes you and I regret that.' Jean took Audrey's hand. 'That was already happening last year, even before I went away. I promise to be better. I do miss you.'

Audrey too began to cry.

'All right then. Apology accepted. But you'll need to help me choose my dress, and help with the other bridesmaids. Oh, lots of things.'

'Well, of course! That's part of the job, isn't it!'

The two of them giggled, as they had done so often over so many years.

'So tell me,' Jean continued, 'what's the exact date? What time of day? And what do you have in your hope chest?'

Christmas Day itself was bright and clear, and the family spent a happy morning in church. This was Jean's first time in church since August, and she dreaded telling her parents – or anyone in Lake View – about this. She hadn't exactly lost her faith, she had never actively had one, but church seemed so important to everyone else that she wanted to avoid the subject altogether.

But it was lovely to sing familiar carols – and oh! – the choir of little children, taught to sing by Audrey. What darlings they were with their adorable voices. Jean sensed warmth, love and fellowship for those few hours. The family ate a delicious dinner and exchanged gifts: a scarf, books, and a fur coat from her parents. A nightdress for her mother, driving gloves for her father, a baseball bat for Larry – all things she had bought at the last minute but which seemed welcome, nonetheless.

However, just three days later Sunday rolled around, with a visit to church expected once again. This time Jean decided she would actively refuse to go and had to steel herself against everyone's reactions.

Jean was still in her housecoat when the family pulled on their hats and scarves.

'I don't think I'll come with you this morning,' she said to her mother, who stared at her with an expression she could not decipher.

'Why?' she asked, more directly than Jean had anticipated.

'Well, it is only a couple of days since I went last.'

'That was Christmas Day and this is Sunday. It's not the same thing at all.'

'No...' Jean's guilt nagged at her.

'Please yourself. We need to leave now.'

Jean could feel the other two staring with disapproval and disappointment. She was doing something wrong, she knew.

Audrey telephoned in the afternoon.

'I thought you'd be at church today, are you sick? I'm worried you're overdoing it.'

Jean wondered what she could be overdoing but decided against telling her friend the truth.

'I am a bit. But really, it's nothing to worry about.'

'We have so little time to talk. You'll be going back in less than a week.'

They arranged to meet up in the evening, with Audrey coming for dinner. Jean was struck by just how well Audrey and her mother got along. The two of them seemed to be far better pals than she was with either. There was a feeling – what was it? Jealousy? Jean tried not to name it more precisely.

Then, soon, it was the last day of 1947. Jean ached with the knowledge that somewhere, in a city a few hundred miles away, some of her friends – including Richard – would be celebrating New Year's Eve with games and eating and laughter. Here in Lake View, however, they would be at a Watch Night service. There would be a potluck dinner, of course, but the main event would involve their attendance at church singing, praying, listening to sermons and waiting for the new year.

The whole thing seemed like a huge pretence. She had to go – what else was she going to do? But it was so different from last year. Even though she had known that things would soon be changing, her new life still hovered some way in the future. Now, however, it had begun.

At Christmas, Jean had hidden behind her parents while their, and her, friends came up to ask about the city, and did she enjoy school, and surely she would be wanting to marry soon and wasn't it rather a waste of money. Then, she had brushed off their questions, but with what felt like hours of chatting and then worshipping spread out ahead of her, she knew this would not be possible on this occasion.

Joe was there with Noreen Glass, no doubt a perfectly pleasant girl but not one Jean cared to know. They nodded, and Joe followed it up with 'good to see you' in a distant and unconvincing fashion. Jean's shoulders drooped sadly but Audrey rescued her, kissing her cheek. Ed just shook her hand.

'Why, hello, Jean.' It was Reverend Parry, the minister of their church, a serious-looking man of about forty who had always been kind to her and, indeed, everyone else. His singing voice was both strong and tuneful, its depth reflected in the way he spoke. She had avoided him this trip because she didn't want to face his questions. But now, it seemed, there was no getting away. He was holding a plate of meat pie and salad, as he took a seat next to her.

'How good to see you. Are you here for long?' Very politely, he forked some pie into his mouth.

'I'll be going back to the city soon.' She smiled.

'It must be very different from here.'

'Yes, very. It's so noisy and crowded.'

'And you are very busy, I imagine, what with all the new people to meet and all the classwork you need to do. I'm sure it seems very exciting.'

Jean's heart sank. She knew exactly what he was implying.

'Don't forget God, Jean,' Reverend Parry continued. 'He hasn't forgotten you.'

Jean looked down at her plate, empty now, seeing traces of mayonnaise streaked with the pink memory of beetroot. Her cheeks glowed bright red.

'We all miss you here. You were a good little helper with the children.'

She nodded slowly, not raising her gaze.

'Why don't you help out with hospital visiting before you go? The community needs everyone's involvement. Some people feel closer to God when they are serving others.'

He put his finger under her chin, and lifted it, staring into her eyes.

'What do you say?'

Jean smiled, but said nothing, as he stood up from the table and went to prepare for the service. Her fingers gripped tightly onto the underside of the rickety chair and did not let go.

As soon as she woke up on New Year's Day, Jean knew that she had to get out of Lake View. Right now. The rest of her family were all around the breakfast table, which made it easier to break the news.

'I'm going back to San Francisco today,' she said. 'There's some painting that I must finish before classes start again.'

Her mother sighed heavily.

'Don't go back yet, please, dear,' she said. 'We miss you. We are your family, and surely that counts for more than whatever art you are doing.'

Dorothy's pronunciation of the word 'art' was cutting. 'You can do it here. Please.'

There was a moment of silence.

'Besides, surely there are no trains or buses today.'

There were; surely, there were? Jean was no longer sure. Her mother's begging did not convince Jean, rather the reverse. Instead, she felt an urgent need to flee, even if she would have to wait another day. All the art materials in the world, everything her mother could provide, would not be enough to keep her.

Jean could not have been more pleased to see Richard when she arrived back in the city. Was it him, or the atmosphere of openness and creativity that she had craved? The art school was closed and would be for several more days, but the two of them took their sketchbooks out to draw from life. The weather was chilly and it drizzled, but they were happy wrapped up in their coats and scarves, only sometimes having to rub their fingers together to stop them going numb.

Then there were the movies. On Saturday night, the day before she knew Betty would be returning to their dorm room, Jean and Richard went to see *Road to Rio* and sat in the back row. It was four months since they had started dating.

Perhaps it was the film – a light musical comedy with Bing Crosby, Bob Hope and Dorothy Lamour, none of whom were especially sparkling in their roles – that led to a complete lack of romance between the two of them.

'What's wrong,' asked Richard as they left the movie theatre. 'Didn't you enjoy it?'

'It was all right. But listen, Richard, don't you like me?'

'I like you fine. What are you talking about?'

'We were surrounded by people kissing, but you didn't make a move on me at all.'

Suddenly, Richard grabbed her and pulled her towards him, kissing her firmly but inexpertly on the lips, his mouth clamped shut.

'Oh,' she said, rubbing her lips.

'Better?' he asked.

'I don't understand.'

With one arm around her back, he drew her towards him, pressing his forehead against hers before quickly moving back.

'No. I can't. I'm sorry.' He put his arm into hers. 'Let me take you back to your dorm.' They walked slowly, both stunned with embarrassment. At the entrance, he turned to her suddenly and said, 'I'm not a virgin, you know.'

'So what is it then? Am I not your sort of girl?'

'You're grand, Jean. It's me who's not right.'

He opened the front door for her, and while she stared back at him, he walked briskly away.

Betty arrived late the next afternoon, but with her parents and sister in tow so there was no opportunity for the exchange of confidences. Nor was there much time for Jean to brood about Richard and his strange behaviour as classes were to begin the next day with watercolour technique, taught by Adrian Nichols.

Richard was already in the studio when Jean got there, but he had chosen a different easel, far from hers. She looked at him, hurt and confused, but he did not meet her gaze at all.

Nichols, a tall, thin man of twenty-eight, did not trouble himself trying to win over the students, as Costello had done. He was a working painter, mostly portraits of society ladies, their children and dogs, and this had coloured his view of people. He had already become a misanthrope and thought everyone lazy apart from himself.

They all sat down with their brushes, paper and erasers, with minimal fuss from Nichols, who only occasionally came over to an individual student to discuss what they could be doing much better. Nothing seemed to please him and when it came to Jean's work, he simply sniffed and moved on to the next person.

Jean noticed something strange about her fellow students – especially the men – that was different. They were unfriendly, ignoring her. She asked another girl, Connie, what on earth was going on. Connie put her right straight away.

'It's obvious, isn't it. You're top of the class with better marks than anyone else. Girls aren't meant to do that. Johnny must like you and maybe the feeling's mutual.'

Connie was clearly no more pleased with Jean's achievements than were their male classmates.

'What a nerve,' Jean thought, more angry with Connie than with the boys. She had done well through talent and hard work. Costello didn't like her in that way, surely? He was so much older than she was.

A few days later, walking along a corridor looking down and with her mind on the precise colours of green in the floor tiles, she bumped into Johnny Costello. Bumped almost literally, as she could see his shoes approaching and they both stopped before they collided.

'Good morning, Miss Woods,' he said wryly.

'Mr Costello.'

'How are you getting on with Mr Nichols, Miss Woods? Are you enjoying his classes?'

Unaware of what might be the right answer, she said nothing. Costello laughed.

'Yes, I thought so. Well, you'll be getting me again in the fall and I hope you'll find that a little more to your satisfaction.'

'I expect so,' she said tersely.

'Work hard in the meantime,' he continued. 'Though you don't need my encouragement to do that, do you.'

He moved away, turning after a few steps to smile at her. What a strange man, she thought, touching her neck which had become unaccountably warm.

• • • ● ●• ● ● • • •

'A fan of Jackson Pollock, hey? Now that's unusual for someone like you.'

Jean looked up from her sketchbook. A woman stared down at her. She seemed to have thrown on a man's checked shirt and jeans, and her wild brown hair stuck out in strands. Jean bristled.

'What do you mean, someone like *you?*' Well, honestly! The nerve of it. 'Why wouldn't I like his work? This painting is fascinating.'

Jean was genuinely entranced by *Guardians of the Secret*, a large canvas that had been acquired by the gallery a few years beforehand. She was contemplating what the figures in it meant and why he'd used that precise shade of blue.

'Of course it is. But not everyone wants to understand it.'

'Well, I do. I'm studying his work: the colour, the meaning, the artistry, the ideas behind it. Why Mr Pollock does what he does and how he does it. Thinking about the way the new generation of young artists create their work and how it doesn't seem to be connected to what we are learning at school.'

'All right!'

Jean, who had been happily making notes and drawing tiny sketches alongside them, sprang up from her position on the floor as if preparing for a fight. The woman laughed, moving away a little.

'Don't hit me! I was just wondering. You're a student at the San Francisco School of Fine Art, right?'

'A painter,' said Jean firmly.

'A fierce painter, it seems, as well as a student,' she retorted, smiling. 'Now don't get cross, I'm happy to meet you.'

'Oh,' said Jean sarcastically. 'Why would that be?'

'Because you're real, you're serious, and you might have something. Besides, I'm at that school too, and students there aren't supposed to like abstract art! They need to be realists, able to draw exactly and precisely what is in front of them. So on both counts, we need to stick together.'

Jean stared at her in disbelief, the various parts of her statement swirling around her head.

'How on earth do you know what I do or don't have?'

'Your sketchbook there...' The other woman paused. 'Also, I've seen you about and you're keen. So why aren't you in the studio right now? Painters need to paint.'

'Because this is good. I want to see why it's good and what I can learn from it. There's a lot in it and I want to absorb it...' She turned towards the woman, prepared to be angry again but instead saw her looking open and friendly, even anxious.

'I'm Helena,' she said holding out her hand.

'Jean.'

They shook hands, Helena impressing Jean by the strength of her grip – neither too forceful nor too limp.

'The thing is, Jean, most girls... their paintings are small. They aren't ambitious, they want to be art teachers, not artists themselves. You're not like that. I can tell.'

Jean wasn't sure whether she should be angry or not at this odd woman's reactions. She wished she didn't feel flattered.

'How can you tell?'

'Listen, it's not some kind of magic. It's your commitment. I've noticed you in the studio, the hours you are there, the way you just paint and paint and seem to get lost in it. You're not here for a husband, are you?'

'Oh, I wouldn't mind.'

'You would mind. Don't look for a husband, please, not yet.'

'Why not?'

'Because it will be all about him. If he's an artist, he'll want you to say how wonderful he is, and how nothing you do will ever match up. He might say how much he admires you and how your work is impressive for a woman, but that doesn't mean he'll be happy when the washing isn't done and you leave sandwiches for dinner because you're in the studio again. If he isn't an artist, and that isn't likely unless he's a poet or a musician, and they're just as bad, then he won't understand you at all and will ask you to stop because he needs you, he can't live without you, and what he has to do is so much more important.'

'All right, I see your point.' Jean paused. 'Are you married?'

'Newly divorced!'

Jean burst out laughing.

'Well that makes sense,' she said.

'I was talking about myself,' Helena continued. 'Obviously.'

She half-sighed, half-laughed. 'Sometimes I wish I didn't have a sex drive.'

Jean's eyes widened, hoping her real feelings – she was impressed – weren't obvious.

'And you're a virgin. Well, well.'

Jean flushed, on the back foot once more.

'All right. Shall I leave you alone to worship at the feet of Pollock, or shall we carry on this conversation in a place which serves alcohol?'

The two women smiled at each other warily.

'But we can't go to a bar on our own!'

'Sure we can. At least, we can go to a bar where there are artists, some of whom are my friends who will stand us drinks.'

Jean smiled to herself. Helena was going to show her how artists behaved when they weren't in the studio. She felt she had been torn away from what she saw as her work, but only a little unwillingly, because she could always come back again tomorrow.

The whole place was small and dark, with men at the bar and people huddled together at tables around the edges of the room. It was too shadowy to see who was at those tables and the level of gloom was surprising when it was still light outside. Jean shuddered happily. Helena took her elbow and guided her towards a group of men at the bar.

'So, boys, this is Jean and she's a painter.'

The three men, all of whom were slightly older than her, looked at her as though she were a little girl blown in from Sunday school. One of them, a rugged, red-haired man, with green eyes, put his knuckle under her chin and raised it so their eyes met.

'Huh,' he said, letting it down again almost immediately.

'That's Hank Stillman, and I was married to him. For my sins,' she said bitterly, leaving Jean a little confused. 'And this is Mitchell. He has a lot of money and is spending it fast.' A tall pale man bowed at her seriously. He was already very drunk.

'Then this here is Jeff, and he's as serious about painting as you are.'

'Jeffrey Haslam at your service, miss.'

She looked across at a skinny, athletic figure, his long, light brown hair framing troubled eyes. Without even thinking about it, she knew he had served in the war. His appearance, though, was the type she found attractive; he raised his glass to her, less drunk than Mitchell, to be sure, and knocked it back. He was a little awkward, moving quickly and inelegantly, but she liked this awkwardness. She liked it a lot. He waved to the barman for more drinks, and beers were put down along their section of the bar.

'Whose side are you on?' he asked, staring deep into her eyes.

'I don't understand.'

'Sure you do.'

'Why does there have to be a side?'

'If you don't know whose side you are on, you don't know what sort of artist you are going to be. I mean, you aren't a social realist, are you? Or one of those ladies who paints flowers?'

Helena blew smoke in his face. 'Don't be like that, Jeff. I found her today studying Pollock.'

'Oh, you're one of THOSE. Well, that's just peachy, because so am I. So are we all.' He smiled at her and tipped back his beer.

'What if I wanted to paint flowers, what would be so bad about that?' Jean thought these superior-sounding people were simply horrible.

'What would be so bad about that?' he mocked.

'Let's go, honey,' Helena said. 'Someone must have said something bad about his work and now he's all twitchy and wants to take it out on someone. Jeff,' she continued, 'Jean is a student who's going to be really great someday as long as a man doesn't shit all over her first. She's still thinking about her direction, which is something you should have been thinking about yourself.'

The two women turned to go, but Jeff grabbed Jean's hand. 'She's right,' he said, almost too quietly to be heard. 'I spoke too soon, and I should have thought some more before I opened my big mouth. Don't go. I'd like to talk with you some more.'

Jean turned to Helena and shrugged. Helena shrugged back.

'Another drink, boys.'

Jean gulped her beer anxiously. She had never had so much as a sip of alcohol before; she was below the legal age, and anyway her parents and most of her community abstained. She was surprised to find that she liked both the taste and the warm sensation of it flooding her body.

'One thing you need to know about being an artist in this city,' Jeff began portentously, 'is that everyone is on some side or other. The art schools, and the teachers in those schools all hate each other. You are at the San Francisco School of Fine Art, and I went there too. We go for abstract expressionism, though most of our tutors don't. They painted social realist murals back before the war and can't accept that the world has moved on. Whereas at the Berkeley Art Institute, they accepted a lot of surrealists, refugees from the Nazis. They like abstracts now, but not in the same way we do.'

Jean felt lost; she wasn't sure what she was meant to think or, worse, what she did think.

'And they all hate each other, of course,' Jeff continued. 'Someone is always fighting with someone else or going back to New York because they can't stand it here. But our school is setting up special painting classes for veterans, so I have to give it that I guess. Some of their work is real good even if it's not what I'd do.'

'You were in the service yourself?'

'Yes.' He ran the back of his nail down her cheek very softly. 'I was in the navy for a while. Still can't swim though.' He smiled. 'Huh. Wish I could.'

'Time for another bar,' Mitchell shouted, and the five of them trooped out onto the street. It was dark now, and through the crowded streets, people pushed and shoved, laughing as they were. Jean was reminded that she had already been on the Fillmore with Jim, Audrey and Ed, and they had been frightened. She hadn't been frightened, but she had been sober; now she was neither.

By 2 am, when they had drunk more beer, the others in their group had melted away.

'Where's Helena?' Jean wondered plaintively. 'I really liked her, and I don't know if I'll ever see her again.'

'She's gone home, I expect,' Jeff said. 'But you'll see her again all right. She likes new kids like you, maybe she wants to be their mother. You're going to come home with me, right?'

'No. No!'

'Oh come on. Don't do this to me.' He stopped. 'Oh brother. You're a virgin aren't you?'

'Of course I am.'

'Of course I am,' he mocked again. 'Of course I am.' He sighed and rolled his eyes. 'Well, you won't be for much longer. But don't worry, little girl, you'll still be one tomorrow.'

Jean hugged her arms about her and looked at the ground. Why had this had to happen and ruin a great night?

'I'll put you in a taxi.'

And as the door slammed on her, and the cab drove off, Jean sank into the seat and cried.

Jeff was interesting, wiry, athletic, and his lips turned downwards at the sides in such a strange pout. He kept rubbing his eyebrow where, during the Italian campaign of '43, the tiniest piece of shrapnel had grazed it and left it permanently hairless. He alternately teased Jean about her small-town past and praised her work for showing something of the world that he didn't even know was there. They ate spaghetti and Chinese food; they drank beer and coffee and beer again.

'You're great, kid,' he said to Jean, rippling his fingers up and down her left arm. They kissed intensely in alleys and doorways and, because this was the fifth time they had been on what – in less bohemian circles – would have been a date, they both decided that enough was enough. Jean would go back to his apartment, and they would have sex. Jean had foreseen this and had signed herself out of the dorm for a night to stay with her non-existent cousin in Berkeley. She hadn't lost her wits, not quite, but she had an overwhelming sense of two things. One, that her virginity was something she needed to get rid of *right now* in order to be a woman. Second, her legs were almost collapsing under the weight of her desire. She had not felt this way before; the hours of kissing she had done with Joe subsumed in her memory into schoolgirl fumblings, feelings so mild as to have come and gone with no trace.

Jeff pulled her to him, and she responded more than willingly. 'Can we go back to your apartment,' she whispered.

A short walk later, they literally ran up two flights of stairs, flinging open the door, tearing off their clothes, and falling onto the bed. Their bodies touched and she could hardly believe how wonderful it was to feel another person's flesh on hers. The penetration part seemed quick. Too quick for her to know whether she liked it and to what extent. There it was, then. She was a virgin no longer, and it had taken what – five minutes?

Jeff collapsed on top of her.

'Sweetheart, are you okay? Did I do it right?' She wasn't sure that the experience should have been quite as abrupt as that.

'Uh-huh. You're great.'

Her body wasn't feeling particularly different to the way it had as they left the bar. She wanted him to touch her some more. Shouldn't there be more to sex than this?

'I think maybe I need to learn more, to get better. I think I need more practice.'

'Oh, honey!' He turned back towards her. 'You're a real dish. You don't need to practise.'

He kissed her neck, pulling away to comment. 'I think you did just fine.' He nuzzled her neck some more and began to stroke her breasts. 'Did you like it?'

Jean wasn't completely sure whether she had or not, but right at that moment, she liked it very much indeed.

'Oh yes, yes,' she said, losing herself in whatever the next few hours had in store.

Jean woke up late in the morning, stone-cold sober and suddenly aware of what she had done. Jeff had gone, leaving her a note. *Beautiful Jean. The milkman has been so you can have coffee and I think there is some bread. I have gone to see Mitchell and will find you later on.*

Calming herself down, she had breakfast and set out to find Helena.

'For the love of all that's holy! Why didn't you tell me about this before you spent the night with him rather than after?'

Helena seemed angry, but she wasn't really. More, she was worried about her friend and her evident naiveté. Everyone slept together these days because why would you deny yourself one of the greatest pleasures in life? There was no need to be prudish. Just because your mother, or your small-town sister, thought you should keep sex for marriage that didn't mean that they were right.

'I don't know.' Jean was shamefaced. She was meant to be a modern woman, a bohemian, but she hadn't considered the practicalities involved.

'You don't want a baby, do you?'

'Of course not!'

'Well, that could easily happen without birth control.' Helena looked at her friend sternly. 'You must know that. You don't think that if you jump up and down afterwards, or do it standing up, or if he says he'll *be careful* [two words spoken with such vitriol] 'that it doesn't matter. Any one of those can lead to you getting pregnant.'

'All right, all right! I got carried away.'

'Well, don't apologise to me. I won't suffer if you're in a fix. That'll be you.'

Tears started to fall down Jean's cheeks, and her friend moved to put her arm around her shoulders.

'I know a place you can go,' she said. 'I'll take you.'

Three hours later, Jean and Helena came out of a rather grand house which was – she now knew – *the* place for treating 'female troubles', or stopping those troubles starting in the first place. Jean had a bag containing a circular rubber item which was called a diaphragm and could be used alongside jellies that you could buy at any drug store.

'It works for me,' said Helena with a laugh. 'It's the best invention ever because you put it in yourself and you don't have to rely on *them* to do anything at all.' Helena explained that because the doctor had fitted it, it was a lot better than the things you could buy over the counter. The jelly was there to make doubly sure.

'Now we just have to pray that you aren't in the family way already,' she continued. 'And make sure the diaphragm is well-hidden in your dorm room. If the college authorities find it, then they could kick up a stink and maybe throw you out. Because, heaven knows, someone else might realise that they can have sex before marriage and nothing bad will happen!'

Still, there was no point in worrying about whether or not she was pregnant for the moment. It was too early for them to go to a bar and celebrate, although probably not too early for them to find one of their male friends already sitting there. So the two of them returned to college and their separate studio spaces.

Later, Jeff came to find her, looking thoughtfully at her work before pulling her away from it. Jean knew that she would not be able to spend the night again for a while

– she had to be back for dinner – but she wanted to try out her diaphragm.

Helena advised her not to tell Jeff what she was doing because men seemed to get a little queasy about the whole event, so she went into the bathroom and put it in without saying anything, adding some jelly.

Jeff took off her clothes in the manner of someone unwrapping a Christmas present and then lay her down on the bed as though he was going to first graze on her, then gobble her up. Sure enough, he began to lick her breasts and her stomach, stroking her between her legs before penetrating her. But as soon as he had done that, he withdrew rapidly, yelping loudly and turning his penis this way and that. He ran into the bathroom; Jean could hear the tap turn on and the sounds of water being thrown at something. A few moments later, he returned, a greyish towel around his waist.

'Jeez. You're using that freaking jelly, aren't you? I'm allergic to it.'

'Oh!' Jean was absolutely crestfallen, as though this whole plan would now fall through and her thrilling dreams would not come to pass.

'Look, honey. I can be careful. I mean I wasn't yesterday, I admit. But I can be.'

'But is that really...'

'It will be. I promise.'

He lay down next to her, and she realised that there would be no more sex this evening. Well, she supposed she could use the diaphragm without the jelly. He probably wasn't allergic to that too, and he would never know that she wasn't just relying on him.

CHAPTER SEVENTEEN

Just for once, Barbara contemplated her good fortune. Such a lovely day, she thought. The roses were tumbling over the fence, the honeysuckle mixing with them, scents combining in a glorious mix. Sunlight made patterns on the lawn and she watched butterflies moving in and out of the shade. This afternoon, the brightly coloured painted ladies would be busy creating a new generation of beautiful fluttering creatures.

Barbara had spent many years in this house and had always given special attention to the garden. For more than sixty years she'd lived here, in this enveloping warmth which now resembled her childhood home more than she would ever have anticipated. Her roots went deep here, and Victor's death bound them even more firmly.

She was well aware that all her family considered her in the early stages of dementia. That, finally, the diseases of old age had caught up with her. After the arguments of the past six months, they were treading on eggshells, thinking her fragile, her children remembering their early years when, to them, she had been just that. Broken. When the fear of being 'carted off' – that laughable term – remained ever present. Barbara realised that the modern world appeared kinder about these things, indeed many things, but she could not entirely believe in the changes. Did she have dementia? She didn't think so. Sometimes, she sensed that she was about to lose herself but then, somehow, she came back. This had happened in the past too, and oh how clearly she remembered that. She didn't want to blame herself for any of it. But there it was; she did.

They will all be here soon, Barbara mused, and she would need to pull herself together, bring herself back from her reflections on the past. Lynne fussed so much, and she could not help being irritated with her daughter. She would be happy to eat the cake, blow out the candles, but really – how could she have reached this age? It seemed quite impossible. Yet facts were facts; she knew the date.

If only they had never taken those tests. If only. Barbara closed her eyes, the sun almost burning her face. Soon, it would be too hot; it wasn't yet.

'Gee-Gee!'

Barbara opened her eyes as her great-grandson jumped down the two steps leading into the garden and ran towards her. She had not seen him since Christmas – *that day* – and he seemed to have grown a foot in six months. Oh, but she must never think this was his fault. She would dismiss that thought, dampen it down and swallow it. Danny knocked the chair as he kissed her cheek.

'Careful!' she said quickly. 'You're going to knock me sideways.'

'Yeah. Sorry!' He looked at her from the corner of his eye, in a way that, to her, was so obviously an assessment of her fragility. Danny took her hand.

'Happy birthday!'

She smiled. He seemed to be getting facial hair. Oh heavens!

'Thank you. I'm very old now, aren't I?'

Danny looked momentarily confused, trying to find the right answer.

'I guess. I mean yeah! Ninety is pretty old. Not that far off a hundred.'

Barbara shuddered, as though clearing the thought from her mind.

'No. Not far off at all.'

He looked at her, then took out his phone to take the first of many photographs. She stuck out her tongue. Click. He uploaded it to Instagram straight away. #greatgran #90 #family #birthday

Barbara smiled at him and shook her head.

'Why do they care? Your friends. I'm just an old woman.'

He looked down at his phone; the picture already getting likes and comments. Several people had added #cute and #OMGsocute. Danny grinned. 'They think you're cute, Gee-Gee.'

Barbara looked at him again, her face screwing up in a mixture of confusion and annoyance. She would not be cross with him.

'Because I'm old?' she said crisply. 'Believe me, there is nothing cute or sweet or adorable about being ninety.'

'Oh look,' Danny responded with relief. 'Here's Uncle Nick and he's brought Joe with him too.'

Nick's son Joe was – to Barbara's eyes – still a child, no older than Danny. The fact that he had recently become a lecturer in sports science; well, Victor would be proud. Barbara was bundled in hugs and smothered in kisses. She was loved; she could feel it.

Yet she knew – of course – that, out of her hearing, her descendants were arguing non-stop. She saw Cathy and Rachel through the kitchen window, Cathy wagging a finger at her daughter. What was that all about? The two were so different. Cathy reminded her of Victor's mother Marjorie; Rachel resembled Barbara herself; Amber – the absent great-granddaughter, new mother, too distracted, too poor, too *something* to make it back to England for this occasion – was more like Cathy. What would baby January be like? And why would anyone call their child *January* for heaven's sake? *April, May, June...* that would have been a different matter.

Cathy disapproved of the name, and she often told Barbara of her feelings. While Cathy agreed with her granddaughter over many things, she was uneasy over the way Amber had completely abandoned convention in favour of van life. The whole family agreed that Cathy felt jealous of Amber, who was doing the sort of things she should have, like taking the hippy trail that was so popular in her youth and still seemed slightly daring. Cathy should have left, Barbara thought. It might have suited her better than the life she had. Was leaving so very terrible? Well – she reflected – it wasn't *now*.

Finally, all potential guests had arrived and Lynne carried the cake out from the kitchen. It comprised a three-tiered confection like a wedding cake, deep layers of pink, yellow and white, with tiny green sugar leaves all over the sides, and darker pink swirls of icing in a froth along each of the edges. Surely none of her family could make something so extravagant? There were two huge candles pressed into the top – a nine and a zero – and more tiny leaves clustered in a decorative heap around them.

Then they were singing happy birthday. Barbara smiled; what a nice day. So why did she feel outside it all? Until six months ago, she had not experienced this distance for years. For more years than she wanted to count. But now, the gap between herself and others – any others, even people to whom she had been as close as can be – had come right back.

'Blow! Blow!' they all shouted at once and she screwed up her face to blow out the candles. She had so little puff these days, and the lack of yoga wasn't helping. She must start yoga again, must. Barbara credited that with keeping her alive. And then, look, they were helping her; with a joint effort, the candles went out after two seconds and the cake was whisked away. This highlight was over so quickly but Danny had taken pictures that had probably already been 'liked' by many patronising strangers. The word 'like', in Barbara's mind, came surrounded by heavy inverted commas.

'Here's your cake, Mum. Isn't it lovely?' Nick handed her a plate with some multi-layered sponge cake, a pastry fork she had never seen before, and a paper napkin with the number ninety embossed on it in gold and silver.

'It was a shame to cut it,' she said sadly.

'That's what cakes are for: eating.' Nick tucked into his own slice. 'Delicious,' he continued. 'I think I'll have some more. What about you, Mum?' Barbara shook her head.

'It's really good, Gee-Gee,' Danny repeated. 'I think Auntie Lynne learned how to make it on some course she did.'

Barbara nodded, poking at the cake rather than eating it. What a silly thing this fork was. So tiny and fragile. And how typical of Lynne to learn such an impractical skill, something of no use in daily life. Perhaps this was how she was going to make some money now that she had decided she was a 'retiree'. Now there was another stupid word. She put her plate down with a sigh.

'Why are you being so salty, Gee-Gee?'

She turned to him and grabbed his hand, tears starting in her eyes.

'Sorry, what?'

'Salty.' He paused. 'A bad mood. Cross. Gee-Gee! This is your birthday!'

'You try being ninety and see what sort of mood you are in.'

He looked at her in bewilderment. Of course, he could have no possible idea what she meant.

Barbara sighed. 'Not Gee-Gee. Jay-Jay.'

She spoke quietly so that he wasn't quite sure what he had heard. Danny looked more than confused, he looked scared. She should not have said that, Barbara thought immediately afterwards. She should not have uttered the words Jay-Jay. She had sworn to herself she never would and for so many years now she had kept her word. She didn't know how or why she had.

'Okay.' He clung onto her hand but looked around the garden for help. At least, she thought, he was putting her quietness, her grumpiness, down to bad temper and not dementia. Being out of sorts because this was a big, and not necessarily welcome, birthday.

Cathy sat on the chair next to her, taking over from Danny as the person holding her hand. She wanted not to tune out Cathy; however, she didn't want it enough. Barbara reverted to nodding and smiling. Like the queen, she thought. She was two years younger than the queen. Two years and two months. Perhaps everyone looked at the queen with anxiety too, tiptoeing around her. No, she replied to herself immediately, they didn't.

Of course, her family would be talking about her health, about Barbara's refusal to take all the pills the doctor wanted her to. As though she had turned her back on life.

That was not how she saw it. Barbara had taken so many tablets during parts of her life, once she stopped, her previous dependence rendered unnecessary by years of yoga – or the menopause, or a pleasant life, or simply the passage of time – she had sworn to herself that she would never take any drugs again. She'd decided that it was her body, and she would not hand control of it over to anyone else. They – her children, her grandchildren, her doctors – could do whatever they pleased.

As the hours passed, they began to leave her alone with her thoughts, to talk amongst themselves. As they left her to it, she recognised this sense of exclusion from years before and was not unhappy about it. She felt tired, but she also knew she was coming to the end of this tiredness. For now, just today, her family could leave and she would carry on sitting out here enjoying the enduring warmth of a beautiful day. Here was peace.

Midsummer gardens are so lovely at night, pondered Barbara. It was a warm evening and she looked at the white roses shining in the gloom. How wonderful that her eyesight remained good enough to see them. Suddenly, gratitude overwhelmed her. She was here; not dead yet. All these people, who had spent the day celebrating, without her having much to do with the occasion, added up to her family. She was wrong, selfish. She had been behaving badly and simply being old was not sufficient reason for that.

Barbara walked slowly back into the house, into the slightly orange glow of her old-fashioned kitchen. She immediately saw Lynne sitting, despondent, her elbows on the table and her head in her hands. She was sobbing. Barbara put her hand on her shoulder and thought that her heart would break for her daughter. Lynne's pain was hers.

'I miss Dad. Whatever was going on, he knew what to do. I miss him so much.'

Barbara bent forward and put her arms around Lynne's neck. 'So do I. Always. Every day.' Awkwardly, she kissed the top of her daughter's head.

'He's my dad. He is, he is. It doesn't matter about anything else. I don't care.' Lynne cried and cried. There would be no end to it. Barbara sat down next to her, and they hugged and wept together.

'Oh, love. I'm so sorry. For everything.' Lynne nodded and wiped her eyes on a piece of kitchen towel. She smiled slightly at her mother.

Barbara reached into the pocket of her slacks and handed Lynne a letter.

'This is just the beginning,' she said. 'I'll tell you whatever you need to know.'

PART THREE

CHAPTER EIGHTEEN

JEAN: SAN FRANCISCO, 1949

Jean had been allowed to work on a large canvas –
higher than she was tall and wider than the span of her
arms. She loved these huge canvases, and could not
believe her luck that she could make any mark on them.

The beaches at the edge of the city reached out to
her the most. The sky encompassed so many different
colours. There was every type of blue. The azure of a
clear day. The indigo of the night sky. The powder blue
of twilight. And the greys – when it rained, when the
fog rolled across the sea, in the shadows of the buildings
creeping onto the edge of the shore.

Then there were all the different shades that the sand
could be. Brown wet sand like coffee, bright gold sand
that never got wet, glittering white sand reflecting the
sun from many angles, mottled sand in heaps and piles
because it had been trampled over by many feet.

All of these, Jean attempted to put on canvas. There
would be time enough for the sea, yet more for trees
and grass and flowers. For now, she concentrated on the
sand and the sky.

She had to do this; she had never felt anything
more strongly. But more than that, Jean knew she was
learning. This might not work, might not be the best that
it could be. Nevertheless, she felt compelled to do it.
Because when she painted and it was going well, Jean
felt euphoric, dizzy. Painting was something she had to
do. This would never be otherwise.

Her style, she decided, was to use wide brush strokes, not small, precise ones, the opposite of her drawings. This, Jean felt, meant the subject and the style working as one. There would be no figures in her paintings, nothing she considered pretty, just big, bold strokes.

There was a sense of freedom that she felt in painting, the putting together of emotion and ideas, all the things in her head put out there for others to see. She hoped that someone else could sense its value too. She could not define it any more clearly than that.

When a painting goes well, when it looks like it did in my mind's eye, then I can't imagine anything better, she thought. Jean could feel the blood rushing through her veins; it was an extraordinary feeling, such a profound sense of being alive, she could almost explode.

This one, she had finished. In a sudden flash, she scrawled two initials in the corner of the canvas: JJ. Rather than Jean Joyce, as an artist, she would become JJ Woods instead. Not a girl painter, or a woman painter, anyone or anything that could be dismissed for its femininity, she would be JJ. A mysterious character who could be whatever the observer wanted them to be.

• • • ● ●• ● ● • •

While the title of the show was 'West Coast: The New Generation', the artists, in general, were not as new as all that. Instead, some of the people who had shown before, whose work of various sorts had featured in exhibitions in 1948, 1940, 1938 even, were demonstrating that they weren't stuck in the past. They were hip to the new style, moving with the times, believing in the future and all it had to offer them. And offer the art world too, of course.

Jean admired so much of the work, so many of the artists displayed here. She was part of something, and she loved that, though not quite as much as she loved art. More to the point, she believed in what they were all doing. Jean wanted to carry on doing it, come what may. Money, respect, love and marriage, she wanted them all, of course, but none of them came even close to this. This was something she was compelled to do. She was an artist and that was that.

It was sad, at least a bit, that her parents had not shown up. That they thought her work ridiculous. But weren't parents inevitably squares? Unless you were very lucky. Though with a flash she realised that maybe there could be disadvantages in having parents who were hip too.

The crowds – too many people pushed into a rundown three-storey building, whose rooms were too small for the large paintings – were milling, and pushing, and shouting. Laughing, too. Jean reeled from the way their loud voices vibrated between the stone floor and the bare brick walls. Her previous experience of shows had been sedate and quiet, almost reverential, with people looking steadily at whatever was on show. This was different. Raucous.

Some of these people were critics, Jean knew, and her career depended on them. Would they ask about JJ Woods, the newest painter of the new generation? Or would it all be nothing much, a disappointment the like of which she had never experienced before? Jean chewed her nails as she waited to find out. Surely she should be talking to some of them, or at least drinking so that her nerves quietened down a little?

Briefly, she missed Jeff, who could at least have stood beside her, drink in hand. He had moved away from San Francisco and taken up a fellowship in Chicago. The artist's life. He'd asked her to go with him and she had said no. Neither of them was surprised and she realised – with no little self-disgust – that he had served his purpose.

'JJ Woods, huh.'

Jean recognised the man, his face creased from too much sun, his blond hair floppy and now almost to his collar.

'Mr Costello?'

'So, I made an impression then.'

'Thank you for coming. I wasn't sure that you... approved of this kind of art.'

'I prefer other things.'

He stared back into her eyes and she shivered, hoping that he hadn't noticed.

'Nevertheless,' he continued. 'I appreciate talent when I see it.' He paused for effect. 'You have a gift, Miss Jean Woods, JJ. I believe I said something of the sort when you were my pupil.'

'And I want to thank you for...'

With his cigarette, he waved away her thanks.

'Come on! You would have done this anyway.'

She stared back at him, as he had stared at her.

'Yes. I would,' she said, continuing to stare at him with a gaze that was almost hostile.

'And who is representing you?'

'Well, no one. Not yet. I'm not ready.'

'You're kidding, right?' Their staring match continued.

'No, I'm not ready.'

Helena tapped her on the shoulder, looking quizzically at the man who seemed so enthralled.

'Hello,' she said with irritation.

'Mrs Stillman,' he said curtly.

'I'll be with you in a second,' Jean said, her eyes flickering in confusion.

Helena moved away, Jean unable to read her expression.

'It was so good to talk to you, Mr Costello,' she said in tones of diplomacy that she remembered her mother using with churchgoers who were reluctant to leave after services ended. Jean held out her hand and he grabbed it, pulling her body towards him and her hand down to his thigh.

'You're not a student anymore. You can call me Johnny,' he breathed sharply in her ear. Jean pulled away slightly and looked at him sideways, with anger.

'All right,' she breathed back. Then, before she knew what had happened, he pulled her towards him again and quickly, using his whole tongue, licked her cheek from the jawline up.

Jean turned around, her blouse tugged by a group of people she barely recognised. When she looked back again, Johnny had gone. There were so many things that could have accounted for the tremors surging through her body that she could not pin down the cause to just one.

• • • ● ●• • ● ● • • •

'So listen, honey, HONEY, listen.'

Johnny and Jean were in bed together; they almost always were. In the six months since their volcanic encounter at the New Generation show – after which they had made love for thirty-six hours straight – they had slept together manically, exhaustively, passionately, in every possible place, means, position, known to man (or so they thought). Jean had not felt herself to be inexperienced or naïve but she had not anticipated making love with someone who had clearly devoted so much of his life to ensuring a woman was happy in bed. Or women, she thought, not wanting to be overly romantic or unrealistic. His enduring injuries seemed to have no impact on his sexual desire or stamina, though afterwards his legs would be too weak to take his weight, and he would reach for one of several bottles of pills on the nightstand.

'Okay, I'm listening.' She smiled, her face just inches away from his. 'You've got me.'

'You really need to paint smaller, you know. I've said it before. How can I convince you? You want people to buy your work, then you need to make sure they can fit it in their damned houses. There aren't enough millionaires in America or galleries in all the corners of the world, that can take things of that size. Damn it, we aren't living in the thirties where they all wanted those murals.'

He had painted those murals, though, and she knew that was the problem.

'I can't do that, baby, I really can't.'

'You don't want to.'

'No,' she said softly. 'I don't want to.'

It wasn't love that felt so obsessive, was it? Surely it must be the sex that consumed her. Sometimes she felt that he devoured her too but it wasn't quite the same. He was trying to swallow her up. She looked at Johnny as he slept, and worried about him. His wartime memories meant he mumbled in his dreams and thrashed about when he should be lying quietly, and physical pain sometimes woke him up. The problems hadn't started then though, she knew. His life had often been combative and his unsettled relationship with his ex-wife Frances dated from before the war. Maybe he was both troubled and trouble too. This feeling in itself made her heart tingle with love, not just desire.

'Surely there are other things I could do to bring us in some money. You don't need to teach if it makes you so miserable.'

It did make him miserable, she knew that.

'Come to the studio with me,' she said softly, once more. 'I'm experimenting with colour, maybe using different, less realistic blues as a background to the darker sands. I want to know what you think.'

He rolled her onto her back, stroking her thighs very gently and then scratching them a touch more deeply

'Soon, honey. But let's just stay here a little longer.'

After she had made them eggs and toast and cleared up the dishes, it was 11.30. Johnny chain-smoked as he looked out of the window at the rain-slicked traffic.

'You could paint this, couldn't you? Your landscapes are too damned... attractive. Beautiful. Beauty's dead, man.'

'Beauty isn't dead! There is plenty left. Not in the city, maybe, but there is beauty.'

'No beauty in the city! Come on. It's more real than those *beautiful beaches* you can't stop painting.'

Jean bit her tongue. She would not stop painting the blue and gold abstracts, what he called 'beautiful beaches'. In any case, she painted plenty of greys with the blues and disagreed with his assessment.

'You could paint them yourself. Why not? You need to get back to your own art. There's nothing to stop you. Even the doctors said so. There are drugs that might stop your tremors.'

He gave some kind of strange roar, so that Jean was frightened, saddened, and confused, all at once. She moved back and the two remained there for a few moments. Jean was worried he would cry and didn't know what she would do if he did.

'Jean, Jean, you're still a little girl, tied to Mommy's apron strings. Too optimistic for your own good, still so damned full of hope. The trouble is...' – he ground his cigarette butt directly into the table – 'you're so full of talent that it flies around in all directions and isn't geared towards doing something that is just *yours*. Don't do the beautiful beaches, other people are doing those. Paint the city, paint the city in the rain as seen by a woman, as only a woman could see it. They couldn't do that. I couldn't do that. But you could, Jean. You could.'

He stroked her hair, a shoulder-length mess of brown waves and wisps.

'You know, when we got together, I thought you'd be my muse. But you aren't. I don't think anyone can be.' He pressed his lips together and Jean could not remember whether she had ever seen anyone looking so sad. 'Instead, I think maybe, perhaps, I am yours.'

• • • • ● • ● ● • • ·

'Now stand there. No...' Larry gestured with his hands, moving Jean and Johnny into the very centre of the staircase. 'Yes, there. There! That's grand.' The camera flashed, and flashed again, as the newlyweds smiled broadly at the young photographer.

Jean knew her parents were saddened by her refusal to marry in church. They accepted that she would not come back and marry in Lake View – she had flat out refused to do so – but, as they said, San Francisco had no shortage of churches. She did not tell them that Johnny had been married before; they realised that as soon as they saw the flower girl, whose serious eyes reflected those of her father. Still, City Hall had a beautiful wide staircase, perfect for wedding photographs. The internal ceiling domes reminded them all of the grandest churches although the number of people walking up and down each side of the couple meant that it was the best day of their lives for others, not just them.

'Shall I toss my flowers?' she laughed, smiling at her mother.

'That's only for bridesmaids,' she said. 'Little Leonore is much too young, and Larry is a boy. What would he want with wedding flowers? No, you can give them to me tomorrow and I will take them to a hospital.'

Jean held a bouquet of large white and cream flowers and Leonore carried a posy of grape hyacinths and baby's breath, echoed in the wedding party's corsages. The bride's dress comprised a New Look suit – a tight jacket with a very full skirt in white silk – an ensemble designed to be completely impractical and unsuitable for wearing ever again. But its glamour pleased her mother, and Jean did want to make her happy. There were many ways in which she had not done so.

The restaurant had been chosen by her father who had visited several times during his youth. It might only have been 11.30 in the morning, but at the Ritz Old Poodle Dog, the champagne was on ice and the bride and groom prepared to drink it in large quantities. Jean's parents had the smallest of glasses each, embarrassed that they should be drinking any alcohol at all.

'This restaurant is more than one hundred years old,' her father smiled. 'Eating at somewhere old, grand and French, well that's just what I want for my only daughter's wedding!'

'The bride and groom,' he toasted, picking up his glass. Johnny and Jean took large swigs of their champagne; her parents sipped theirs very slowly. Teenage Larry and ten-year-old Leonore, Johnny's daughter, gulped their sodas as if there was nothing very important about the occasion.

Johnny stood up. 'I would like to toast you, my dear parents-in-law, who will be my parents too because mine are gone.' He sipped. 'First, to you, Mrs Woods, who has made Jean the beautiful woman she is today, loving and kind, tender and so good to me. Thank you.' He raised his glass; they sipped. 'Next, to you, Mr Woods, for giving me your precious daughter to look after. I promise I will do everything in my power to honour that sacred trust. I love her.' They sipped again.

'Hey, hey, I'm right here,' Jean laughed, tugging at Johnny's sleeve. She didn't feel like laughing but she would do it anyway. Was this the wedding she really wanted, with no friends invited? It had seemed like a good idea when they discussed it.

'For the rest of your life,' Johnny said, leaning forward to kiss her.

Then they fell silent, none of them knowing what to say next, especially Jean, who was sure that both her parents were about to cry. She felt overwhelmed with love for Johnny; she had experienced so many doubts but at that moment they were all far away. She was unable to say anything at all. Leonore, her cheeks red, traced little circles on the tablecloth with each finger in turn.

'Well I never thought you would get married,' said Larry. 'I didn't think anyone would want you!'

They all laughed, although Johnny made boxing fists across the table towards the boy.

'Anyone would want her! Everyone! I'm so glad she wanted me.' Johnny smiled, his eyes narrowed at Larry, as he took Jean's hand and held it on top of the tablecloth.

The waiter arrived with the first dish of the restaurant's De Luxe Dinner: mixed greens with crab meat. Oh, Jean thought, this is truly heavenly! This was going to be a meal she would never forget.

It had been during the third night of a heatwave, with dogs barking in the distance and thin white drapes swaying in the whisper of a breeze, that Johnny asked Jean to marry him. They were in bed together, sweat hardly drying on their bodies after hours of love-making, shadows coming into the room falling across their faces as they gazed into each other's eyes. She had not made an active decision, more a feeling that marriage marked the next step to be taken and she would be taking it. So she said yes. How are you meant to feel about a man you are going to marry? Her body was delirious with need and surely that was love? Her desire to take care of him, to ensure he wasn't in pain, overpowered her.

Their wedding day lasted a long while, Jean felt. She had heard many women saying theirs was over in a flash but she was only too aware that, after the lunch when her parents and Larry had gone sight-seeing, and Leonore went back to her mother, that she and Johnny would be back in the bars drinking some more, while their friends laughed.

But Jean didn't think her friends would be laughing wholeheartedly. They might shake their hands or hug them, buy more drinks, but they would be nervous about this marriage. Helena, in particular, now Jean's closest friend, did not trust Johnny. Early on, she told Jean there were things about Johnny that Jean really did not want to know. 'Don't tell me then,' said Jean. And Helena kept quiet.

In the middle of the afternoon, Johnny bought a bottle of good whisky and took it round to the first of his friends' studios.

'Surprise!' Johnny said to his friend Maxim, who had been a young muralist with him in the 1930s. Maxim was covered in paint, but he wiped his hands on his overalls to grasp Johnny.

'You haven't done it, have you?' He smiled. Johnny took Jean's hand and pulled her arm towards Maxim. 'So, you have! Congratulations. Well done, old man. And I hope you'll be very happy, Mrs Costello.'

Jean scarcely knew Maxim and was surprised that he was the first of Johnny's friends they visited. They all drank a toast in celebration, Jean worrying about wet paint and her white suit and unable to sit down. Nevertheless, there was another drink, and then another.

'He hated Frances,' Johnny said as they left. 'But he's going to love you!'

Jean reeled. 'I don't see why.'

'Because *I* do,' Johnny said, kissing her cheek.

Five in the afternoon, and another studio. This belonged to Ned, a sculptor in wood, a man Jean had never even heard of. There was more kissing, more whisky, more congratulations. This time, the studio was covered in fine sawdust, too dirty for Jean to sit down on the hard chair Ned offered. Her feet were hurting in her delicate satin shoes. Oh, but there was so much whisky!

At around eight, they went to the usual North Beach haunts to find Helena and some of her young fellow artists. 'We're married,' shouted Johnny to the bar. Some dozen people cheered and shouted indistinctly. Helena was not there, although some of the others in her set were, and the owner bought them all drinks. What had happened to Helena? Jean needed to know. She was not at the next bar they went to, nor the next. She had to talk to her friend.

Eventually, so much later that Jean could not put a time on it, nor on what had happened in between, they found themselves in a crowded nightclub on Fillmore Street. 'We're married,' Johnny said to the orchestra leader.

'Uh-huh', he said, before launching the band into a swing version of the wedding march. There were so many, too many, people in the club. Jean started to slide towards the floor, and Johnny picked her up and walked her towards a taxi.

They spent their wedding night in a gloriously swanky hotel; a grand and spacious room with a chandelier and velvet chairs. Yet they scarcely made it through the door, too tight to notice their surroundings. Jean fell asleep on top of the covers, still in her white satin wedding corselet. That night, unlike all the nights since they had first kissed, they did not make love.

According to Johnny, Jean's first task as a married woman would be to find them an apartment. His place, where they'd spent their time before, was not suitable for two people to live in any kind of domestic bliss, bohemian though they might be.

'We need to find somewhere for a kid, don't we? It can't sleep here with us.'

'But we don't have a kid, Johnny. We might not have a kid for a while yet.'

'Don't you want one?' he said, his face screwing up.

'Sure I want one.'

'But...'

'But not yet. This is all so fast. Besides, I need to work on my art first.'

'*I need to work on my art first!*' His mocking repetition stunned her into silence. She was too hurt to respond in kind. Or at all.

'All women artists have to find a way to do both. If they can't, then they give up the art.'

'I will find a way,' she said firmly.

'I know you will,' he said, putting his arms around her. 'You're a great artist, or you will be.'

But in the end, Johnny found them an apartment. He had wanted two bedrooms, which to Jean simply meant more housework. She would have to do this herself because they couldn't afford to have anyone come help with it. Much to her astonishment, though, Johnny found a huge ramshackle building for rent – eight rooms with no obvious purpose for each of them – at the north end of Fillmore Street, in an area of empty warehouses far beyond the jazz clubs. And she loved it because he persuaded her with her own arguments: she needed to work on her art, and he would help her do that by ensuring she had a studio in her own home. The rooms were large, the light in at least some of them was ideal. They didn't need to use all of them right now. He set to work painting the walls and finding furniture in thrift stores. It would be more expensive than his small apartment, sure, but not so very much more expensive because of the state it was in.

Jean loved her studio – its high ceiling, its big windows, its worn concrete floor with unspecified stains hinting that it had been a factory at some point in its existence. Soon, she was spending all the time she could there, her hair tied up in a scarf, wearing an ancient sweater of Johnny's and shorts when it was warm; workmen's dungarees in the cooler weather. Soon, the paintings began to stack against the walls.

In the evenings, excited and tired, she would drink whisky with Johnny and they would take their drinks to bed with them. But Jean was not a natural cook. She would burn food, forget that something was on the stove and not remember until she could smell it. She would try so hard to make something delicious – a fish pie, or the sort of casserole her mother had made without having to think about it – but it would turn out all wrong. The fish would be overdone; the potatoes too salty; vegetables turning to mush in the pan. Eggs she could sometimes manage, but only barely. That was the first thing she had learned to cook for him. Fried eggs sunny side up. How hard could that be? Too hard sometimes, it seemed, when they turned out like rubber or had whites which were almost raw.

'I have no clean shirts! For Pete's sake, Jean. We aren't bums. I need to meet my students today. And if I didn't have this job, how would you ever be able to paint all day and night?'

'I'm sorry, Johnny. I forgot.'

'You forgot, huh. So don't forget. Just don't forget. I don't want a wife who can't do any housekeeping at all. Jeez. How can we live like this?'

'I'm trying, you know. I really am trying. But I'm naturally messy. All my family say so. My room mate said so. I was in trouble with the housemother of my dorm for leaving wet towels by the shower.'

It was important to Johnny that he continue teaching. It was not that he found it tremendously fulfilling – although he did find the discussions with potential artists quite invigorating – but it was at least something to do. The school authorities also seemed to think he was rather good at spotting and developing talent. He had spent five years teaching now and was no nearer returning to any kind of art for himself. He would look at his students' work and feel... nothing much. Some were good, some not, though of course none of them was a patch on Jean. She would not do what he advised, though, and that was a constant source of frustration to him.

But, after a couple of months, she had some good news.

'Oh, Johnny,' she ran up to him, hugging his waist tight. 'Look at this letter. It's from that gallery – the Cheltenham in Sausalito – and they want two of my paintings! I can't believe it. Not when I don't even have an agent yet.'

'That's swell,' he said tersely. 'How much are they offering?' He looked at the letter, in which the figure of fifty dollars seemed to flash out at him. Two paintings for fifty dollars, neither of them especially small in size. It did not seem enough. Johnny earned five thousand a year more or less, but as he was now supporting two households, he did not consider himself a wealthy man. He thrust the letter back at her. 'They need to pay more. Why don't you have an agent yet? I'm going to call them and say I'm representing you.'

'Oh no, don't do that. They might say no.'

He shook his head at her. 'You have no idea, do you? They want your work. This is why you need an agent. Everyone does. Women particularly. Your sex just can't stand up for itself.'

It took a matter of a few minutes' telephone call for the gallery to double the offer after he said he represented Jean – but not that he was her husband. This did not make things any easier between them.

'I just wish you had been happy for me, Johnny. That was what I wanted. The money doesn't matter.'

'Sure it matters. How can you say it doesn't matter? Money always matters. It's only when other people are looking after you that you can say that.'

Johnny sighed, lighting a cigarette for himself and then, after a few minutes, one for Jean too.

'You would get more money, too, if you painted as I advised. But oh no, you don't want to do that. Still, you believe the money doesn't matter.' He smoked in silence for a few moments, looking at Jean who was still holding on to the initial letter. 'Even besides the money, though, you know what I think. What you are doing now is a waste.'

Jean thought – as she always did – that Johnny should stop thinking about her art, and start thinking about his own. This wasn't simply to deflect attention from herself, although it was that too.

'You should start your own work again,' she said carefully. 'I know that you want to.' Jean felt frustrated that he would not paint, would not look beyond what he saw as his failure because his body was incapable of doing what it had in the past. There was so much he *could* do, so many different types of art, so much painting that did not involve climbing ladders and sitting on planks for hours. Where he could avoid vertigo and manage the tremors. He was still physically strong in many ways, still had the eye of an artist. Nevertheless, she could not make him do what she wanted, just as he could not make her paint the way he thought she should.

'Cut it out,' he shouted. 'You don't know anything. You will never know anything.'

Jean bit her lip. She knew bringing this up was never a good idea and she had promised herself to avoid the subject.

He stood up, turned on his heels, and walked out. Although she was several storeys up, and to the back of the apartment, she could still hear the slam of the front door, so loud and strong that the whole building rattled. He did not come back until two the next morning, then so insensibly drunk that he collapsed loudly on the floor of the kitchen. Why had she mentioned it? He was never going to agree with her suggestions, however gentle. Besides, what did Jean know? She doubted herself in all sorts of ways. By the time he had sobered up, they had made a tacit agreement that this was something they would never talk about again. They also made an open agreement: he would act as her agent. Clearly, she needed one.

Months later, when they had seen the paintings hanging in the gallery and subsequently sold on, Johnny began to talk with increasing urgency about another of his wishes. At night, he would whisper in her ear, sometimes so quietly she could barely hear it, sometimes when he thought she was already sleeping. 'Give me a son.' Each time, she would turn to him, stroking his back and welcoming him into her body. She still craved him, but not in the same way as she had before. Perhaps it was his anger, sometimes directed at her, and sometimes towards the world as a whole. It was as if she was there to make him feel less alone. That with her, and only during the period of love-making, he was whole. Without her, part of him was missing and that part was not her, not Jean. It was a part of him, and she was able to fill the broken parts of him with herself.

One early morning, a bright day in November 1951, she was awoken by him stroking her back and kissing her neck, turning her towards him.

'Darling,' he said, kissing her neck once more.

'Wait a second,' she said, rushing into the bathroom to pee. While she was there, she also thought to check that her diaphragm was still in place, just as she usually did in the morning. But somehow, her fingers must have dislodged it. She got back into bed with him, smiling as she lay back down. He put his fingers inside her, soon pulling his head away and staring at her quizzically.

'What's this?' he said, his fingers prodding and pulling now, not erotic at all.

'Johnny. You know exactly what it is.'

'Ah, right, your diaphragm. I'd forgotten about this... thing. You've been using it all this time?'

'Of course I have.'

'But why? We are married. Even if you'd got pregnant months ago, it wouldn't have mattered. I would have taken care of you.'

'I already said. I wasn't ready. I needed to work on my art.'

'Sure, sure. You needed to work on your art. Well, now you're working on it.'

Johnny pulled her to him fiercely and kissed her hard.

'You're mine.'

'Yes,' she breathed.

'I want you.'

For Jean, this was the reverse of desire. She felt afraid, not just of Johnny but of the future of their marriage. Why did she not want the same things as he did? He thought she should go along with his wishes – of course he did, that was husbands, wasn't it? Why were her own wishes so very different?

'Yes,' she breathed again, not meaning it.

Suddenly, he reached inside her and pulled out the diaphragm. Looking at it with a mixture of disgust and bafflement, he threw it as forcefully as he could across the other side of the room.

PART FOUR

CHAPTER NINETEEN

The further north you travel in the UK, the cooler it becomes. This summer, Karen thought, that was just as well. London – where she first encountered these family historians – felt uncomfortably warm, with the high temperatures making her tour group flag. While it was cool inside the national archives at Kew, the coach in which they went outside the capital, their hotels, the events painstakingly organised with local history groups were hard to enjoy. Those small community venues were airless. It didn't help that many of the group lived in parts of the world where air-conditioning came as standard, where everything was built to anticipate the heat. In Britain, no one ever anticipated extremes of weather, no matter how often they occurred.

On the train between London and Edinburgh, a faster and more pleasant option than driving, some of the tour group dozed off, others sorted listlessly through the reams of paper they had collected. Karen wasn't surprised; she was exhausted too and looking forward to lots of lovely sleep. Her own involvement with the group would end in a few days, and she would have a longed-for break with her sister's family in the countryside near Glasgow.

Before that, there were many hours to spend on the gently lulling train and when almost everyone was asleep, she checked her emails. She was surprised to see one from Rachel, and that she had copied in not only

Lynne but several more people who Karen assumed had to be other relatives.

'There has been a new and exciting development. Please get in touch as soon as you are available to work with us again.'

Well! Karen shook her head in pleased disbelief, her curiosity piqued, but still determined to stick to her guns that she was not currently available. She would be professional; not over-keen.

'That sounds intriguing,' she wrote. *'I'm looking forward to getting involved again as soon as I finish my current project.'*

She closed her laptop and glanced out of the window as the train approached Berwick-upon-Tweed. Karen wondered if she should wake up the tour group to look at the unexpectedly blue sea and welcome them into Scotland, but her decision was pre-empted by a big crash as cups fell from the refreshment trolley when the juddering train propelled someone into it.

Her co-leader, John McDermott, was about thirty and an expert in male line or surname genealogy. Many of the group were interested in where their male ancestors came from, and whether or not they were connected to famous clans. John would take the lead when they were looking around some of the Scottish archives.

'Ladies and gentlemen,' he began theatrically. 'We are about to enter Scotland, from whence many of your descendants hail. You will see the buildings appear strikingly different from those down south.' John was entirely predictable: he would make a joke soon about everything being fried (Mars Bars) or pickled (the people). Less than a minute later, he did. Karen closed her eyes to distance herself, but all the tour group laughed.

'When we disembark from the train, your luggage will be taken to the hotel which is just around the corner from the station. You'll probably be happy to stretch your legs and get a breath of fresh air after this long journey, especially because there's a very welcome drop in temperature from London.'

There was indeed a drop in temperature – but not as much as they had all hoped. Still, they could have a quick walk, a quick rest and a quick lunch before their minibus arrived to take them to their first Scottish archive.

Most of her charges had gone into the building, and Karen was just looking around for any stragglers when the shadows shifted before her.

'Karen Copperfield, as I live and breathe!'

Karen turned around to see a small, wiry man of around her own age, his hair entirely shaved from his scalp to make him seem bald. Had he been using a tanning bed, she wondered? She didn't remember him being this particular shade before.

'Duncan. Hello.'

Karen felt her hands tremble; she clasped them together.

'And what are you doing up here?'

Ah – not a barbed question at all, she thought sarcastically.

'I'm leading a family history tour,' she said coldly, wondering if he noticed her tone.

'You haven't applied for that job then?' he asked, his eyes narrowing. Karen thought that whatever job it was, he must have applied for it himself.

'I have my own business now,' she said. 'Working as a genealogist, in particular helping people with genetic mysteries.' She made inverted commas over 'mysteries' with her fingers.

'Interesting. Interesting.' He gave the second 'interesting' far more emphasis than the first.

'I'm not looking for academic work anymore,' she continued dryly. 'So if you are going for that job, I'm sure it will be yours.'

'No.' He laughed. 'I'm on the interviewing panel. But it's the sort of job you would like. You have the right experience, the ability to bring sociological and historical context to genealogies, blah de blah.'

Did her shudder show, Karen wondered? She hoped she had hidden it well enough; there was no point in having a scene here, right in front of these grand buildings. This Duncan, this shit of a man, had run her down both in her presence and behind her back in her previous job as director of community history at the Midlands Centre of Continuing Education. He had explicitly rubbished her research, her social skills, her ability to attract and retain both audiences and donors. This Duncan, Dr Duncan Cameron, one-time colleague and many-time competitor for a tiny number of jobs, had made her employers so much more inclined to make her redundant when the centre lost its funding. She had loved that job in continuing education, working with people on their individual and local research projects, giving talks to the public of all ages between five and death. But that was then.

Now Duncan Cameron undertook the work that she had done, with more success too – as anyone could have predicted. He was a snake. There were many reasons not to pursue a career as an academic, and quite a few of them were embodied in this... creature in front of her.

'Excuse me, Dr Copperfield?'

A tour member to whom she had not yet spoken touched Karen on her arm. She felt like kissing the woman but instead just turned and smiled.

'Ah yes, I was talking to an old colleague but we have come to the end of our chat.'

Duncan ran his eyes up and down the woman, registering her evident glamour and affluence. Turning back to Karen, he smirked.

'Good to see you,' he said, as though trying not to laugh. 'And the best of luck with your... projects.'

Karen turned away from him without a word, her fierce gaze directed at the middle distance. She took a couple of deep breaths before pressing her shoulders down and smiling at the tour member.

'I'm so sorry, I don't remember your name.'

The other woman smiled.

'What a horror!' she said, nodding towards Duncan's back, as he walked into a café.

'Thank you for rescuing me!' Karen said warmly. 'I'm very happy he's now an ex-colleague, not a current one!'

The two of them laughed.

'I know that we only have a few days left,' the woman said politely, 'and I wanted to talk to you about my mother. She was born in California a hundred years ago but her parents came from Dumfries and I can't find any trace of them.'

'Of course! That's what I'm here for. One of the things, anyway.'

'There's more too. But I decided to see what I could find out on my own before I came to you.'

'Good plan.'

Karen was so pleased to be talking to this woman. Many of the group were interesting; most of them were older than she was, some of them much older, although a couple had younger relatives in tow. But this woman, though older than Karen, had a cosmopolitan and sophisticated air that the others did not. She looked glossy, well put together, as if she dressed in outfits rather than clothes. Karen liked glossy. She was far from glossy herself and possessed few clothes that together could form an outfit. Even her once-expensive suits appeared frayed and shabby.

'I'm Elle Starchild,' she said, shaking Karen's hand.

'What a lovely name!'

'There's a story behind that, of course. But I can tell you about it later.'

That later was immediately after dinner. Several of the tour group were in the dimly lit, low-ceilinged bar drinking cucumber martinis – a light and delicate drink with a hint of gin – something that couldn't be called a martini in any usual sense of the word.

As Karen walked in, Elle stood up and waved at her.

'Is now good?' she asked.

'It is.' Karen smiled back, edging herself into the leather banquette next to Elle, and waving to the waiter for a drink.

'My problems have been around the surnames of my grandparents,' Elle began. 'I have been searching for Campbells and Browns. There are so many of them. And many of their Christian names are John and Mary. Can you imagine! The horror!' Her expression was lively, almost as though she were going to burst out laughing.

'Yes, I can see how that might be a problem.' Karen nodded wryly. Elle was perhaps older than Karen had reckoned, but her make-up was sublime. Her jewellery comprised large silver discs, both around her neck and in her ears. They stood out perfectly against her simple red linen dress.

'As a result, my research has stalled before it even started.'

'So what do you know already,' Karen asked, setting aside the unwanted straw from her drink, and taking a sip.

Elle clasped her hands on top of the table.

'My mother was born in 1918 and died twenty years ago before my interest in genealogy began. I don't remember my grandparents at all. I think they emigrated from Scotland around 1911 but I'm not sure whether or not they married here or in the States. It's a challenge!'

'And have you done a DNA test? That might help, especially with such common names.'

Elle nodded sadly. 'Yes, although that left me more confused than ever. No one seemed to be close cousins but I found a few people.'

'In the meantime, you'll be visiting some churches with baptism records that might offer the odd clue. Have you talked to my fellow tour leader?' Karen gestured towards John McDermott, who was standing at the bar and making people laugh, though surely he was off duty now.

'Yes, briefly. He said he will talk me through the baptismal records and help if there is handwriting I can't decipher.'

Elle set her near-full cocktail glass on the table and moved it in circles, staring intently at it.

'I also thought I should discuss something else with you.' She looked up at Karen with a direct stare that made the younger woman blink.

'Yes?'

'Now I am sure you can't talk about this with me because of confidentiality, but I am distantly related to someone who has been in contact with you: MerryD, Meredith. You will remember that she had a cease and desist letter, from an organisation she didn't know.'

'Okay. But as you say, I can't talk about that.'

'Nevertheless, Meredith was not your client, that was Lynne, and neither Merry nor I can figure out how she is related to us, as presumably she is. But,' Elle continued, raising her finger to indicate a pause as she sipped her drink, 'I did not get one of those letters. That means – we presume it means – that Meredith has a connection to Lynne that I do not.'

'But you haven't worked out what it is?' Karen asked.

Elle shook her head.

'I know that I am related to Meredith through my father, but I have not investigated that side of my family at all. I was estranged from my father and, for a long time, even thinking about him made me shudder.'

'So whose surname is Starchild?'

Elle looked at Karen from beneath slightly raised eyebrows.

'Well, it's mine, of course. I created it.'

Elle sighed, a flash of sadness running across her face.

'I forget that everyone is so much younger than I am. This was something that women did in the 1970s, a few of us anyway. We wanted nothing at all to do with men, particularly fathers. And while lots of women took their mother's first names, adding 'child' to the end of them, I wasn't on good terms with my mother then either. I liked the sound of 'Starchild' so I've been Starchild since 1974.'

'I've heard of this,' said Karen, 'but never met anyone who has done it.'

Elle smiled. 'Very confusing for future genealogists, I'm sure!'

Karen laughed.

'I wanted to tell you this,' Elle continued, 'in case it helps Lynne's search in the future.'

Elle didn't know about the new situation, then. Karen wouldn't enlighten her.

'Well thanks. There's so much to unravel just to do with the letter. Obviously, whoever the letter is coming from is very targeted with their correspondence. It's not just scattergun: they have already pinned down the connection.'

'Yes.'

Elle smiled again. 'You were one of the reasons I took this trip rather than any of the others,' she said. 'Meredith told me you were a good person. I knew you would understand.'

Understand what, Karen mused briefly. Was she a therapist? Perhaps so.

'After the 1980s, my life changed a lot,' Elle sighed, 'I had been living in a women's community, working on the land. Then I went on retreat in New Mexico, started working at the retreat and eventually owning it, and others, with the man I later married.

'In the few years before he died, I reconciled with my father and he left me some money as part of his estate. I suppose I could look into his family tree now. But I feel everyone neglected my mother because she was just the first wife. I was her only child and I want to make it up to her somehow, now that it's too late.'

'I understand,' said Karen, wondering if she did.

The Skype call was a shock. While Karen was in her predictably neutral hotel room, the other side of the call came from a living room full of wall hangings and colourful paintings featuring concentric circles. There were three members of the Pendleton family – Lynne, Rachel and – to Karen's bemusement – Cathy. While she had met Lynne and Skyped Rachel, this was the first time she had seen Cathy. She looked nothing like her managerial daughter, that was for sure. Instead, she had a cloud of white hair held down by a headband covered in fabric flowers. What appeared to be a scarf was knotted around her bust to form a multi-coloured bandeau top.

'Hello,' they all waved at her, and Rachel, who seemed to be taking over, introduced Cathy as 'this is my mum. We're at her house.'

'Before we go further into our research,' Rachel said, 'we need to tell you that Barbara, Gran, is now on board with it all. Or she says she is. I think it's all very traumatic for her.'

The other two women nodded.

'She gave me the letter she was sent,' Lynne said. 'So let me read it out.'

Lynne inhaled from the pit of her stomach.

> *'Dear Mrs Thompson,*
> *'We apologize for contacting you out of the*
> *blue like this but we wonder if you can*
> *help us. We assure you this is not any kind*
> *of a scam; we do not want anything from*

you, apart from your insight into a family mystery.

'Last month, my sister and I took familial DNA tests and two people, Catherine Mortimer and Nicholas Pendleton show up as being close connections on our father's side. We had never met or even heard of them before and although we tried to contact them through the DNA site, we don't think they saw those messages.'

'We have now,' Cathy interrupted.

'Our father, who died in 2004, often spoke warmly about his sister Jean who he had not been in touch with since the 1950s. But he did not tell us anything else about her, or why they had not been in contact since that time. We wonder if you have ever heard of her? Our father was Larry Woods, from Lake View, California, born in 1936.

'We enclose a picture of our grandparents – Walter and Dorothy – with a toddler who is probably Jean. We think this was taken in 1931. The other photographs are of us, Michelle and Jennifer, from 1977, and Larry, taken in the same year. Do you recognise any of us? Do you know how we could be related to you?

'If you would like to get in touch with either of us, please do email, or perhaps Catherine or Nicholas would email, at this address. Or telephone. As you can see, we live in California but we could call you back. Or contact us by post. Please. We would appreciate any help at all.

'With warmest regards,

'Michelle Woods Conrad and Jennifer Woods Garber (Jazzbabe260)'

There was a few minutes pause.

'Wow,' said Karen. Then again: 'Did you ask Barbara about this?'

'Not yet,' said Lynne. 'We wanted to ask you what we should do. After her birthday party, she said she would tell us anything we wanted to know but when I did ask her specific questions, she shook her head and cried. She said she was so sorry that Larry had died and that everyone else involved had probably died by now too. She didn't say she would *never* say anything more, but just that it was all too much to talk about in one go and she was so very sorry.'

'What about making contact with Michelle and Jennifer?'

'Not yet,' said Cathy. 'We're a bit scared, really.' Karen didn't believe that Rachel would be included in this 'we', that she would be scared of anything so mundane as unknown relatives. Nevertheless, Rachel was clearly anxious that things should not go wrong this time, that everyone should remain on good terms – or at least appear so.

'Right,' said Karen. 'I must tell you something that I discovered myself and that Rachel might suspect too.'

Rachel nodded – in agreement as well as confusion.

'I looked for the parents of a Barbara Thompson, born in British Columbia on twenty-sixth June 1928. As you pointed out, Rachel, it was not possible to know the details of her parents' births because they would only be on a certificate ordered by post. However, I did find an online death certificate for a Barbara Thompson, who died aged four days in 1928. Then I found a gravestone for someone of that name, also in British Columbia, who also died aged four days. I'll send you the link. So it's very likely that your mother took on the identity of this person at some point before she married Victor.'

The three women looked at her, open-mouthed. Karen noticed that they were all holding hands; her own feelings were mainly of compassion, with the smallest tinge of power that she recognised but pushed away. What a mess! She left them with their thoughts for a few moments.

'So was she, is she, this Jean Woods?' Lynne sighed, her voice breaking.

'I can't guarantee it,' said Karen. 'She may not be. But it is a strong possibility. What I would advise you to do is, firstly, to ask your mother if she can tell you anything more and secondly, to get in touch with this Michelle and Jennifer Woods. I would say to take all of it very slowly.'

The three women still looked very shocked.

'Before computers, and when even long-distance phone calls were expensive and hard to arrange,' Karen continued, 'many people did change their names simply by giving false information. It was much easier to do in those days. But Barbara did not just make up a name when she married Victor. She had a birth certificate, which all of you have seen and, presumably, she has kept it since at least the fifties, possibly earlier.'

'There's another thing,' she continued. 'This letter is the sort that people write to unknown relatives when they don't want to scare them off. The chances are that they already realise your mother is Jean Woods and are trying to figure out what she knows first. They also have no idea what sort of physical or mental condition Barbara is in although they do know that, whether or not she is Jean, she is likely to be very old.'

'But I don't understand,' said Lynne. 'How could they have found our address?'

'It's easy enough. There's a huge amount of historical information online and publicly available evidence of Pendletons living at this address over several decades – for instance in the telephone directory. They would see that a Barbara Pendleton is still listed on the electoral register. If you really want to hide, you can, but unless you actively try to cover your tracks, you'll be easy to trace. And I assume that your mother wasn't trying to hide, once she had changed her name.'

She looked at the link for the photograph of baby Barbara's grave: a tiny grey angel, its wings wrapped around its little body. There was sadness in every curve of the sculpture. Barbara Thompson, 26 June–30 June 1928. With Jesus.

'And there's something else too,' she continued. Was she right to continue with this? Surely she had no choice.

'Lynne, you will remember, of course, about the cease and desist letter you had. You knew that someone called MerryD had one too?'

'Yes.' Lynne sighed.

'Well, I recently met someone who knows MerryD, Meredith Dyson, and is related to her, but maybe not to you. She didn't get one of those letters, however, and she doesn't know for sure why. Now don't worry, I didn't talk to her about you, because you are my clients, and our contract stipulates confidentiality.'

'Tell her anything, this woman. Anything at all. I can't bear it,' Lynne spoke, barely taking a breath.

'So to be clear, this is something to do with your birth father's side, Lynne, not your mother's.'

'Yes. Of course.' Lynne's free hand, the one not holding Rachel's, batted the air back and forth.

'Bear in mind, though, that the cease and desist people may come back.'

'Oh, whatever. I'll get a solicitor. I need to find out who they are.'

'Right. I will take a look at both sides of your family. But you deleted your account, didn't you? That makes things difficult because the information will have gone permanently.'

'No.'

'Sorry?'

'No, I didn't delete it. I removed you from being the manager and I listed it as private, so no one else could see it. Then I never looked at it again. But I considered, well... deleting it was too final. I knew I might want to look again later.'

She sighed.

'I'll go into my account. Start it all again. Why not?'

There was more than one tragedy here, Karen thought. But how many? And what, exactly, were they?

CHAPTER TWENTY

During the early and middle months of her pregnancy, Jean had been creative. She felt fecund in every sense, ripe with possibility. A human being was developing inside her and painting upon painting accumulated in the studio. She could see a body of work growing alongside the baby. Much to her surprise, she even started baking, her ability to combine flour and fat to make pastry somehow appearing out of nowhere.

At the beginning of her eighth month, however, all this ground to a halt. Jean was acutely aware that soon she would have a child to look after, while at the same time her body was behaving in a way over which she had no control. Sleeping began to be difficult as the lively infant inside her wriggled and punched when she tried to rest.

There was another problem. At the very beginning of her pregnancy, she stopped drinking alcohol. No one told her to; her body simply revolted against the taste and the smell of it. But Johnny began drinking for two, starting as soon as he woke up and only stopping when he passed out.

Johnny was various sorts of drunk: too loving, too loud, too miserable, too angry and too physical. Physical in many senses.

When she first told him of her pregnancy, Johnny had been very affectionate, stroking her stomach and tenderly pinching her cheeks. He even became more positive about her work, not just the genius he thought she had buried, but her work here and now. His love-making, which had been frenetic and intense, became more gentle and obsessive in a way that was more about him than her.

Something of him was growing in her and he loved that as much or more than he loved her. He was proud too; yes, proud. Of both of them and the new life that would be appearing before too long.

Soon, though, he began smashing his fists into the bar and throwing glasses at walls. Shouting at strangers, asking people why they were staring at him, approaching them aggressively. Once, he pressed his fingers into her arm to make a point, leaving marks that stayed there for days.

Jean was not sure about how she felt about this, not at all, apart from a growing sense of unease. In a way she was wrapped up in herself, moving away from him as she grew in other ways. They stopped talking, though profound conversation had never been something over which they spent many hours. It was not as if she was frightened of him, scared that he would beat her – she wasn't. But she knew a part of him was increasingly disturbed and she didn't know what to do. She wondered how he'd reacted when his first wife had been expecting.

So, at eight months pregnant, Jean found herself on the bus, going back once more to visit her parents. She needed to get away from Johnny and their apartment, littered with empty bottles and so full of cigarette smoke that she could not breathe. It was everywhere; why had she never noticed it before? It filled her lungs, making her wheeze as if she had asthma. Yet she'd enjoyed smoking before. All this was strange, as if her body no longer belonged to her. Perhaps it didn't.

It was years since she'd last taken such a long bus trip. It must have been to visit her parents that time, too. This trip, no men tried to pick her up or make off-colour remarks. She was a pregnant woman, her wedding ring and huge stomach making her of no sexual interest to anyone. Instead, people helped her, smiled, acted friendly in a disinterested way. Here was a married woman who would soon have a baby. Wasn't that exactly how things should be?

Despite that, when Johnny smashed the canvas over her head, she knew it marked the end of their marriage. Why had he done it, why? Her cooking had improved, she tried hard – and succeeded – to be happy that, after all her attempts to prevent it, she was going to have a baby. She stopped talking about his art and what he should be doing. He was pleased about that. But in one way, she had not done what he wanted. She still painted beaches, landscapes, sky, beauty.

Four days before – four days that felt like four weeks – he'd come back from a night on the tiles. Another one! Recently, there had only been late nights for him. She stayed behind, painting, worried that soon she would be unable to carry on.

It was one in the morning and she was still in her studio when he returned from a drinking bout. She had not quite finished her current painting, still a little unsure as to whether another, extra, blue was needed to create the precise gradations of colour that she wanted. Jean perched on the edge of the chair, staring at her work, lost to the outside world. The door to her studio banged, but she remained oblivious to it.

'Jean.'

Johnny put his hand on her shoulder and she flinched.

'I didn't hear you come in,' she said.

'Why aren't you in bed, for Pete's sake? The size of a house and you're still here painting. What do you think you are doing?' Right next to her, he bellowed directly into her ear.

Jean turned to face him.

'I want to finish this one. I don't have much time left.'

'Oh, this is ridiculous. Your bloody obsessions. I shouldn't have married an artist.'

'Well, I shouldn't have married at all!'

Making a sound halfway between a roar and a growl, Johnny picked up the painting and threw it at the wall, a corner damaging the plaster. No damage seemed to have been done to the painting, so Johnny punched his fist straight through it. The canvas tore unevenly, past repair, as Jean gasped 'No!'

'Ah,' he yelled contemptuously. 'That's better.'

He grabbed the painting by the sides and forced the tear over her head, ripping it further. It looked like a huge necklace and all he did was laugh. His visibly shaking wife stood there, apparently unbroken, as she stared back at him.

So that's it then, Jean thought. She steadily lifted the painting off her shoulders, tears in her eyes. Johnny sat down on a hard-backed chair, the one she often sat in to contemplate her work. He lit a cigarette and began smoking it, staring at the floor. His tremors were bad; they had been diminishing but now she could see the cigarette moving from side to side. The high-ceilinged studio seemed particularly empty, despite the canvases stacked against the walls, Johnny's shouting still echoed around the room long after he'd quietened down.

Jean grabbed her keys and stormed out. She hoped with all her might that she could wake up Helena but wasn't sure that she could, nor, indeed, that she possessed the energy to reach her apartment. Just put one foot in front of the other, she thought, concentrate on doing that and nothing else.

Thirty minutes later, having ignored the cat-calling of young men in cars and the kind words of a concerned old man walking his dog, she somehow found herself ringing Helena's doorbell. A third-floor window banged open, and someone leaned from it to shout, 'Cut it out!'

Jean stepped into the street and tilted back her head.

'Can you let me in? I need to see Helena.'

The man banged the window shut again; almost immediately she heard him clattering down the stairs, three at a time.

He opened the door and ushered her in quickly, taking in her appearance with a quick 'Jeez'.

'Mike? It is Mike, isn't it? I need to see Helena.'

'Yeah, well, she's asleep but come in anyway.'

Jean trudged up the endless stairs at about a tenth of Mike's speed, stopping at every third step and leaning against the wall.

By the time Jean reached the apartment, Helena was standing sleepily in the doorway. They both put out their arms.

'Johnny?' she asked.

Jean nodded. 'I've had enough,' she whispered.

Helena's expression, while trying to remain caring and concerned, nevertheless implied 'it was just a matter of time' as she put her arm around Jean and steered her carefully towards the couch.

'What happened?'

'Not now, Helena. I just need to sleep.'

With only one bed and one bedroom in the apartment, Mike said, 'I'll stay out here. Don't worry.'

While Jean fell into a dead sleep almost immediately, her tossing and turning in Helena's too-small bed, and her frequent trips to the bathroom, meant that none of them had a good night.

Mike went off to work early in the morning, leaving the two women to talk.

'You aren't going to stay with him now, are you?'

'No... but...'

'But nothing. He did this once and he will only get worse. You remember I told you that I'd heard things about Frances. Well, he hit her really bad when they were breaking up. Did you know that?'

Jean shook her head.

'No,' she said very sadly. 'I know you warned me about something but I didn't care to be told about it.'

Helena put her hand over Jean's.

'Love. It will kill us all.'

What Jean needed most was to see her mother; missing, even craving, her physical presence. No matter that they had not met since the wedding and barely exchanged letters either. Thankful that her change purse was in the pocket of her paint-spattered maternity smock, she went to the post office to use the telephone. Setting up a long-distance call seemed to take hours and she hoped she would not have to use the restroom before the operator placed it.

'Mom, it's Jean.'

'Jeannie. How are you? What's wrong?'

Well, of course there was something wrong. There were five weeks before her baby was due, the only event that might properly lead to a phone call.

'I need to come home, Mom. I've left Johnny.'

After a few seconds pause, Dorothy said clearly, 'Oh no, that can't be right. What happened?'

'He's bad news, Mom.'

Please, please don't ask me anything else, Jean thought. She did not want to explain anything to her mother, anything at all. She simply needed to be back in Lake View.

'Oh dear.'

'I'm getting the bus as soon as I can, which is in two days, and I am staying with a friend in the meantime. I can't go back to our apartment so I have nothing to wear and very little money.'

'Oh dear,' she said again. Jean could hear the desperation, even panic, in her mother's two polite words.

'Well, that's all for now because this is an expensive call. But I'll see you in a few days. Goodbye.'

As she replaced the receiver, she picked up her mother saying in the distance, 'Shall we wire you some money?'

Jean pretended not to hear, although she regretted that immediately. She would have been very happy if they had sent it, rather than borrowing it from Helena. Too late now. She went over to the counter to pay cash she could not afford for the call she'd never expected to make.

On the bus, of course, she was uncomfortable. It was hot, airless, and bumpy. Her stomach lurched and she hoped that she would be able to last the two hours between restroom stops.

The house looked the same as it had four years before. How odd, she thought, that so much had happened to her since her last trip to Lake View, and yet everything here remained entirely unaltered. There were literally roses around the door.

Only her mother was waiting when she arrived.

'Well now, Jean,' she said as her daughter came through the front door. 'This is a poor state of affairs, isn't it?'

Jean put her head on her mother's shoulder and sobbed. She was still crying when Larry came home from school. He seemed to have grown about a foot since she had last seen him eighteen months before.

Larry's first reaction was exactly what she expected.

'Boy oh boy. You're so fat!' The kid's eyes looked about to pop out.

'That's what happens when you are expecting. Do you want to feel the baby moving?' Jean took his hand and put it gently on her stomach.

'No, ugh, no!' He pulled it away as though her stomach could burn him. A few seconds later he thoughtfully, carefully, replaced it.

'Say! There's a baby in there. It's kicking me!'

Jean grinned at him. 'You'll be an uncle soon. Isn't that amazing?'

He shook his head in disbelief. 'Huh.'

'Not so disgusting then?' She smiled wryly.

'I don't want to think about it.' He wrinkled his nose. 'But I can show it things. It will be fun when it's older.' Jean grabbed his hand and kissed it; Larry looked embarrassed but did not pull away.

With their mother hurrying him upstairs to change, Jean and Larry had no further chance to chat.

'You mustn't go outside,' Dorothy said. 'People will ask too many questions. You are too far along to be travelling without your husband.'

'Oh come on! I need some fresh air. Surely I can go out in the yard? I'm not going to a nightclub!'

Her mother set her lips firmly together.

'You should be with Johnny. He can't have done anything as bad as all that.'

'Mother! He drinks all the time, he's never sober.'

'Drink is a terrible thing. Terrible. You aren't drinking alcohol, are you?'

'Not right now.'

'I was worried at your wedding; I had never seen you drink before and nothing good ever comes of it. Still, you made your bed.'

Jean started to cry as her mother sat on the chair next to her, wiping her hands on her apron.

'Johnny loves you. That's very plain.'

'I know he does, but...'

'Of course, he shouldn't drink. Perhaps Reverend Parry can talk to him.'

The idea that the family's minister should give her atheist husband guidance about anything made Jean shudder.

'You may not like that,' said her mother disapprovingly. 'But God has given him wisdom to help the rest of us.' She paused again. 'Has he hit you?'

Jean struggled with herself.

'Not exactly. There was a painting...'

'He hit the painting?' Dorothy sounded astonished, exasperated.

'He punched through it,' Jean explained, or tried to. 'Then he destroyed it some more by putting my head through it.'

Pain and confusion flashed over Dorothy's face.

'Did he hurt you?' she asked.

'No... I went straight round to my friend Helena's. I was very shaken. It was horrible, Mom, horrible.'

'Oh dear, oh dear. So you haven't seen Johnny since?'

'No,' Jean said sulkily.

'But he probably wants to apologise. I'm sure he regrets doing that.'

Jean was not at all sure that Johnny did, or would, regret it. She said nothing as her mother hugged her tightly. Jean sensed her mother's heartbeat and felt such relief with Dorothy's arms around her.

'Don't worry, Jean. All couples go through this sort of thing. It will sort itself out.'

'All couples? Even you and Dad?'

Dorothy said nothing but rubbed her hand slowly up and down Jean's back.

After a few moments, she said, 'Pregnancy is difficult for everyone. You need to remember that.'

Perhaps her mother had already discussed Jean's situation with her father because, when he came home from the factory a few hours later, he seemed completely relaxed and cheerful.

'Hello, dear,' he said. 'You're looking very well. Blooming.'

'Thanks Dad. I must say, I feel like a whale. Or possibly a balloon that's been blown up too much and is about to pop.'

'My first grandchild, eh.' He smiled with bemusement. 'It's good to see you, and the bump.'

Around the dinner table, nobody spoke about Jean and her situation. Instead, they talked about Larry's science project and the successes of the canning factory. Walter was happy to be expanding his business to employ some of the Mexican men who were moving to the area. Most of the women he'd employed during the war no longer worked at the factory. Instead, many more tiny children went along to the Sunday school classes which Dorothy ran.

Audrey was also involved with the Sunday school, bringing her small son Brian with her. Jean felt bad about Audrey; she had abandoned Audrey before her wedding to Ed and had left his sister Yvette to serve as maid of honour. Despite all that she had said to Audrey about how she'd love to do it, she had run off and left her. Jean felt a sick sense of shame as her parents talked about a friend who had once been so dear to her.

After the meal, the whole family watched the brand new television. Jean was transfixed. This was the first time she had seen a set outside of a shop window and the dark images coming out of the tiny screen were rather disappointing after the huge clear close-ups of the movies. But still, it was enthralling to see newsmen as they talked, rather than simply hearing them.

Perry Como had a show straight afterwards, sponsored by a popular cigarette company. This was an irritating follow-up – but its fifteen minutes of light music ended soon enough. Too soon, in fact, as at eight o'clock, the doorbell rang. Jean thought nothing of it, until a tall man came into the room, casting a shadow on the wall and hiding her mother behind him. Somehow, Larry and her father seemed to fade away, without any indication of how or where they had gone.

'Reverend Parry,' sighed Jean. She had been slumped in an armchair but for this, she knew she had to assume a fully upright position.

'Hello, Mrs Costello,' he replied. 'Your mother asked me to come for a chat.'

Of course she did, Jean thought. Why had she not anticipated this... intrusion. Religion answered all of her mother's questions. If there was something difficult happening, God – in the shape of one minister or another – would know exactly what to do. Very briefly, she felt embarrassed about her clothes: a tatty man's shirt and a worse skirt, which Helena had abandoned after the elastic gave out.

He shut the door firmly as he smiled gently at Jean.

'I see.' Jean knew part of her brain was shutting down, in a sort of panic.

'She tells me that you have left your husband because of his drinking.'

'In short, yes.'

'So what happened?'

Jean took a reckoning of Johnny's misdemeanours in the search for something suitable.

'He wants to control everything I do. I don't know. It's hard to explain. I am a very bad housewife.'

'But he's your husband. Of course he wants you to do as he says. Marriage is a sacred partnership.'

'We didn't marry in church,' Jean said crossly.

'That doesn't matter,' he replied. 'It would have been far better if you had, but nevertheless, you are joined together. Why won't you do what he asks?'

Jean was shocked.

'But he wants me to do things I think are wrong.'

'Are they immoral or illegal?'

'No! Of course not!' Jean burst into humourless laughter.

'You need to bend to his will. That's what the Bible says.'

Jean could sense her body go rigid.

'According to him, he knows best about my art.'

'My dear Mrs Costello, are you still doing that? Well, when little Johnny comes along you won't have the opportunity for art. Instead, you'll be bringing up the next generation, which is where woman's real gift for creativity lies. If you spend too much of your time and attention on interests outside your family, it will suffer.'

Reverend Parry seemed rather skinny, his ribs clearly visible through his grubby shirt. Was there no Mrs Parry,

Jean wondered, or did she too fail in her womanly duties?

'You know,' he continued kindly. 'If you are finding your household tasks too difficult, there are always classes you could take. Don't you want to look after your husband?'

Jean was not sure she did want to look after Johnny, or any man, in that sense, but could not expend the effort it would take to say so. She nodded.

'Of course, he must stop drinking. Would you like me to talk to him about it?'

Jean wondered dizzily what would happen if he did.

'I don't think he would take any notice,' she said.

'In that case, I won't do so. But the offer stands.'

He took her hands in his; they were rather cool, considering the temperature outside.

'Shall we pray about it?'

Oh why not, Jean thought bitterly.

'All right.' As he talked over her, Jean saw herself floating outside her body. After the praying had finished, she had no idea at all what he had said.

It was no surprise at all when, around noon the next day, Johnny turned up outside the house in a rather beautiful car Jean had never seen before.

'Hello, darling,' he said. 'I've come to take you home.'

Her parents stood by the front door, Walter with his arm around Dorothy. Jean sighed.

'Who told you I was here?'

'It was obvious, wasn't it? Where else would you be? Women always go back to their mothers when their husbands behave badly. I behaved badly. I apologise.'

Jean nodded. She felt huge, exhausted, defeated.

'I promise not to drink anymore. I'll stop. You need me. Our child needs me. Please.'

He looked at Jean's parents over her shoulder as they embraced. Jean wondered whether they had called him, remembering that her mother had told her, only yesterday, that a heavily pregnant woman should not be seen without her husband. With Johnny in evidence, Jean's condition was not something that needed hiding.

Walter smiled at Johnny.

'Now, won't you come in and eat lunch before you go back to the city? I can't leave my son-in-law standing on the doorstep.'

'With pleasure, sir.'

Johnny moved inside the house. Was he really calling her father 'sir', she wondered? Or had she misheard?

Her parents laughed along with Johnny as he talked to them about the car, the journey, and his students, and Jean sensed relief in their voices. It being Saturday, Larry was also around. Jean noticed his silence, but no one else seemed to.

'Everything will be all right,' he whispered as they finished their lunch. 'I can look after you and the baby if Johnny turns out to be no good.'

Tears came into Jean's eyes and she hugged him tight.

'I'll come to see you soon,' she said.

Johnny looked grand inside the automobile. Jean gazed at his bronzed arm against the steering wheel, the tiny hairs golden, and remembered how magnetic she had once found him.

'Nice car, huh. I haven't had one since I was injured. I thought I couldn't drive again.'

'Yes, it's real nice.' Jean had nothing to say; she wasn't sure what type it was and she didn't care.

'I figured we needed an automobile with a kid, you know. Makes it easier when you don't need to take a bus. The doctors said...' He paused. 'If I don't drink, I can drive.'

'Sure.'

'Nothing more to say for yourself, Jean? You run away from me and you have nothing to say? No apologies, no I'm sorry, I love you, please forgive me?'

'I'm tired, Johnny, so tired.'

'It takes two to make a marriage, you know. Perhaps your clergyman told you that.'

'Huh,' said Jean. She smiled slightly.

'I was wrong, but you were wrong too. I've said I will give up drinking and I mean it. The doctors said that it only makes the vertigo and the shaking worse. But you also have to change your ways. Look after yourself, for instance, and not spend every minute painting. You'll have our son to look after soon and you're risking his health as well as your own.'

'I know, Johnny. I'm sorry.' Her voice came in a whisper, she was so done in.

'All right then.' He nodded.

He had his eyes on the road, his hands on the wheel, his concentration somewhere else altogether. Jean felt herself dozing off when suddenly he spoke out loud and clear.

'Never do this again, Jean. Never. You hear me. I mean it.'

His voice sounded cold and strange.

'I cannot have my wife running away. What do you think it looks like? Promise me you won't.'

'I won't,' she said in exhaustion, leaning her head against the cool new leather of the seat.

CHAPTER TWENTY-ONE

KAREN: SCOTLAND, JULY 2018

It wasn't surprising that Lisa and her husband Keith were together, Karen thought. Anyone would love him, the great cuddly bear of a man. Even when he didn't have his arm around her, Lisa looked as if she was wrapped in warmth when she stood next to him. His appearance was so stereotypically Scottish with his red beard and his wild red hair, he clearly belonged in a kilt. He had worn one for their wedding but never did so again, at least not in Karen's presence.

Keith's parents lived just north of Glasgow, in a beautiful area between lochs, and he was spending ever more time there. He both wanted to and needed to after his father twice found himself lost around an area where he had always lived. His mother was becoming increasingly anxious about everything and started telephoning her only son in the middle of the night.

After the intensity of a week's tour-guiding, Karen looked forward to a few days' rest, a brief period of hiking and sleeping, talking to her sister and perhaps playing football with her young nephews. But her sense of relaxation did not last long.

'So here's the thing,' Lisa said, as they walked through the forest towards the water. Karen could smell the trees and had missed their calming influence.

'Keith and I have decided to leave London and come to live up here.' Karen stopped walking and turned to

face her. 'It's his parents. You know, you must have seen.'
Karen nodded; she had.

'They need you.'

'Well, they need Keith, and if he comes here then, of course, I will too.'

'Of course.'

Karen and Lisa looked at each other sadly and hugged. Karen felt low, so low as to be almost on the floor. Nevertheless, she carried on with the walk in the tranquil countryside as she put her hand on Lisa's shoulder.

'How do the boys feel about it?'

'They're a bit sad over leaving their friends at school, but you know... they're kids.'

'And me. I hope they're a bit sad about leaving me.'

'They don't anticipate leaving you because you're an adult who will be here whenever she likes.'

'Lisa! It's a long way from London. Come on!'

'So why don't you come up here too. It would do you good.'

Karen pressed her lips together. Her sister might be right.

'You can do your work from anywhere with an internet connection, can't you?'

'Hmm, suppose so.'

'It's lovely here, isn't it? Compared to where you're living now.'

'Ha!' Karen murmured. Lisa's logic had wrong-footed her, as usual. 'But, you know, I would feel exiled from the capital.'

'Snap,' said Lisa brusquely. 'Because, of course, I'm conflicted over this. That's obvious. Still,' – she smiled again – 'think about it. Coming up here, at least for a while, might be a good move. It doesn't have to be permanent.'

They carried on with their walk, the trees rustling, the tourists not so plentiful as to annoy them, the odd local nodding hello and commenting on the weather.

Karen put her tiredness down to the fresh air and after a dinner with more meat than she was used to and several glasses of wine, she collapsed into bed. The room smelled of lavender, of home. Why could she not make her small flat welcoming in this seemingly effortless way?

'Kiss, kiss, I miss my sis,' she said to herself balefully, feeling exhausted and drained of any further emotion. When did they come up with that as a sign-off to their phone calls? Too long ago to remember, Karen thought. And while she wondered for the umpteenth time whether online dating would ever be a viable proposition, she allowed loneliness to settle in the pit of her stomach.

Who was in her life anyway? Lisa and her family, now moving hundreds of miles away; Anna, even further away and constantly busy, and Ben, quite near and more or less available. Aside from that, there were acquaintances and contacts, and a few nice but distant relatives as well as the more unpleasant ones. But what about the other people who had floated in and out of her life? Where were her friends? Mates, buddies, companions? There had been too much work in her life. Even when she had not been working, she had been thinking, obsessing, about the work she wanted to do or ought to be doing.

Insomnia slammed into her again. She had been dog-tired but ruminating had woken her up. In past times, cigarettes would have provided relief; perhaps work served as a substitute for all the other addictions that might conceivably take over her life.

'Oh why not,' she thought, Googling Jean Woods. This was just a casual thing – not the right way of researching at all. Karen and the Pendleton family hadn't even formally signed a contract yet. She would not sign into any genealogy site; she would not.

But who was she, this Jean Woods, born in or around 1928? General search engines offered no instant answers, not for any part of California, or British Columbia, or Vancouver. Jean Woods, of course, was a common enough name. But this Jean Woods could not have been a dog breeder, or a housewife who died in 1965, or a teacher beloved in her small town who left behind many grandchildren when she died in 1988. She needed more information if she were to get good results.

Karen sensed her brain stirring; she needed to get to the bottom of this, and there were many possibilities. She decided to search for the Woods family of Lake View, California, to do her search properly, breaking her own promise to herself. Simply by searching on Ancestry, she found Larry Woods' sister in two minutes, three minutes tops. Karen shook her head in awe.

The extraordinary thing, she thought sadly, was that the most hidden of family secrets were no longer guaranteed to stay buried in the past. Barbara had expected to keep her identity as a British yoga teacher born in Canada, now living uneventfully in a small town in England, a woman whose main claim to any kind of fame was how late in life she carried on teaching. She expected to remain unchallenged as Barbara Pendleton, née Thompson, until she died, surrounded by her family who most certainly loved her.

But DNA, and the ability to search for so much information online, had put a stop to that.

Barbara's original name was there, plain as day: Jean Joyce Woods, born June 1928, only daughter of Walter and Dorothy Woods.

And that was just the start of it.

CHAPTER TWENTY-TWO

JEAN: SAN FRANCISCO, NOVEMBER 1952

Three months, just three, yet Jean could scarcely remember a time before motherhood. She had never been so tired. It was more than simple exhaustion; rather, every ounce of energy had been drained out of her body, leaving her like a corpse. Yet she could not, must not, give in to this; Gary needed her.

Ah, little Gary. A sweet and darling baby, a perfect combination of Jean and Johnny who alternately wailed and grizzled night and day. Crying herself, Jean would look at him in his cradle, unable to pick him up and comfort him. Yet Johnny would come in after his day at work and sweep Gary into his arms, cooing at him and, increasingly, making him giggle. One tickle under the chin would do it, or he would sing lullabies until Gary fell asleep. Jean would fall asleep too. But whenever she woke up again, she would feel as if she had not slept a wink.

Then there was the feeding. She started off feeding Gary herself but the nurse soon decided that he was not getting enough milk from her, and so in came the formula. Johnny happily gave him his bottle.

Johnny loved the baby, how he loved him. Jean felt abandoned, as though she had done her bit and now was no longer necessary. Johnny had desperately wanted a son, she knew, far more than a daughter. He'd taken little notice of Leonore at their wedding and had taken little notice of her since. Still, Johnny brought her to see Gary, rubbing into the faces of both Leonore and Frances the idea that this new child was far superior to the one he already had.

The noise, oh God, the noise. It frustrated Jean beyond endurance, the crying drilling into her brain. Yet she had to endure it, every other mother did, there was no alternative.

Frances was a good mother to Leonore, involved and protective, always loving, like Jean's own mother with her children. Jean was Gary's mother, wasn't she? So why did she feel so detached? The whole thing seemed to be happening to somebody else. When she looked at this tiny, wonderful person she'd created she did indeed feel awe, just as everyone said she should. But what then, what next? She was a worn-out husk, unable even to decide what to eat.

Johnny, rather to Jean's surprise, took over everything. He found Mrs Littleton, a warm, kind, capable woman, recommended by the doctor. Gary's *other* mother. Finally, Jean could sleep as long as she wanted. This, it turned out, was all night and most of the day as well.

Early in the new year, Jean returned to the studio. Sometimes, she could hardly stand but even when she felt almost unable to hold a brush, she managed to put a mark on the canvas. The colours she chose now were different, and this pleased Johnny.

'Yes!' he shouted as he saw her start to work again. 'THIS is what you should have been doing two years ago.'

She painted the canvases in monochromes using all the greys. Charcoal, smoke, slate, pewter, fog, nearly black and barely shadow. She added white and black, huge swathes of them. These paintings were bleak, a reflection of the contents of her heart. Johnny, on the other hand, saw them as cool representations of the human condition. He hugged her to him.

'Being a mother has made you a real artist,' he boasted, looking at her work. Never mind that she was incapable, unfit for the role of mother in any real sense of the word. It was as if he was talking to somebody else, someone that he knew and she didn't.

Jean hated this; the grey was all-pervasive. Her brain, not just the canvas, was full of fog. She could do nothing. She was nothing. She spent days in her studio looking at the greys she had already painted.

Finally, she took a red, a bright, blood red, and splashed it over first one, then all, of the canvases stacked against the wall.

'I'm so sorry, Mrs Costello. My daughter and my granddaughter are both sick and need me. I hope you understand.' Mrs Littleton bowed her head sorrowfully, acknowledging that her absence sure would be a pity but there it was.

Jean did understand, of course she did. In theory. The 'nervous tension' that everyone decided afflicted her should be gone now, shouldn't it? If she needed a babysitter, surely there was nothing to stop her from hiring one. Jean controlled the panic that must show on her face.

'Really, you mustn't worry about me, or us. Gary will miss you, as will I. But your own family must come first.' The two women shook hands warmly and Jean paid her an extra week's money just to show the sentiment was genuine.

Of course, she did feel 'better'. Of course. She slept for weeks on end, had some completed work in her studio, she ate properly. She talked to Johnny, visited some friends, welcomed her parents and brother when they wanted to look at Gary. But was she 'better.'? Definitely not.

The grey paintings – apparently enhanced, rather than destroyed, by the red – were growing in number.

They were stacked against the walls of her studio, ten deep in places. But she did not love them. She knew what it felt like when she had painted something new and beautiful, that came straight from her heart. Oh the joy of it! The intense involvement. Jean remembered that dimly. Now, her heart was grey and cold and the work reflected that.

The next sitter – a young girl, not an experienced woman recommended by the doctor, but a relation of the landlord – could not have been more different. Giggly and wearing tight orange slacks and an oversized sweater, her hair cut very closely to her scalp, Ronnie had only recently graduated high school. Jean was astonished to see her arrive in a car – her own car, no less, that she had bought with her earnings as a waitress. She looked like a kid. But children cared for younger children; she had done so herself. Right now, Jean felt both too young and too old to be a mother.

'Hey, cute boy.' Ronnie smiled. 'He'll be fine with me.' Gary grinned back at her and Jean, anxious and guilty, made her way to the studio. She stared at a canvas for an hour, wondering if she could paint anything. Nausea rose in her stomach; should she check how Gary was doing? She went upstairs into the kitchen, where Ronnie sang to Gary while he ate his mashed potato.

'We're doing swell, Mrs Costello,' said Ronnie, reassuringly. 'Gary and I have really hit it off, haven't we?' He squealed and moved quickly back and forth with his mouth open. Jean suddenly knew that Ronnie, young as she might be, had been warned that she was a wreck who might collapse completely at any moment.

'That's grand,' said Jean. She smiled back at Ronnie and stuck her tongue out at Gary, who screwed his face up to cry. 'Well, I'll just get a glass of water.' She took her water back into her studio, guilt and relief churning together to make her queasy once more.

Ronnie turned up more or less on time for a while; she clearly liked Gary who squealed with delight to see her. But three weeks later, Jean jiggled a teething Gary on her hip as she drank her morning coffee. Where was Ronnie? This was too bad. An hour later, Ronnie's mother telephoned. Ronnie had been called away for a college interview. She'd be back tomorrow. Jean was uneasy; to the best of her knowledge, college interviews did not happen without warning. There would be no painting today at any rate. Instead, she would take Gary out in the stroller.

A mother with a baby, taking him for a walk, that was exactly as it should be. People smiled at her. She wondered whether she could take him to visit one of her friends. Helena, for instance. She had neglected Helena, who had written with her new address and to say she was in the early stages of pregnancy herself. The trouble was that Johnny did not like Helena, or Mike, who she'd married a few months before. Johnny had never gone so far as to forbid her from seeing them; he would not have done anything so, as he put it, Victorian. Nevertheless, he would roll his eyes and make contemptuous comments. 'No talent, no-hopers,' he called them. 'You deserve better.'

What that meant was that they only saw his friends, and even then not often as none of them had small children in tow. Besides, she had 'nervous tension' and he had sworn off alcohol. So they stayed at home much of the time, not speaking or doing anything much apart from reading.

But Ronnie did not come again the next day, nor the one after. On the third, Jean received a letter apologising for her absence and saying that she had taken a job in San Diego. For the love of all that's holy, Jean thought, San Diego? Why would she do that? But she knew the likely answer: adventure, excitement, the thrill of something new. The college interview was probably a lie. So, back to the beginning. Would she ever again paint anything?

When Johnny came home that day, Jean was sitting slumped on a wooden kitchen chair, staring at Gary, still holding Ronnie's letter. The boy lolled in his high chair, dried tomato sauce all over his face, his hair, and his clothes. Gary had been crying, had sobbed himself to sleep, his small gasps transforming into hiccups.

'Jean!'

She jumped. 'Oh! Johnny.'

'What on earth's going on here? For God's sake pull yourself together. Look at the state of the boy. He's not safe with you. Never mind loved or happy, not even safe!'

Jean handed Ronnie's note to Johnny; the rest of her body still frozen.

'Dammit!'

He took a washcloth and gently began to clean Gary's face. The child barely stirred while his father changed his diaper and all of his clothes, before taking him into his bedroom and laying him down in the crib. Johnny stormed back into the room.

'Jean. What the hell is wrong with you? Do you *want* to be sent to the funny farm? *Do you?*'

'I can't...'

'You can't *what?*' His voice had risen higher so that he was screaming at her.

'I know the doctors, we all, agreed that you had nervous tension but maybe you are actually fucking nuts. How long have you been sitting there?'

'A while.' She shrugged. Why did she feel so anxious when they talked? She was incapable of keeping ideas in her head long enough for them to be spoken out loud.

Johnny rubbed two fingers on either side of his eyebrows. He looked across at Jean, and up towards the ceiling. The paint was flaking at the top of the walls and he could see cobwebs stretching between the corners of the room; the dinginess no longer a necessary part of an artist's life but disgusting. Unspeakable.

'All right,' he said.

Jean was still sitting as she had been for hours when Johnny came back into the kitchen, two bags packed.

'I'm taking Gary to your parents,' he said. 'I don't know what else to do. Then I'm going to come back and find you someplace else to live.'

He glared at her, a mocking pity on his face. 'Frankly, Jean, you can go hang as far as I am concerned. Gary will be better off without you.'

CHAPTER TWENTY-THREE

JEAN: SAN FRANCISCO, NOVEMBER 1953

One good thing Johnny did, Jean realised much later, was make her see a psychiatrist. Jean had met few women doctors, and they specialised in the treatment of babies and children. By contrast, Dr Levenson's patients were women: usually mothers. Mothers who experienced difficulty in doing what they must. For some, their failures lay on the wifely side. They didn't want their husbands to touch them or they wanted it too much, too often. All those female flaws, offences that lay with women, not men. Thankfully, Dr Levenson didn't consider sex was one of Jean's problems.

Nor did she think Jean was merely suffering from nervous tension. Dr Levenson's area of research dealt with women who had become disturbed as a result of pregnancy and motherhood, women like Jean, and she wanted her to undergo psychoanalysis. But first, because Jean's mind needed to be fixed in the short as well as the long-term, she recommended a drug called isoniazid, which was starting to be used as a treatment for depression and anxiety.

And what a relief it was! The fog began to clear and Jean stopped being worried about everything all the time.

Jean, alone, had moved to a much smaller apartment, where she might work in the kitchen, and live, eat and sleep in the only other room. Even the bathroom stood out on the landing but that was all right. She would move away from the monochrome and red paintings that she didn't love, and turn back towards something more, well, joyful. Soon, when she began to paint again, this is what she would do. She had not felt joy for what felt like decades. Now, possibly, the pleasure was starting to creep back.

But before she could experience any real happiness, she needed to see Gary. Whenever she thought about him, piercing guilt repeatedly stabbed at her. She had failed him. Dr Levenson had told her that her own mother was probably at fault, something that Jean found hard to believe. Her father must be an inadequate parent too, according to the doctor. Oh but Jean hated the very idea! She would rather blame herself. Or Johnny. Nevertheless, the drugs allowed a chink of light into her darkness and made her believe that looking after Gary herself might be a possibility. If only she didn't feel so queasy all the time. That, said Dr Levenson, was a side effect of the treatment that she would come to accept.

Johnny kept the new car after he moved Gary to Jean's parents, and then Jean to her own place. He stayed in their old apartment and hired some decorators to make it the sort of place a successful, caring father would live. Johnny was changing; it was all of a piece with his stopping drinking. He was an adult and a father of two with responsibilities that he had never taken seriously enough before. His previous attempts at adulthood had been crushed by the war and the injuries he incurred as a result. That experience had taught him the nearness of death, and that precious little mattered. Certainly, he no longer valued his own art. But he was growing away from that misery now. He knew that he would probably live for years and that other people, particularly his children, depended on him.

Jean heard this from her psychiatrist; she and Johnny no longer spoke. He gave her an allowance each month, and she imagined that he paid her parents for Gary's keep. All other information about him comprised gossip and rumour. She didn't think he had taken up with anyone else, not really, and anyway she wasn't sure whether she even cared.

Her real concern lay elsewhere. Jean managed to buy a second-hand car: a dark-green 1948 Ford Deluxe Coupe, a pre-war style that no one seemed to want anymore. Jean hadn't driven an automobile since she learned in high school but she would not be able to visit Gary in Lake View, and maybe even take him back to the city with her if she could only go on a bus or train. There would be too much to carry. As she felt more alive, her yearning for him grew. He was her son, after all. Her baby. She would go there now.

During the last few miles of the drive, nausea started to roll over her in great waves from deep within her stomach, forcing their way right up through her body. Oh no, she thought, pulling over, opening the car door and jumping out just in time to heave onto the road. Jean pressed her head to the side of the seat, empty inside, her head spinning. If only she had some water. There was hard candy in her pocketbook; that might help. She sucked at the lemon drop but still, as it grew dark, Jean smelled the vomit that had somehow made its way onto her shoes as well as the exterior of the car. She must keep going.

She pulled up outside her parents' house and looked at the lights glowing through the curtains. The air seemed colder here than in the city, and Jean worried that her clothes were not warm enough. They weren't expecting her either. Still, it was too late now and Gary would be inside, his little face smiling.

'Hello, Larry.'

Her brother opened the door to her, his expression a mix of surprise and confusion. Then, together, happiness at seeing her and distaste at her smell.

'Jean! Okay!'

He called back into the house.

'Mom. Dad. Jean's here.'

Her parents came to the door, smiles and embraces disguising their bewilderment.

'It's good to see you,' her father said, kissing her cheek.

'How are you feeling?' asked her mother, guiding her into the kitchen.

'Oh, you know. Better. But the doctor has given me pills and they don't agree with me. The driving made things worse.'

'Sit down and have some water.'

Jean drank gratefully.

'Is Gary asleep then? It's been so long. I miss him.'

There was a pause, while the other three tried not to exchange glances.

'What is it?' Jean shouted in desperation. 'What's wrong?'

'Gary is with Johnny,' her mother spoke slowly. 'We figured you knew. Gary only stayed here for a week, three months ago. Johnny thought, Johnny *said*, that there was no point in writing to you because it would only upset you. That for you to get better, you needed not to be disturbed.'

'But you are angry with me, aren't you?' Jean barely breathed. 'I believed that was why you didn't send any letters. Anyway, what is there to say?'

'You are my daughter,' Walter said slowly. 'There is plenty to say.'

Dorothy, desperate to be excused from the crime of giving Gary away, looked firmly at Jean.

'After all, Johnny *is* his father,' she continued. 'He has someone reliable to look after Gary while he is at work. He's not a bad father, is he? I would say he was a good one.'

'But I am his *mother*. His ***mother***.'

Walter moved over to Jean and put his hand on her shoulder.

'You never thought I should marry Johnny,' she sobbed. 'Or be an artist. You thought I should stay here and live your sort of life. You wanted me to marry Joe.'

No one spoke. Larry took her empty glass and filled it at the faucet. At seventeen, he realised that everything was just plain wrong. What had happened to his sister?

Jean was the only one shouting; she realised that. Oh, but the disappointment. She couldn't bear it. Her child was not there. Johnny had Gary now; her boy was lost to her.

'I must go back to the city,' she said. 'But I need to sleep. Before I came here, I had started to feel better, but now. Well, I don't.'

'Of course, dear. I'll make up your old room.' Dorothy was pleased to have something practical to do, a necessary task, in the absence of saying anything worthwhile or helpful. She thanked God for that.

'Would you like me to run you a bath?'

Jean nodded, silent. To Dorothy, she handed her clothes, somehow dirtier than she realised, bathed, and then got into bed. It was just 9:30, so early. She had eaten nothing, but the residue of the pills and the nausea remained. As she fell into a deep sleep, she could hear them speaking about her, and then one side of an angry telephone call.

The walls of her childhood bedroom pressed against her, crushing her on that too-narrow bed. Yet that was what she wanted too. When she'd visited before, she'd felt only claustrophobia. Now, there was also love and warmth. Until, that is, she awoke at three, gasping for breath as if the spirit of Johnny had clamped his hand over her mouth.

In the bathroom, she splashed some water over her face and then trudged downstairs. First, she went into the kitchen to eat some ham from the refrigerator and drink some soda. Then, she sat in the living room, next to the television – a larger one than on her previous visit – staring as the moonlight played over the slightly open drapes, moving onto the family photographs on the wall and the glass of the framed painting she had done in junior college. There had been so many versions of this room, she remembered; different colour schemes, furniture, wallpaper; so many versions of herself too. The family had moved here when she was a baby, when the house was new. They had grown up together. But she experienced no sense of nostalgia about it, neither the house nor her childhood. Everything passed.

Jean went back to bed, pulled the cover over her head and slept until noon. She had nothing at all to say but was happy that her mother had washed and ironed most of her clothes, and made her eat some eggs and toast. Larry cleaned her car inside and out. Still, she needed to be gone. She would not take another tablet until she was back in the city; she could not risk the sickness happening again.

All three of them hugged her as she sat back in the driver's seat, grey and drained. What was the point of any of this, she wondered? Nothing. She wanted to sleep forever.

Impossible.

Johnny was in their old apartment, just as she'd thought he would be. And by his side, wearing fleecy pyjamas with dogs on them, stood Gary. He held his father's hand and looked up at Jean with dismay.

'Hello, wife,' said Johnny. 'I wondered how long it would take. Your mother telephoned.'

Jean looked at Gary, so sweet, leaning against Johnny's leg.

'Why didn't you tell me you had Gary here?'

'I'm protecting him, surely even you can see that?'

Jean did not want to cry. She would not cry. She *would not.*

'He was protected at my parents' house.'

'Huh. Well, I don't want him to be raised by them. They hardly did a great job on *you*, did they?'

She reeled. He was still able to shock her.

'I didn't realise you disliked them. I had no clue from your behaviour.'

Johnny shrugged and then smiled down at Gary.

'This little man needs to get to bed.'

He lifted the boy to his hip in a way that Jean had not seen him do before. Gary leaned more closely against his father, sucking his thumb. 'Give Mommy a kiss,' Johnny cajoled. He angled the child towards Jean, but he turned his face away. She kissed Gary's cheek, wondering if she could carry on standing.

'Night night, Mommy.' As the person she used to love spoke, in a sing-song, mocking voice, Johnny took Gary's hand and waved it limply at her.

While Johnny put Gary to bed, Jean went into the large living room and sat on the couch. It seemed new, a bright plaid yellow and orange. When had all this furniture, this smart light paint, this lovely clean apartment... when and how did it happen? It was only a few months since she moved out. Why had she been unable to achieve anything like that herself? Her inadequacy floored her, her lack of skill in all the areas that mattered.

Could things get any worse? It seemed so.

Johnny came into the room and pulled up a chair opposite her.

'You're seeing that head-shrink, aren't you? She still bills me, at any rate.' Jean nodded, eyes cast down. 'Well, look. You can't see Gary until you are completely better. If that ever happens, which I doubt. I won't let you. Take this evening, for instance. He felt scared, poor kid. What was he going to think, you turning up out of nowhere?'

'How can you do that?' Jean did not trust her ability to speak, her voice barely louder than a whisper.

'Easily,' he said coldly. 'I'm his father. I can do whatever I damn well please.'

Jean looked at him blankly.

'I know that you aren't going to divorce me and sue for custody because quite frankly you haven't got a hope in hell. Have you?'

Until that very minute, this thought had not crossed Jean's mind. But now it did, and she saw that he was right. She would not have a hope, in hell or anywhere else.

'So you need to leave me to be his only parent until and unless you prove to me that you can be the mother he needs.'

'Did you do this to Frances too?'

'Do what?'

'Take Leonore.'

Johnny looked baffled.

'Of course not. Frances was all right with Leonore. You are not all right with Gary. Frances has never been fucking crazy. She's a normal woman, not an artist. God! Remind me never to marry an artist again.'

Jean's limbs seemed entirely disconnected from the rest of her. Was blood still flowing around her body? She supposed it must be.

'I don't care about art anymore.'

'Right! Right!' He laughed bitterly, contempt and disbelief fighting for the upper hand. 'What about that show you have lined up? All those Death/Life paintings.'

'I hate them. I don't know why I did them. I want to go back to what I painted before. Or...' she stopped, no longer certain of anything. 'Maybe I don't want to be an artist at all. What good did it do me?'

Johnny looked at her with derision.

'I don't want a show. I wasn't ready when I did my first show and I'm still not ready. I'll never be ready.'

He rolled his eyes.

'Now listen to me, you stupid woman. You have a show booked for January. The pictures are right here in the studio. It is going to happen whether you like it or not.'

Jean stood up and ran downstairs, slamming the apartment door behind her. It was only then that she realised that Gary was still with Johnny, and she had not even said goodbye. She drove a couple of blocks before she began to shake so badly that she had to stop.

An hour later, she got out of the car, her head spinning. She felt dizzy. So dizzy. She managed to walk the rest of the way to her apartment, just getting inside the door before she vomited again.

It was no good; nothing would be any good ever again.
She took the bottle of isoniazid and emptied her tablets
down the toilet.

Family Tree: Costello-Woods 1954

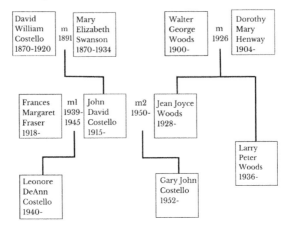

PART FIVE

Chapter Twenty-Four

Jean: San Francisco, April 1954

Helena's kitchen was messy. The room measured some twelve feet square; Helena and Mike spent most of their time there and so, obviously, did Bobby and Billy. The walls had been white when they moved in but eighteen months of smoke and inadequate cleaning had put paid to that. The mess encompassed oil paints and leftover baby food, piles of clothes waiting to be washed alongside other piles of pencil sketches: it was all there together in total confusion. Was it warm, happy, creative domesticity, or every woman artist's worst nightmare? Jean didn't know. Probably both.

'So, spill,' said Helena sharply. 'Something's up. Tell me now.'

She sat on a stool in front of Jean, her legs apart, her elbows on her knees. As always, Helena spoke directly.

Jean sighed, pressing her lips together. 'I think I'm pregnant.'

Helena sighed sympathetically. 'Whose is it?' She paused, alarm crossing her face. 'Oh God, it's not Johnny's is it? Please don't tell me you're back with him?'

Jean said nothing, shook her head and looked down, so that Helena didn't know whether she was saying no it wasn't Johnny, or sorry to say, yes it was Johnny after all.

'How far along are you?'

'Not long. I mean, I might not be pregnant. Six weeks. Two months?'

'So you probably are. Do you think you are?'

'Mm.'

'Mm?'

'Yes, I expect I am.'

'Oh dear.' Helena reached out to give her a quick hug. 'What are you going to do?'

'I don't know.' Jean paused. 'I can't go back to him, I just can't. You know what he's like. And anyway, I don't want a baby, any baby, certainly not this one.'

'But what happened? Why did you go to bed together? I thought you hated him?'

Jean shook her head, tears starting to run down her cheeks.

'All right, I'm sorry. You needn't tell me, it doesn't matter.'

Helena took two cigarettes and lit them, passing one to Jean who inhaled deeply and tipped back her head, pursing her lips to blow the smoke firmly towards the ceiling.

'Men are bastards,' said Helena contemptuously. 'They have no idea what women have to go through.'

'Not Mike, though. Mike is just fine,' Jean spoke decisively, equally contemptuous in her way.

'No, he isn't. Oh well, maybe. Maybe he's okay.' Helena moved to hug her again, putting down her cigarette and wafting away the smoke. 'Jeannie, dear Jeannie. What are we going to do with you?'

'I need to go to that woman you took me to before.'

'You mean Nurse Wright?'

Jean nodded, the movement almost imperceptible. 'I have to get rid of it.'

'Yes.' Helena sighed. 'It's horrible, but I guess the alternatives are worse.'

Rustling from the tiny bedroom next door indicated that Bobby and Billy were about to wake up from their nap. Sure enough, they soon started gurgling and laughing with each other. Then one began crying, with noises that might have been 'Mamma, Mamma' before rushing into the kitchen. Helena scooped him up into her lap.

'Yes, I'm here honey.' She bent down to kiss him. 'What's wrong?'

Too young for proper words, he stretched out his arm towards the table, making sweet little mewling sounds. Helena poured out some milk for Bobby, and then another for Billy, who came in, rubbing his eyes. Jean looked at them with a pang as they drank. The boys were so very cute, she could have scooped them up and devoured them. Helena noticed her yearning.

'Perhaps you would love this child if you had it.'

'Not considering its father,' said Jean firmly. 'I would hate it every time I looked at it. Remember what happened with Gary. This would be much worse.'

Helena stretched out her arm and pulled Jean close, like she had with her sons.

'Call Nurse Wright to set up an appointment,' Helena said. 'I'll come with you if you like. It's not something you should go through alone.'

'But getting rid of a baby is illegal.'

'Of course it's illegal. You already knew that, didn't you?'

'Yes,' Jean mumbled. She sighed and then sighed again.

'But your life is worth the risk.'

Jean nodded miserably. Her heart pounded and she hadn't even made the call yet. But the thought of having a baby, any baby, under these or any other circumstances was horrific. Oh boy, she felt wretched.

She didn't want to be in the warm fug of domesticity anymore and so she walked out of Helena's apartment and towards a road, any road, where adults ruled and children were old enough to be at school. Jean staggered to the nearest diner and, settling into a booth, ordered a coffee. She took a sip. Was coffee the reason for her nausea and the tugging sensation in her stomach? Maybe. Perhaps it was a whisky that she really needed, but surely not at three in the afternoon. Her hands shook. Maybe she felt anxious, scared of the future, scared of what had happened, disgusted and repelled. Maybe her hormones, her body had taken over so that she lacked the slightest control over her emotions. Thoughts and feelings were at war in her brain.

Jean became aware of rocking back and forth, like a small, disturbed child. That was what she felt like but suddenly it was clear that she appeared like this too. Someone tiny and obvious, too young to be in a diner alone. With difficulty, she stopped the rocking. She reached inside her bag for the piece of paper with Nurse Wright's number written there. Surely her name wasn't really Nurse Wright? She turned it over and over with the fingers of one hand. This soothed her.

'More coffee, miss?' The waitress looked down quizzically, as though this would make everything all right. Jean nodded, an automatic reaction. She lit a cigarette and inhaled deeply. The waitress's curious glance continued.

'You okay?' Her eyes narrowed.

'Quite all right, thank you.' Jean felt humiliated.

'Well, if you're sure.' The woman walked away, sneaking glances at her every few steps or so.

Jean consciously pulled herself together and sipped her coffee. She no longer wanted the coffee. But she drank it anyway, finishing the cup and slapping some coins onto the table.

Back on the sidewalk, the sun had come out and, although it was mid-afternoon, seemed unusually high in the sky. Her stomach churned, oh boy did it ever. The walk to her apartment seemed far longer than fifteen minutes and she thought she would fall over before she got there. Her limbs were weak, like she had flu.

Climbing the stairs, Jean was scarcely able to fit her key into the lock. She reached her bed and fell forward onto its softness. Suddenly, could it possibly be? Her underwear stuck to her thighs. She staggered into the bathroom. Finally, after far too long, bright red blood. Jean put her hands to her face and sobbed.

CHAPTER TWENTY-FIVE

LYNNE: SWINDON, ENGLAND, AUGUST 2018

Why didn't Nick have any interest in their family history? Lynne could not fathom her brother's reactions. Who would not want to know that their mother was really someone else, who had lived a hugely interesting and intrepid life under another name? It beggared belief. This represented the most extraordinary thing that had ever happened to Lynne, or Cathy. Or, indeed, Nick. But he'd said, very explicitly, I don't want to know.

Several weeks had passed since Karen told Lynne, Cathy and Rachel that their mother and grandmother, Barbara Pendleton, did not start life as Barbara Thompson in rural British Columbia, but was, instead, Jean Joyce Woods, JJ, a once-esteemed artist. Cathy told Jennifer and Michelle, and they, too, seemed bewildered. They dimly remembered a man introduced to them as Uncle Gary, who was staying with their grandparents. But they had no idea he was Jean's son and had not seen him since they were small children.

None of them knew what to do next.

Should they talk to Barbara?

Should they try to find out more about why she went missing, without asking her directly?

Should they try to find out more about her life?

Everyone stayed stuck, waiting for something, anything, to happen. After what felt like an onslaught of information, of having the ground crumble beneath their feet, they were unable to act.

Karen had drawn up a basic family tree for them, using what they knew about Jean and what DNA confirmed about their maternal side. Jean Joyce Woods, born 1928, and taking the professional name JJ Woods, married John Costello in 1950. The couple had a son, Gary John, born in 1952. Larry Woods was Jean's brother and, as they wrote in their letter, Jennifer and Michelle were his daughters, now in their late forties and their only maternal first cousins.

But tens of second cousins now appeared as genetic connections, along with hundreds of third and fourth cousins. They didn't want to look further down the list of fifth to whatever other degree cousins. Every time any of the Pendletons went online, more people seemed to have taken DNA tests and found connections to lives and families that they had never dreamt of. They could not work out how these unknown people might be related to them. It was all too much.

There seemed to be no DNA connections to Gary, however. The most likely reason for that, Karen told them, was because he simply had not tested. They should all upload their data to other familial DNA sites just in case. As far as she could find out, Gary was still alive; at any rate, she could find no proof or reason to assume otherwise. At sixty-six, he could be living anywhere and doing anything.

In the end, Barbara herself broke the silence.

The weather had been worryingly hot, too much for all of them, and it had been doing this for months. Endless days of sunshine whereas, usually, one or two at a time would be England's lot. This was climate change, everyone said so, but on 9th August something longed-for happened: rain. The temperature dropped and everyone breathed again.

'Better now, Mum?' Lynne asked as she made them both some tea.

'I'm happy it's a bit cooler this morning, aren't you? The air's fresher.'

The grey sky started to spit and spot on the garden table; suddenly it was pouring with rain.

'Oh look, I'd better shut the windows.'

'No, that doesn't matter. Come here.'

Barbara patted the chair next to her.

'This has gone on for too long and I'm feeling stronger now.'

Lynne pulled the chair away from the table nervously.

'You fuss a bit, but you don't flap around me like Cathy does. She flaps so much, she could almost take off like a helicopter. Or a chicken!'

Lynne thought this quite funny but felt uneasy too. She was going to be the recipient of confidences and would have to pass them on, with all the repercussions that would entail. She pulled the seat cushion beneath her.

'I realise you have worked out who I used to be. I'm not entirely deaf; I can hear your conversations sometimes. But I never expected any of this to happen. My life in the years before you were born was dreadful. I married a man I was... not exactly afraid of... but he was very difficult. I loved him to start with, of course.' Barbara stopped, remembering.

'When I met your dad, oh he was so lovely. Such a gentleman. A sweet, generous person.'

'But, Mum, I don't understand. You were a successful artist.'

'No. Definitely not. My husband. Mr Costello.' Barbara practically spat his name. 'He was a Svengali. He knew what he wanted me to be and he was damn well going to make sure he moulded me in that image.'

Barbara paused, unhappily.

'This is the ninth of August and I always remember this day. My little boy, Gary, was born on the ninth of August. He'd be sixty-six today. Johnny Costello stole him.'

'Stole him?' Lynne's voice was shrill; the sound bounced around her head, hitting it from the inside out.

'You remember how I got when I had my babies. You were old enough to realise how I went away, was given pills and electric shock treatment. The same thing happened with Gary too. Of course, these days it would be called post-natal depression but not then. I don't know if Mr Costello took advantage of that, or if he really thought me a terrible mother. But anyway, I had no one to help me, my mother lived far away, his mother – she died years before. I was still trying to be an artist too. Who knows why. That never gave me any happiness, not after I became a mother anyway. I suppose it did to start with.'

'Oh, Mum.' Lynne started to cry, but Barbara didn't.

'He took Gary and called me unfit. Everyone probably agreed with him and Gary cried when he saw me. I thought it was too late to be a mother to him and I was probably right. Maybe he was better off with Johnny.

'Anyway, when I got pregnant with you, I had to get away. Then I met your father, and we married, and my life, your life, was a good one. I didn't have depression with you, you know. Perhaps that was relief. But then later, with Cathy and Nick, I felt so sad and guilty about Gary. I wonder what sort of life he has had.'

'Is Johnny Costello my biological father then?'

Barbara lay back and closed her eyes.

'Not now,' she said. 'Later.'

CHAPTER TWENTY-SIX

KAREN: LONDON, ENGLAND, AUGUST 2018

Dear Meredith, (Karen began her email). She paused. Clearly, Meredith felt happy to be in touch with her because Elle – mysterious Elle, connected with all this somehow – had said so. Nevertheless, it was very disconcerting.

I am once again working on my client Lynne Pendleton's family and she has given me permission to find out as much about your family connection with her as I can. I attach the information we do know (her mother turns out to have been an artist who went missing in 1954) but I still have no idea as to who might have sent this cease and desist letter. This is definitely connected with her paternal, not maternal, side as her brother and sister have not received one.

We are still trying to work out the identity of Lynne's biological father. It seems likely that he was her mother's first (and I have to say only legal) husband, a man called Johnny Costello. However, DNA links to him are not obvious given the people who have tested so far. I am trying to work out who among the many cousins might be connected to him but I have not managed to do this yet.

Meredith replied in the time it took her to type a response.

Karen! This is amazing! I have to pass this information on to Elle! She will be astonished but I will let her tell you herself!

All those exclamations. Meredith's shock radiated through it. And in the time it took Karen to stand up and stretch, Elle was calling on WhatsApp.

'Hello, Karen.'

How could she look so glamorous, Karen wondered? It was six in the morning in New Mexico.

'This is scarcely believable. My original name was Leonore Costello. My father was Jean Woods' husband, Johnny. My goodness. I thought he killed her!'

Elle seemed to be on the point of fainting. She sat down in a deep armchair and shut her eyes, breathing slowly.

'I'll just take a moment.'

'Of course.'

Karen was shocked too, as surely her research should have given her at least a hint of this possibility?

'Is this woman my sister?' Elle breathed eventually.

'Perhaps. I can't say any more than that. I can't find a DNA connection between the two of you on the sites where she has her data.'

'I only have it in one place.'

'You can upload your raw DNA data to some other sites. But of course, Lynne may not be your blood relative. Because she and Meredith received one of those letters, and you didn't.'

'Yes, I know. I just don't understand that.'

'Still,' she continued, her age showing now to Karen's eyes. 'I misjudged him my entire life. Wouldn't see him for years because I thought he murdered Jean. My mother wouldn't see him either. He was violent towards her when they were married but I don't expect anyone thought he was going to kill her. I mean, different times... He'd been in the war, a hero. Drank too much and behaved like a macho shit. People didn't like it but they didn't hate it enough to stop him. He never acted violently towards me but then he didn't pay me much attention either. Not like John.'

'John?'

'John, his child with Jean. My half-brother. He was a doting father to him and I suppose I was jealous. Perhaps that made it easier for me to believe my dad was a murderer when he always denied it. And, might I add, denied it loudly and at every possible opportunity, complete with polygraph tests.'

'Wasn't he called Gary?'

'That's his official name but Dad always called him by his second name: John. Or rather, he called him John Junior.'

Karen reeled internally but said nothing.

'Is he still alive?'

'Thankfully, yes. But I want to talk to him a bit more about this first. In the meantime...'

Elle breathed deeply and slowly.

'Give me a little while to process this. There's a lot to take in. I can tell you more, and of course, I'd love to meet Jean's family, but right now. Right now, I need to calm down.'

Meredith emailed shortly afterwards.

I'm at work now but I know that you spoke with Elle. This is awesome. FWIW I uploaded my DNA on every site I can find and Elle and I have a similar amount of shared DNA to the one I have with Lynne. I think the walls are tumbling down.

Karen sat at her computer and opened up the family tree she had started making, trying to figure out the lineage of William Prior, and how he might be Lynne's biological ancestor. There was so much information. It was exactly like doing a jigsaw puzzle, she thought. But what did the missing pieces look like? What were their shapes and colours?

Meredith's line had become clearer since Karen had first started on it some months before. Right at the top, the furthest she needed to go back at this point, there was William Prior, Meredith's great-great-grandfather, born Glasgow and lived 1850-1920. William married Harriet Jackson in 1870, and she gave birth to Henry in

1871. Henry, by that point living in California,– married Selina Swanson in 1890. Their son Frank, born in 1895, married Hazel Wainwright in 1918 and they had Marcia – pretty late! – in 1944. Marcia was Meredith's mother, giving birth, like her own mother had, aged forty-four. There was Meredith. Clear enough.

It was hard to see how Lynne could fit in, but she would be there somewhere, as would Elle. One of the women in that tree, one of the sisters as yet untraced, had – 120 or more years ago, married a Costello. Johnny came along in 1915, and his daughter Leonore Costello, Elle, in 1940. So Karen would start with William's marriage to Harriet in 1870 and see whether either of them had a sister who might be a likely candidate. And then whether any of their descendants had sisters marrying a Costello, and so on down the family tree until she found the right person.

This might be easier if enough useful people had tested and uploaded their DNA onto all the sites but it wasn't obvious that they had. Still, Karen had plenty to be getting on with as she searched through the records, adding everyone's details onto her spreadsheet.

Several hours later, the most likely candidate sprang towards her: Selina Swanson's sister, Mary, married a David Costello in 1891. Their youngest son was John David Costello, born 1915. So there he was! Karen put her head on the desk, feeling a mixture of satisfaction and exhaustion. There was a definite connection of some sort or other. She would find more about this later.

Before that could happen, her email pinged. Elle had sent her a link to a YouTube video.

I'm still absorbing this information and don't want to talk anymore today, she wrote. *In the meantime, please take a look at this and share it with Lynne and her family.*

It led to an episode of a US TV series from 1987 called *Still Missing* which dealt with people whose disappearances were particularly notable and had never been solved. The emotional music, the frightening graphics, the general air of doom formed a key part of those series, Karen knew. But whose needs did they serve? Probably not those of those missing and probably dead, or anyone who cared about them.

Photos of Jean as a young woman, her art, her parents, and Johnny, glowering in what Karen could imagine had been considered a very sexy manner, all featured ominously on the blurry screen. Karen had, by now, seen most of them on the internet. But there was more. She must show this to Lynne. Whatever happened after that was up to the Pendletons.

PART SIX

CHAPTER TWENTY-SEVEN

JEAN: NORTH FROM SAN FRANCISCO, JUNE 1954

She had no obvious plans, nothing concrete or considered, nothing conscious. Nor was she in a state of panic. But she had a car, and what she needed was to drive.

The wrecking balls were out in her neighbourhood and many buildings were coming down. She felt for them. Her own hopes for what the city would offer had been demolished too. There would be new homes, new futures for some, just as the city promised, but they would not be an improvement on what had gone before. The loss of what was past seemed too great.

Jean pointed her car north, towards the Golden Gate Bridge and Highway 101. For hours there was a clear route, nothing to slow down her drive, the occasional road sign indicating how many miles to small towns she had never heard of and the way edged by looming trees. She drove straight through Oregon, a state she did not know. It was all so beautiful, Jean was shocked by it, by the mountains and the wilderness. Awed too. But she had no wish to stop. She needed desperately to put San Francisco far behind her.

How were her parents, she wondered? When would they start to think about her again? Jean wished their last meeting had been warmer, that her mother and father hadn't kept on about marriage being a sacred pact, that she and Johnny were joined together before God. How she had failed them! The comfort of her parents retreated far into the distance. The comfort of God, something she had not considered for years, retreated even further.

Finally, after many, many hours of driving, she saw signs to a big city she'd heard of: Portland.

Without thinking about it, Jean knew she had to stop. Her heavy arms would not stay on the steering wheel. Just outside Portland, she pulled into the U-Rest motel. There was nothing remarkable about it: a few white-walled chalets standing around a small and dusty lawn. A middle-aged woman, with a hairstyle dating back twenty years, gave Jean the key with no more than a grunt. The woman's even grumpier husband glared at her, as though she was obviously up to no good. Why would a single woman, flustered, in need of a good wash, with her blouse rumpled and skirt tight across her stomach, be driving alone?

Jean didn't even go into her chalet before the need for food overcame her. The chicken pot pie at the motel's coffee shop was barely edible. Yet she could not have eaten it more quickly. Her whole body craved sustenance, and now that she had eaten the pie, it wanted, with equal urgency, to sleep. She staggered back to the room and lay down. Eight in the evening. Was that too early to go to bed? Oh, what did it matter? The hideous bedcover smelled of soap, a strange mix of bleach and lavender. Jean did not wait to get beneath the sheets, or wash; she put her head on the pillow and was out for the count.

Five hours later, her eyes sprang open. Outside, as if from a long way off, she heard a car being parked, followed by a chalet door clicking shut. Three in the morning. Humanity existed despite her, going about its business, moving on.

Jean pressed her hands to her mouth and inhaled sharply. Suddenly, she knew what she must do now.

• • • • •• • •• • • • • •

The tiny wooden church had come straight from fairyland. The sunlight filtered through the trees surrounding it, shadows flickering across the graves, the whole ensuring the greatest sense of hallucination. How had she found it? She was driving towards Vancouver, had surely almost reached it, but this was somewhere unexpected, rural. Perhaps it didn't exist at all outside her imagination; intense fatigue genuinely destroyed her certainty. Still, there it stood, as different as possible from the churches in California. Those had a kind of spurious grandeur; this one looked more like a stretched-out hut, a low-roofed barn, sitting in a field. Yet she didn't go inside. She wasn't seeking anything she would have recognised as spiritual succour.

Jean wandered around the graveyard. It held twenty rectangular plots, some with commemorative stones and some not, but many with a kind of concrete border. Would she end up here, she wondered? Around the edges of the plots were lawns. Not the type that were the basis of the large burial parks she knew, but overgrown grassy areas in which she imagined small creatures hiding from predators.

She found herself drawn towards one plot in particular: a concrete slab topped with a small marble angel, its baby arms hugging its knees close, its intricately feathered wings covering the entire body. A cherub. The statue reminded her of Billy and Bobby, both of them angelic only in sleep, her body convulsing at the connection with this tiny angel of death. On a raised wedge, the engraving said: Barbara Thompson 26 June–30 June 1928 Beloved daughter of Donald and Martha (nee Gregson)

Yes. That was the one.

Jean looked around her for anything to put on the grave. She owed it to the baby, to the child's parents. What could she give them? The place had no flowers. Then she thought of Jeff putting a stone on his uncle's grave to show he was remembered forever. She found one stone, and another, and another. Barbara Thompson would not be forgotten.

The town hall was easy to find, on the main street which somehow looked different from the main streets in small-town America. Perhaps that was due to the number and variety of trees: tall old trees, small newly planted ones, deciduous and evergreen. It was quiet, as though everyone had gone home for lunch. The heat somehow made the silence deeper, more profound. Where were the cars? The one diner was almost empty, two young women sitting at the counter and a waitress standing, staring out of the window towards her.

Had anyone here known Barbara Thompson or her parents? Jean hoped not.

She walked towards the town hall, a small building attempting to be grand, a reminder of its counterpart in Lake View. San Francisco seemed immune to such nonsense; things were either truly grand or made no attempt at it. Neither building was that impressive, of course. The young female clerk waiting, bored, at the reception desk seemed all too aware of this.

'I'd like to order a replacement birth certificate please,' said Jean pleasantly. The clerk waved her through towards the back, paying her no attention at all.

Jean repeated her request to an older, more tired woman behind a dark wooden counter. The woman, holding a printed form, dragged herself up from a hardwood chair and handed it to Jean.

'For myself,' she said. 'We lost the other one.'

The woman nodded. 'That will be a dollar, please.'

Was that expensive or not? Jean had no idea and really, what did it matter? She filled in the form with the scant details from the gravestone.

'I don't know the answers to all of these questions because my parents died some years ago,' she said, her lip drooping with the prospect of tears.

The woman looked down at Jean's handwriting; she had attempted to disguise it, without any idea why. The clerk took the form and went into an office further back, while Jean sat on a bench breathing in the dust and hearing some shuffling and indistinct voices some rooms away. The clock ticked and Jean wondered if she had stopped breathing altogether. But then the woman returned, the door swinging back and forth behind her.

'That will be fine,' she said, taking down a large book from a high shelf.

Jean sat on her hands while the woman put the blank certificate into a typewriter and copied over the information from the book. Was her rapid breathing betraying her? It seemed not.

The woman ripped the certificate from the typewriter with a flourish, signed it on the bottom, and blotted it. Then, she took a metal stamp from the side of her desk and clicked it smartly.

'There you are, Miss Thompson. Marrying soon?' Her voice rang out terse, disapproving.

She cast a glance across Jean's stomach. For a second, Jean felt confused. Then she smiled, in a way she hoped was sheepish.

'That's right,' she said. 'I'll be married in the city but I knew that this is where...' Jean ran out of words; there was nothing left and she might cry, from relief as much as anything.

The women nodded at each other, and Jean took the certificate. She sensed the older woman staring, but never mind. Jean looked down at her certificate. She was Canadian now, the daughter of a farmer of Scotch descent. This made her smile: Scotch, like whisky, when surely it should have read 'Scottish'. If it weren't for the fact that even the thought of drinking liquor made her queasy, she would have gone to a bar and raised a glass to her old pa.

• • • ● ● • ● ● • • •

It was still sunny as Jean drove north through suburban Vancouver and crossed the Lions Gate Bridge. More mountains, she thought briefly as she stopped to pay the toll. She had never seen anything like their grandeur. They were not her destination. But where was? Surely it must be up here somewhere, this community San Francisco artists talked about? She hadn't dreamt it, had she? Jeff had talked about a man who... but that was five years ago. Then, Johnny's friend Ned had mentioned a writer... Jean started to doubt herself. She was clutching at wisps of things she barely remembered. Were her hopes for the future really based on a place she had chosen almost at random?

Jean turned east along the road to Dollarton, the sun high above the inlet. The road stretched out in front of her. If she could just see someone, anyone, to ask. But the area seemed deserted. There were trees, a foreshore with rocks, and a jetty stretching out, but no one was fishing from it. Nor were there any boats. She stopped the car and picked her way through the saplings to stand next to the water. Jean retained enough agility to sit on the ground and she did so, picking up a pebble or two to throw at the sea. It was damp and muddy on the ground but warm, with the only sounds those of the water and various birds whose songs and screams she could not identify.

She had never been much of a planner, just done what she thought best. She had not intended to come here, not at first but she'd had a compelling need to get away. Jean possessed no maps, no clothes, little money, not enough of anything. She pointed her car north and drove. Everything was on the spur of the moment and only occurred to her the second before she did it. In truth, her desire to retain a bohemian life in some other, less known place was no more than a fantasy.

Maybe Johnny was right, and she had a screw loose. Well, so be it. She was not going to make herself and this new child safe. It would all end now.

Jean felt entirely at peace as she lay back in the sun with overwhelming contentment that it might all soon be over. She lay down and began to doze.

'Look, look, it's a mermaid.'

'But she doesn't have a tail. She's wearing a skirt so she can't be a mermaid.'

Jean opened her eyes to see two grimy children looking down at her, both wearing pale T-shirts and shorts, and no shoes. They carried buckets with crabs writhing in them.

'Oh, hello,' she said, pulling herself up to sitting.

'Hello,' the taller one said.

The other continued, 'Are you a mermaid?'

'No. But what a grand idea.'

'Well, bye then.'

They ran off, leaving Jean on the ground. Her peace had gone and she started to feel cold. Where should she go, what should she do? She began to struggle to her feet. At least she could sit in the car.

As she brushed herself down, a woman around her age came running towards her. Wiry red hair flying, man's shirt billowing, long bare legs extending from bright green shorts, she looked anxiously at Jean, as if she were a firework set to explode at any moment.

'Thank goodness, not a mermaid! My Davy was convinced that you were a mermaid even though you said you weren't. But Judy said she thought something must be up with you and I should take a look.'

'Eileen,' she said, offering her hand. As Jean shook it, she saw that it wasn't much cleaner than the children's.

'Jean. Wait, no, Barbara.'

'Make up your mind! Or rather, call yourself anything you like. Who cares?'

'Barbara. Thank you.'

'Are you lost then? Or are you going somewhere? Where are you heading?'

Now that Jean was required to explain herself, the whole enterprise sounded ridiculous.

'I had heard that there were artists here, people living a different kind of life. Squatters.'

'That's us, I guess. At least, our shack is over there. And there's a few more that-a-way, more when you go further east.'

Eileen looked at Jean quizzically.

'Threw you out, did he?'

'No, I left. It's complicated.'

'Never mind. Let's have some tea. I need a break.'

Jean couldn't believe that she had missed their cabin, as they called it. It blended in very well with the trees, made from timber that had weathered and faded into the same colour, even though traces of paint remained from the wood's previous incarnation as doors in now-demolished houses. There were windows, too, with large panes of glass, and a canopy sheltering a terrace that looked over the inlet. For a split second, it seemed like heaven.

Eileen had an open fire and she set a sturdy black kettle on the metal trivet balanced across it. 'We'll have crab for dinner tonight. The children have caught more than we need and you're very welcome to join us.'

'Thank you.' Jean was too moved to speak above a whisper.

Eileen poured boiling water into a teapot and the two women sat on rickety chairs looking at the fire, and the sun, which was starting to set.

'My husband is helping Charlie, he's lived here forever, mend his shack today. But he'll be back later.

We've only been here for two years ourselves.' She smiled at Jean.

'It's beautiful here now but you wouldn't want to be here in the winter. Oh dear, no. And definitely not with a baby. Nothing is ever dry, everyone gets coughs and colds, you're never warm, and there's mud everywhere.'

'So what do you do then?'

'When the weather's really bad, we stay with my brother in town. He says we're always welcome but we still feel anxious about it.' Eileen sipped her tea and continued.

'Every time we go, we almost expect that it won't be here when we get back, see. That we'll be evicted and this lovely cabin burnt to the ground. They want to expand here, build houses that folk like us couldn't afford even if we wanted to.'

'Why do you stay here then, if it's such a worry?'

'I love it here, I love nature. I want my children to as well, I want them to be free. The people here are different, eccentric like us. We can live a simple life but it's not for everyone.'

She was quiet, both women were.

'There's all sorts of people squatting here. Folk from lots of places, some of them are artists or they just don't fit in.'

Eileen smiled. 'I'm not an artist but I don't fit in.'

Jean smiled back. 'I used to be one but I'm not anymore. Still don't fit in though.'

They drank more tea as Jean recounted her life. She told Eileen how she'd moved from small-town California to big-city San Francisco, her painting, marrying Johnny and having a son she'd left behind.

Eileen's husband, Frank, came back around six. He was a muscular, tanned man, brimming with energy. Perhaps Johnny had been like that once, Jean thought, before war and envy consumed him.

She fell asleep next to the fire and Frank carried her to the couch indoors, covering her in an old woollen blanket that smelled of a dog they seemed not to have.

Jean woke as the sun rose, her body stiff from sleeping on thin cushions that were not designed for proper rest. She went outside to relieve herself. There was mist across the water, and a fresh, damp odour, redolent of fish but also trees, or plants she did not recognise. She knew nothing about the countryside, she thought. The peace here broke her heart. It was tragic it could not be hers.

Suddenly, out of sight, birds started to shriek. As she looked down the cove, she noticed more shacks, built on stilts to keep them out of the water. Rough-hewn ladders lay against one side and Jean imagined trying to scale them to get indoors. Even now that would be hard but in a few months? Or with a tiny baby? It would be completely impossible. How had she considered it? Living in a rundown building in San Francisco was one thing but at least there was plumbing. She did not have to collect drinking water from a spring and bathe in a rock pool.

She sat down on a log and wept. The sun rose, flickering long shadows through the trees. What should she do now?

Jean wandered back to the cabin, where Frank was re-setting the fire.

'Sleep well?' he asked.

'Yes, thanks.' she replied. He gazed at her in gentle disbelief.

'It's early but I can fix us some breakfast. If you're expecting you need to look after yourself. There's water for washing in a bucket over there' – he pointed to a fenced-off area – 'so you do that, and there'll be eggs and coffee before you know it.'

At six, after they had eaten, he went off to help Charlie again and Eileen came out to eat her own breakfast.

Jean watched the sun move across the inlet.

'Shall I brush your hair?' asked Judy. 'It's all tangled.'

Jean sat on a chair, looking out at the sea, while Judy, who could not have been more than ten, brushed her hair gently and consistently in a way that she remembered her mother doing years before. Its repetition soothed her and she returned to the couch.

At around noon, she woke again to the sounds of Eileen and the children throwing stones into the water. They turned to wave at Jean as she walked gingerly down the wooden steps to the foreshore.

'We're seeing who can throw the farthest,' said Davy. 'It's Mum so far.'

Jean smiled, as Eileen walked towards her.

'How're you feeling,' she asked. 'Better?'

Jean nodded.

'Good.' Eileen put her hand on Jean's shoulder and they climbed the steps to sit on the terrace.

'Now,' she continued. 'I found this place in the newspaper. I'd heard about it before from a friend whose sister needed help. I think they looked after her all right. It's a charity, not a bad one. Perhaps you could telephone them...?'

'Elizabeth House,' the advertisement said in discreet lettering. There was a pen and ink drawing of a large, somewhat elegant, building, and underneath were the words: *Home for Girls and Women*.

'You can stay with us as long as you like,' said Eileen. 'If you want, we will help you find your own shack and make it right for a baby. There are good people here who will be on your side and do whatever they can.' She pressed Jean's hand. 'But I wouldn't advise it, really I wouldn't. Not on your own. Not with what you said about your other baby. It's too hard.'

Jean nodded, looking at the paper. 'Yes,' she said. 'I see this might be a good idea.' A strange sensation of relief, hope and despair overwhelmed her.

'There's no telephone hereabouts, or for a couple of miles, but you can drive to the gas station,' Eileen continued. 'The kids and I will come too. I need some things from the store so you'd be doing me a favour.'

They piled into the car and the children sang loudly in the back. When Jean telephoned, the woman at Elizabeth House was straightforward, matter-of-fact. There would be a bed available for her in two days. Miss Thompson had struck lucky. Usually, they had a waiting list. She should present herself in the afternoon, along with her birth certificate if she had it. Jean was pleased that, however impulsively, she had arranged for the very thing that would prove her new identity.

She went back into the general store, where Eileen and the children stood talking to the woman behind the counter.

'All set?' asked Eileen.

'I can go on Wednesday,' Jean said looking over at the small selection of women's clothing. 'I need to buy a few things. I came very unprepared!' Her voice cracked and wavered, astonished at her stupidity and its display in front of total strangers. She bought some underwear and stockings, a blouse and skirt which would soon be too tight, and a toothbrush, toothpaste, towel and soap. She had little money left.

'If you like,' said Eileen as they unpacked some provisions in the cabin. 'We could buy the automobile from you. Our car is only on loan and we can't be out here with no vehicle. We'd give you a fair price.'

Of course they would, Jean thought to herself. These people were so good she wanted to cry. There was no one really decent in San Francisco, except maybe Helena. She was decent. But not selfless, not in this way.

'Thank you. I need the money more than I need the car right now.'

Two days later, after a quick wave to the children, and a sad hug from Eileen, Frank drove Jean into Vancouver. They agreed he would set her down a few streets away from Elizabeth House, no nearer, just in case they noticed him and asked awkward questions.

He pulled up next to a house with a large garden, one that looked similar to Elizabeth House but where enthusiastic teenage boys were playing tennis, then sat in silence for a minute. 'You still don't need to do it, you know, if you don't want to,' he said. 'If you can figure out a way to be happy living in the mudflats with us, we'd be glad to have you.'

Jean twisted around in her seat and looked at Frank. 'This is the only sensible decision I have made in years. But thank you from the bottom of my heart. You and Eileen have been so kind and I will never forget it.'

'Well, good luck then.' She got out of the car and, by the side of the road, they embraced briefly. Frank handed Jean the small, shabby case which he and Eileen had found for her and she watched Frank drive away in the car, her car. The car that represented freedom; the ability to get up and leave. And take Gary back from her husband. None of that was a possibility any longer. But this was not the time for warm or tender feelings. For now, she must gather every ounce of strength she possessed to ask for help.

From this moment on, she was no longer Jean Woods. She was Barbara Thompson, daughter of Canadian farmers, a woman who had never left British Columbia in her life.

CHAPTER TWENTY-EIGHT

LYNNE: SWINDON, ENGLAND, AUGUST 2018

'Mum.' Lynne sidled up to Barbara, who was sitting on the sofa doing the crossword. Lynne noticed that she had already completed half of it.

'Yes, dear?' Barbara looked up and smiled.

'There's a video about you on YouTube. About you going missing, I mean. About *your case*.'

'My case?' repeated Barbara with quiet wonder. 'There's a *case*?'

'Yes.' Lynne paused. 'It's part of a series called *Still Missing*.'

'Oh my goodness!'

'Mum, you don't have to see it if you don't want to. It might help but... you don't have to.'

Lynne realised that the grabbing of the hand, the sudden way of addressing Barbara like a toddler, infantilised someone who had clearly led a whole other life her children had never discovered. But her mother's hands felt frail and bony, her skin thin. Guilt rose in Lynne's throat. What was she doing inflicting this on someone of her mother's age? Barbara had not seemed so terribly old just a few months ago. She'd given every appearance of winning in the genetic lottery, or whatever those paramedics had said.

'No,' Barbara said firmly. 'I want to see it. I must.'

'But it might upset you.'

'I expect it *will* upset me and I will cry my eyes out.' Barbara's words seemed to tumble out of her. 'But you can't shield me from my own life. Things happened. Now that this has all opened up, I need to find out what they said about me after I had gone.'

She pressed Lynne's hand in a quick, sharp squeeze. 'Turn the bloody video on. Let's get it over with.'

Lynne settled her laptop on the coffee table opposite her mother and opened the link, putting it to full screen.

'Okay?' she fussed.

'Yes, yes, let's just watch.'

Lynne clasped Barbara's hand, feeling her mother tremble despite her determined stare.

They both leaned back on the sofa.

It started with the expected theme tune, the loud, flashy graphics. *Still Missing* in white, slightly out-of-focus text. It all happened so long ago; even this documentary was over thirty years old.

'San Francisco, California and it was just a regular June day when twenty-six-year-old mother Jean Woods Costello got in her Ford Deluxe Coupe and drove out of the city. A private detective hired by her parents tracked her down as far as the Canadian border, but he never found any definite evidence that she was alive after that. Tonight, we look at the evidence: Was Jean running away from her life, or did she meet with foul play?'

On screen, the background showed a too-bright travelogue of San Francisco in the 1950s. People on the streets looked strikingly formal, women with hats and gloves, even furs; buildings from perhaps the early 1900s – Lynne noticed a Woolworth's – but there were none of the skyscrapers that Lynne assumed would have taken over in the twenty-first century. Then, suddenly, the screen filled with a grey and black painting, a huge canvas with a large dribble of red down one side.

Barbara sighed deeply, as the off-screen commentator continued. 'Using the name JJ Woods, Mrs Costello had already made a name for herself as an artist. But her most recent show, six months before she disappeared, had not gone well.'

Then she gasped. The painting had been replaced by the face of an old man, haggard, but all too easily recognisable. The titles read *Johnny Costello, gallery owner.*

'I first met Jean when she was one of my students. Her talent was obvious even at that stage. She was always a serious artist, very committed, without a doubt the most gifted student I ever had.'

'Give me the laptop,' Barbara said quickly. 'Give it to me.'

Lynne unplugged it and put it on her mother's lap. Barbara paused the video.

'Maybe I need to take this slowly. Let me keep it here so I can turn it off if I need to.'

She sighed and turned to Lynne. 'I'm glad you're here,' she said to her daughter as she restarted the video.

'As for her character, though. Well, I think everyone would agree she was very highly strung.'

'Bastard,' Barbara hissed. 'That was your fault. I wasn't highly strung before I met you!'

'So what about Jean Costello's background? Where did she come from?' queried the solemn voiceover.

The screen changed to a black and white montage: a lake, with mountains in the distance; a large warehouse, with the words Woods and Son painted on it; then a sepia photograph, the family portrait of Jean with her parents and brother that had been sent to Barbara by her nieces.

'Jean grew up in Lake View, California, the first child of Walter and Dorothy Woods. Her father owned a canning factory and her mother was a homemaker, active in the church. They were a comfortably off, happy family.'

Then, there was another set of photographs: Lake View High School, a grand white building, with columns out front; a banner, which said Farewell Seniors 1946, and a picture of a teenage Jean in a long dress with many layers of pale tulle, a tall young man standing beside her.

'Mum!' Lynne burst out. 'Oh my God!'

'Shh!'

A blonde woman smiled out of the screen. Aged around sixty, her hair piled astoundingly high on her head, she was smartly dressed, with pristine make-up and a gleam in her eye. Barbara let out a 'ha' of pleased surprise. The subtitle simply read Audrey Barker.

'Jean was my best friend in high school. She was very creative and quite determined with it. Not like most of us, who mainly wanted marriage and children. For most of the time I knew her, she was a great girl. Lots of fun, attended church, sat on high school committees, liked sport. But she grew away from Lake View very quickly and I hardly saw her after she started college. Our lives went in different directions.'

'Church! I don't remember you ever doing that.'

Barbara paused the video again.

'Well, I did. That was a different life. Everyone went to church. It was only a matter of which church, which denomination.' She sighed. 'I have only good memories of Audrey though. We had a lot of fun back then. But...' Barbara pressed her lips together. 'I hated the smallness of Lake View. So I let her down. I abandoned her.'

She sighed again and pressed play.

Next, there was Larry.

'Jean was nine years older than me, which was too much of an age gap for us to be close. But one of my earliest memories is when I fell over in the street, cut my knees real bad on some glass, and I yelled my head off because of the blood. Jean looked after me real good, even better than my mother. I didn't think anything of it when I was a kid, but maybe I remember it now because of the reputation she had later on. Johnny put it about that she was a bad mother and even my parents thought she wasn't capable of looking after a child.'

'Oh, Mum!'

Lynne shook her head. How could Barbara bear it? She pulled her mother's hand towards her lips and kissed it fiercely.

Larry continued. 'I remember her leaving home for college and never really coming back. How upset our parents became because she had changed so much. They had been proud that she was going to art school, even though it meant she was moving away. But they saw her as a good daughter, the sort who would always put them first, and then her husband and children first, and of course she would come back to Lake View. But then she didn't. She wanted a different kind of life. I didn't realise that, but it hurt my parents very much. They didn't understand it at all.'

Lynne looked sideways at her mother; unsurprisingly, tears covered her face. But more than that, she looked stricken. All the pain she had not shown, or perhaps even felt, for so many decades. Barbara squeezed her hand again. 'Shh,' she said before Lynne had a chance to make any comment.

This was followed by a montage of buildings where Jean had gone to college, pictures of art students – some, to Lynne's eyes, very overdressed, others downright shabby – and a few of Jean's early paintings. The series finished with photographs of the vibrant San Francisco counterculture of that era, ending with the famous City Lights bookstore.

Another woman came onscreen, a very different proposition to Audrey. She had brown hair, short and fluffy, and thick eye make-up. Her long wooden earrings seemed a mist of tiny twigs, a huge matching pendant dangled over her black sweater.

The screen read: Helena Margetson, artist.

'I first came across Jean in 1948, when we were both students. As soon as we met, I realised she was a committed and exciting artist, with a very developed technique. She was at the cutting edge of the art scene out west. The fact that she was a woman made this even more unusual. It was extremely hard for women to have any kind of impact within the art world back then.'

Barbara stopped the video. 'Just a moment, dear,' she said. She shut her eyes. 'Oh, Helena,' she murmured, before pressing play once more.

'Her first paintings were in a group show in 1949, and soon after that she was much in demand by private collectors,' the unseen narrator continued. 'Then in 1950, she married Johnny Costello, who represented her, and encouraged her in her art.'

Barbara pressed Lynne's hand rhythmically, squeezing it more and more fiercely. Lynne could almost feel the anger pouring with the blood through her veins. How could such fury exist after so many years?

'He remained a well-respected painter at that time...'

'That's a lie,' shouted Barbara.

'But, although he had been a successful muralist in the thirties, after the war things were different. The art world had moved on and many of the men who had been successful sought solace in the bottle.'

There were some photographs of large murals, a small man stretched out on planks laid precariously between stepladders.

'Huh,' said Barbara.

'He also taught a few classes at the San Francisco School of Fine Art.'

Helena continued. 'I knew Costello slightly because he had taught me but also, everyone in the San Francisco art scene had some kind of connection with everyone else. He had a reputation as a hellraiser, not good around women, and I tried to warn Jean not to get involved. But she fell in love with him and that was that.'

There was a photograph of a young Barbara, encased in a cream New Look suit, and Johnny, his arm around her unnaturally small waist. She looked straight ahead, while he looked down at her protectively. 'They married in 1950,' said the narrator.

Once more Helena continued, 'He believed in her art, but I don't think he believed in her as a person. He thought he knew best. Still, I don't know if she would have painted quite so prolifically without his backing. I'm just not sure. She worked obsessively but after her first show in 1949, it never seemed to make her happy. She could not achieve what she wanted.'

A subtitle announced that Jean and Johnny's relationship had deteriorated after the birth of John Junior in 1952.

Photographs of a boy at various stages flashed onto the screen, as a baby, a toddler, a determined boy with a baseball bat, and a teenager with long brown hair flopping in front of his face, as he looked shyly up at the camera.

'Ohhh! Freeze it, freeze it!' Barbara's hands came up to her mouth. 'It's Gary.' And then, more softly. 'Gary.' Lynne put her arms around her mother. 'I always wondered what he looked like, how he had turned out, was he happy? I put him to the back of my mind. I had to, don't you see?'

Lynne didn't see, not at all, but there was time enough for that.

'They are calling him John Junior, Mum.'

'John was his middle name. Giving a boy his father's name isn't that unusual and was common enough back then. But changing his name after I'd gone, how could he?' She paused. 'My husband was like that, though. You do see, Lynne, don't you?' Barbara grabbed Lynne's hand very tightly.

'So he *is* my brother, then?'

'Yes, he is.' Barbara smiled slightly. 'Let me try to watch this to the end without stopping. I'll never finish it otherwise.'

They continued to watch, as the talking heads presented themselves one after another.

Johnny: 'Jean did not cope well with motherhood. Maybe now we would say she had post-natal depression but she didn't know how to care for a baby. She had help, sure, but despite that, it didn't work.'

Helena: 'Jean couldn't find a way to balance her responsibilities and that was the real issue for her. She wanted to carry on painting and she was a wife and mother too. It was very hard back then. Everyone thought that women's first and only responsibility was to their families and everything else must take second place. That tore her apart.

'We (that is, my then-husband Mike and I) saw less and less of her after she married Johnny. Then they broke up and after that, I saw her more. There is no doubt, though, that she was near a breakdown. She may have been in hospital but I'm not sure about that.'

Johnny: 'The whole situation was completely impossible. I know some people thought I was unsympathetic [he shrugged]. But, you try it! Jean would just sit there while John cried. So I took John to stay with her parents for a while until I could figure out a way to look after him myself.'

Larry: 'I was around sixteen at this time and I didn't really understand what was going on. I remember that at one time she came to our house looking for the baby but Johnny had already taken him back to the city. She was in a bad state then, very dishevelled and upset. Sick, I guess. She needed someone to help her out and there wasn't anyone. She wouldn't stay with us. We were all worried about her and worried about the baby too. Not that Johnny wouldn't care for him properly but that we wouldn't see him again. In fact, my parents didn't see him between 1955 and 1968, when he came looking for them. I'm still angry about that. Losing both Jean and Gary broke them, really.'

Johnny: 'I made a home for him and hired a housekeeper. You have to see that he was only a little kid and there had been so much upset and disturbance for him already. Jean only made matters worse when she did see him and I didn't want her parents interfering. He did see them when he got older and later they had other grandchildren anyway.'

Lynne could sense Barbara tensing and shaking with anger at his arrogance. She also wondered, is this my *father*? Was my mother making sure I was safe from him? Or saving herself? She tried hard to quieten her rapid-fire questions and concentrate on the video.

Helena: 'The last time I saw her, that was May 1954. She thought she might be pregnant, and that frightened her, but after a week or so she telephoned me to say she wasn't. I've never been certain if that was true or not. I wonder if she realised she was pregnant and decided she couldn't cope with another baby and was going to end it all. Or maybe she told Johnny and he... I don't know. I have never known. I only have my suspicions, as do the rest of her friends and family.'

At this point, the narrator interjected: 'While her husband has always denied playing any part in her disappearance, just after the war he was well-known to the police for his violence due to a string of violent offences committed when he was drunk.'

The screen flashed with newspaper front pages from 1945 and 1946, a rapid and indecipherable succession of headlines about violence, war, heroes and artists.

'I should have known,' said Barbara. 'Why didn't I listen to Helena? Everything could have been so different.'

Johnny: 'I had been badly injured in 1944, and after that, I couldn't paint as I had done before the war. That turned me into a drunk for a few years, I don't deny it, and I did things I regret. But I turned my life around and stopped drinking completely before Jean and I broke up. I told her parents I would do that and I kept my word.'

'In public,' Barbara spat. 'Only in public.'

Larry: 'My parents were worried sick when she hadn't been in touch for a few months. After Jean moved into an apartment on her own, she didn't have a telephone and she didn't reply to any of their letters. They blamed Johnny for not looking after her, for not caring even though they were still married. But they also thought...

that she had turned her back on them and everything they stood for.'

Lynne turned to look at her mother.

'Had you turned your back on them?' Barbara looked at Lynne. 'They had turned their backs on me, or so I thought.'

Johnny: 'By early July 1954, I started to hear that Jean hadn't been seen for a while. I covered the rent for her apartment, and her landlord called me up asking if I knew her whereabouts. I asked around various friends, and no one had any idea. Then I rang her parents. Of course, they rang the police who told them I needed to come in and declare her missing which I did. But after that, nothing. For months, there weren't even any rumours.'

Johnny's face vanished, to be replaced by black and white footage of men in long shorts running along an athletics track. Background music, somehow both poignant and sinister, swelled over it, before the voiceover continued:

'Then, in a surprise twist, some old friends enjoying a rare night out without their children spotted a woman they thought just had to be Jean.'

Audrey: 'Late in 1954, my husband and I were at the movies when we saw Jean in a newsreel of a sports event in Vancouver. Without doubt it was her. We told her parents who saw the newsreel for themselves and were convinced she had made it that far, although none of us can understand why she'd have gone there. But the private detective they hired couldn't trace her further than the Canadian border. We at least are satisfied she got as far as British Columbia! But not everyone is convinced.'

Larry: 'My father paid for a private detective because of what Jean's friends said. But as for her being alive and in Canada, well I doubt it. I have always been suspicious and I think she may not have made it. She was a lost soul, so unhappy, and Johnny did not treat her like he should have. In any case, why would she go to Canada? She didn't know anyone there. But then I was a kid, with no insight into the details of her life. The whole thing makes no sense.'

Johnny: 'Look, I know her folks thought I was responsible, but I wasn't. I took several polygraph tests, my choice, not the police, and they all showed me to be innocent. The police never investigated me. They believed she left of her own free will, whatever had happened after that. In 1958, I hired a private investigator myself but he could find no trace of her.'

Even after that, the narrator intoned, her family weren't so certain.

Larry: 'When she was dying, my mother said that she thought Jean was still alive and didn't want to be found, that she had given birth to her and she'd know if she had died. I didn't take any notice but maybe she was right. I just wish I knew.'

The voiceover continued:

'Jean Costello was officially declared dead in 1961. But what really happened? Did she make a new life for herself in Canada? Or did she, or someone else, make sure she did not have that opportunity? If Jean was still alive today, she would be fifty-nine. Her son, John Junior, who declined the opportunity to take part in this programme, is thirty-four, and has spent his whole life wondering what has happened to his mother,' the narrator added.

Barbara turned to Lynne. 'I used to be called JJ. John Junior is also JJ, isn't he? Oh, the horror of that man, the horror. I had forgotten that I hated him but I am remembering it now more strongly than I remember ever feeling it before. Even in 1954, I didn't hate him as much as this.'

Lynne was shocked at the strength of her mother's grip and after a few moments, she unwound Barbara's fingers and went to grab two glasses of water. Barbara was leaning her head on the back of the sofa, her eyes shut. They restarted the video.

Helena: 'There has been much more interest in female artists in recent years and I think, Oh, Jean, if only you'd stuck it out a bit longer! All the work you might have created!'

Helena had tears in her eyes, leaning back so that they would not spill down her cheeks before she continued. 'Jean's paintings, including those in the show of January 1954, are starting to sell for quite substantial amounts of money. Costello still owns many of them,' she said shakily.

Helena got up from her hardwood chair and turned to point at a large canvas behind her. It was a joyful piece, with blue, yellow and green coming together in a splashing jumble of colour.

'She gave this one to me, though, a painting that she did around the time we first met. And as long as I have it, I will never forget her.'

Barbara froze the screen, and reached out to it, touching her fingertips to Helena's face as she began to sob.

'Darling Helena, my dear and lovely friend. I am so sorry I betrayed you!'

Chapter Twenty-Nine

Karen: London, September 2018

Karen pounded the treadmill, her feet thumping ever faster on the moving belt. If she kept on doing this for long enough, then her anger would abate and she could get on with... whatever. Slap, slap, went her feet. The heavy beats from the gym's sound system helped her along, as she watched the rain trickle down the full-length windows.

The phone rang; Lisa.

'Wait a second,' she said as she pressed the 'cool down' button, and then the emergency stop, on the machine. 'Yes?' she continued, catching her breath.

'Look, I'm sorry, okay. I've been really busy.' Lisa sounded both apologetic and exasperated.

'You know how much I hate it when you don't return my calls.' Karen felt as if her fury about this had been building for days.

'It's just... there is a lot to do up here. My parents-in-law and the boys. It's all falling to me, of course.'

Karen knew that Keith was a good man: nice, funny, warm. But he had one significant flaw: he worked almost all his waking hours, even though he didn't really have to.

'Come up here,' Lisa wheedled. 'Please. Live near us in Scotland. You know you want to.'

Karen sighed heavily. She didn't. She only wanted to be near her sister or, failing that, to have the amount of contact they used to have. It hurt that she was no longer, or not currently, one of Lisa's priorities.

'But I need to be down here.'

'Why though?'

Why? Karen asked herself. Because her life was in London, however lonely she might be, however expensive and far from the centre the available accommodation. She would not go and hang around her sister's family, be the spinster aunt, simply because it was convenient. It felt like a trap. A quiet, beautiful trap where her only reason for being there was her blood relatives. No, she would always be an urban person, not wanting the type of conventional life that seemed to be all there was on offer in smaller, quieter places.

'Because...' she stopped. 'Look, I'm at the gym now. I'll call you later.'

She turned the treadmill back on. Karen was a big fan of basic gyms, the sort that offered good machines, a couple of classes, and no frills whatsoever. That love came partly from necessity. She no longer had the money for the ones that provided piles of fluffy towels, where the monthly fee would probably be more than her earnings.

Back in the mists of time, when she was acting like a successful investigative journalist, while in reality walking the tightrope between having a job and not having one, she had belonged to other, more glamorous gyms.

What a waste of money that had been! The basic gyms had other advantages too, over and above the cost. Karen felt at home amongst the ordinary people at her gym, who weren't bankers, or television presenters. So what if there were drug dealers and gangsters? They didn't register her: she was too old, no kind of threat or interest to them, and she only noticed them in passing. Anyway, better them than the two-faced vipers who poisoned those who couldn't help them. Why had she chosen two careers where everyone was so cut-throat, she wondered for the umpteenth time? Journalists and academics had to fight their perceived rivals for the tiniest shot at glory. At least genealogists were kinder people, weren't they? She hoped she was right in that.

Karen visited her local My Gym three times a week, more if she was particularly stressed, because it gave her something physical to do. To bend and stretch her body in a way that did not involve hunching over a laptop. Succeed at something different. And that had been significant when she knew she hadn't succeeded at anything, really.

She pressed the cool down button on the treadmill for the second time. Nothing could be done about Lisa, she realised. She would just have to be sad and feel the loss of her sister. Karen's anger dissipated; the running had worked.

In the changing room, she was sitting on a bench, towel-drying her hair when a woman in swirly pink and purple Lycra leggings and a navy padded jacket came to sit next to her. She was younger than Karen, maybe in her early twenties, with her hair pulled back tightly from her sharp face.

'You're Karen Copperfield, right.'

There was no question in her voice; she had caught her prey.

Karen moved away from her instinctively. She did not recognise this woman and, although she was not physically threatening, this was surely designed to be intimidating. The communal changing room was empty – not unusual at 3 pm when most women who used that gym were either at work or collecting their children from school.

'Who are you?' she asked abruptly.

'That doesn't matter. We need to talk.' The woman sat too close.

'Here? Really? I don't think so.'

'This is as good a place as any,' she replied. Karen could not see her arms through her jacket, but the muscles in the woman's legs were taut, athletic, much younger than hers.

'Are you trying to intimidate me, because it isn't going to work?' A lie, of course. Karen shook as she pulled her jeans onto her clammy legs.

'You are researching the family tree of William Prior and have already been sent a letter demanding that you stop.'

'I'm not talking about any of my clients with you,' Karen said brusquely.

'I am working for some wealthy people and they would very much like to talk to you.'

'No. Get out of my way.'

The woman was of average height, similar to her, with dyed black hair and matching eyebrows. Karen wondered whether her previous assumption could be wrong. Maybe she had seen her before. Perhaps she even used this gym as a matter of course. She leant against the door to the changing room as someone on the other side tried to open it. The throbbing house music coming through the loudspeakers ensured that her words could not be heard by whoever was repeatedly typing in their passcode and pushing at the handle. She shook her head and laughed.

'You think I'm going to hurt you! I don't need to do that! But my client knows all about you. And this is your last chance, isn't it, Doctor, to have a career. You're getting a bit old to start again, aren't you?'

Karen rolled her eyes. 'In that case, you will realise that I don't give up.'

'But it's easy enough to ruin a reputation, isn't it? In a field where you have to be discreet and people are telling you their secrets.'

'WILL you get out of my way!' Karen stretched her arm out and, pushing her to one side, she pressed the green exit button that opened the changing room door. The cheek of it!

The woman clutched at the door handle.

'My client wants to meet you and has an offer that you'll find very interesting.' She thrust a business card towards Karen. 'Anyway, we'll be in touch.' With that, she pushed open the heavy door and vanished.

Once out of the building, Karen looked up and down the street, but there was no sign of her. Perhaps she had literally run away. She leaned back against the wall and looked down at the pink card: Christie Lebon, it said in bold black letters. Close Protection Solutions. There was a mobile number but nothing else. A pink card? To appear extra-feminine for your potential clients? Karen scoffed but stuffed the card in her pocket anyway.

Back home, a quick internet search revealed nothing at all about Christie Lebon. Ah well. Instead, she sent a group WhatsApp message to Anna and Ben, which started *Adventures in genealogy.*

A woman threatened me in the changing room at the gym today. She said she wasn't, but she lied. Appaz, her client had an offer I'd find very interesting and I was too old to start a new career. What do you think of that?

Anna videocalled her back immediately. 'Wow, no. Do you know anything about her?'

'Only what's on her business card.' Karen gave the details. 'She has no internet presence as far as I can tell but she must exist somewhere.'

'Be careful, Karen. Don't take unnecessary risks.'

'Not this again, please.'

'Anyone threatening you is worrying. So worry about it. Take steps.'

Karen sighed. 'I'm just freaked out. Nothing bad happened. No one beat me up. I'm an ordinary person with no power to do anything. If they wanted to hurt me, they'd have done it.'

Anna smiled at Karen, so close on the video app but so very far. Everyone who loved Karen wanted to protect her but she wasn't having it.

'I'm so sorry I can't be there with you.'

'Yeah. Same.'

Karen sighed. The women in her life were never there for her, not really. It was their physical presence she wanted, not a shield or support from what they saw as the frightening world. She didn't see it like that.

Ben took longer to respond to her message but at least they lived in the same city.

I'll be round in a couple of hours, he wrote. *Don't freak out. You can stay with me if you want.*

I'm fine, but come round, yes. Yes, please.

Look after her Ben, LOL. Anna responded to them both.

Ben came around with a bottle of wine and a gourmet pizza. Karen wasn't too happy about that; in her small flat, the smell of the pizza would be hard to get rid of. It was lovely to eat it, though, and drink the wine.

'Now, Karen,' Ben said as he took her hand after they had finished. 'With all the love in the world, what are you doing? Remember what happened, why you left journalism.'

'These people aren't gangsters. I'm not trying to bring them to justice. I can't be a campaigning journalist and want nothing to do with that life anymore, as you well know.'

'But you are uncovering people's secrets, and presumably threatening their wealth or status. Just like you did before. How is this any different?'

'Oh, Ben, this is nothing like that.'

'Isn't it?'

'No, it isn't.' And she hugged him very hard until he laughed and left her to her empty flat.

Two days later, Christie was back, this time ringing Karen's doorbell at the unintimidating hour of eleven in the morning. Perhaps she had rethought her attitude because she seemed friendly, warm even. Apologetic, as Karen stood on the step, glaring.

'Please, Karen. I'm not trying to threaten you but my client really wants to talk to you. In person.'

She gestured towards the taxi behind her.

A glossy blonde woman of indeterminate age exited the cab elegantly, as though she had taken lessons in it. She smiled. Karen registered that her vertiginous high heels flashed red soles and her black and white suit must be Chanel. The woman reached out her taloned hand.

'Dr Copperfield,' she said in a manner that Karen registered as professional. 'I'm Gloria Costello, head of the Woods Costello Foundation. We need to talk.'

CHAPTER THIRTY

Barbara's house was more or less what Karen had expected. It was the type of three-bedroom property that had been built in its millions across Britain in the 1920s and 1930s. Semi-detached, suburban; though Swindon was not really big enough to have suburbs, and the Pendleton home was within walking distance of the centre. Eighty or ninety years after they had been built, most of them were unattractively modernised, the wooden windows and doors replaced with plastic double-glazing, the front gardens paved over for parking.

In her sturdy, middle-management car, Rachel collected Karen from the station and, as they drew up outside, she could tell the house had seen better days. The pebbledash across the top of the building had become patchy and the once-pink paving slabs at the front of the house were discoloured and cracked. The property needed the kind of complete renovation people in their eighties or nineties were unlikely to provide.

Rachel smiled at Karen, recognising her appraisal. 'Gran won't let us touch the house,' she said. 'She doesn't want the disruption. Nothing's been done to it for at least fifteen years but it's comfortable enough once you go inside.'

They slammed the car doors behind them, as Lynne, Cathy, Nick and Nick's yapping terrier came to greet them.

'It's good to meet you at last,' he said half-apologetically.

There had been no explanation for Karen about Nick's prior absence and now presence. She imagined he found the whole idea of his mother having a previous and unknown history simply too hard to handle. Everyone reacted differently to secrets. Perhaps Nick had taken a while to even consider Barbara as a person with a past, complex existence.

They moved into the dining room, a small, wallpapered space entirely filled by a wooden table and six chairs, and Karen spread her paperwork over the table.

'So this is where you start to get some proper answers and unravel what has been going on with parts of your extended family.'

They examined a roll of paper spanning the width and half the length of the table. Lynne, Cathy, Nick, and Rachel sat on one side of it; Karen was with Barbara on the other.

'So complicated! Oh, Mum...' Cathy sighed, as though it was her mother's fault.

Karen smiled brightly at Cathy's brittle irritation.

'A lot of this tree is not Barbara's at all, but Johnny's. He had three marriages altogether, and children from all of them, so naturally there are many branches to his tree!'

'I've also needed to go back a few generations to work out who Meredith Dyson is, and her precise relationship to Lynne and also to Elle, Johnny's daughter from his first marriage.'

'Such a silly thing to call herself,' said Barbara. 'When her real name is Leonore, I mean.'

'So,' continued Karen without breaking her stride. 'Meredith's and Lynne's DNA suggests they are both at a similar distance from a direct ancestor of Johnny's, without being close relatives themselves. I traced back both of their family trees and discovered that person. Their biological connection is through a woman called Delia Swanson, who was born in 1851. It is not directly via William Prior as that... letter suggested.'

They all looked at her, baffled.

'Frank Prior, William Prior's grandson, is Meredith's maternal grandfather. Frank's mother was born Selina Swanson and married Henry Prior. Selina's sister Mary is Johnny Costello's mother. They are both Delia's daughters.'

'How are we ever going to remember all of this?' Nick wondered aloud.

Karen smiled. 'Yes, it is a lot to take in. That's why I've got it all printed out here.' She pointed to the relevant section of the paper.

'Meredith is also connected with Elle, Leonore, but that is quite a distant connection. And there is an anomaly there because Meredith and Lynne share a greater amount of DNA than do Meredith and Leonore.'

Karen sipped her tea.

'I know, though, that you want to find out why both Meredith and Lynne were sent a cease and desist letter.'

They all looked at Karen expectantly.

'What I haven't told you yet is that I have been... contacted by someone who knows quite a lot about you, Lynne, but is missing some vital information.'

She paused.

'By the time Johnny died in 1996, his estate had become... if not substantial, then at least very healthy. Gloria, his ex-secretary who he married in 1970, has invested well and has proved as good or even better at buying art than he was.'

'A businesswoman then?' Lynne asked.

'It seems so, yes. Johnny and Gloria also had two sons who worked in Silicon Valley, in the late nineties and early noughties, and moved into arts philanthropy, which is why they set up the Costello Woods Foundation.'

'They're rich,' Barbara said slowly. 'Well, good luck to them.'

'But it is important that you realise he only started his gallery in the first place on the back of your paintings. Without you, all of this money, the business, the foundation, it wouldn't have happened. So potentially some of that money is rightfully yours.'

Barbara sighed heavily, shaking her head.

'Mum...'

'Let's just listen, shall we?'

Karen continued.

'One thing we were never sure about was why Lynne and Meredith received cease and desist letters, asking them to stop research on their trees, when other family members didn't. The answer to that seems to be in Johnny's behaviour.

'Gloria had worked for Johnny for ten years before they got together. She knew he had been married to you, Barbara, or rather to Jean. Gary and Leonore were recognised as his offspring. But he always suspected that he had more children. Not with you, but from the time when he was a big drinker, both the period after he had separated from Frances, Leonore's mother before he went off to war, and then after he left hospital a few years later. No one had ever come to him claiming to be his child, though he was still nervous that they might.

'But then he died, and no one thought any more about it. Not until familial DNA tests came along.'

'After that, the Costellos started to get nervous that there would be people who had a financial claim on Johnny's estate, and as a result on the foundation as a whole. That was why they issued those cease and desist letters. They hired a genealogist to keep track of people uploading their DNA.'

Karen paused once again.

'The foundation knew all about Leonore and Gary who received money in Johnny's will and had no interest in his work. Everything was settled over twenty years ago. But Gloria was not sure how any other genetic descendants might react.

'However, this much is clear. She doesn't realise that you, Barbara, used to be Jean Woods Costello and that you are still alive. Your nieces are not in contact with the Woods Costello Foundation and, because Gary has not done a DNA test, which would show a connection to both them and your other children, no one has put two and two together.'

'I see,' said Barbara thoughtfully.

'That is despite Gloria turning up outside my house with a minder and sending me, Lynne and Meredith, possibly other people too, those rather threatening letters. She has worked out that there is *someone*, without realising who it is. I think she suspects Lynne is one of those children that Johnny might have fathered, but not that you are Lynne's mother. She is charming herself, even if she employs people who try to be... less so. Also, if she had known anything about genetic genealogy she would have hired someone to work out precisely who was related to whom and how.'

'You should have said you were being threatened,' said Cathy. 'We could have called the police or something!'

'It didn't come to that,' Karen said. 'Gloria, or rather her... close protection person and lawyer... were verbally intimidating, but there was nothing the police would be interested in. Gloria did try to buy me off. Bribe me, if you like!'

'What did you say?' Rachel asked, as though there was a possibility that Karen would accept.

'Of course, I refused! And said that I never discussed my clients and was not starting now.'

'It does, of course, throw into question the whole issue of whether or not Gloria has ever been legally married to Johnny. I know you, as Jean, were declared dead in 1961,

Barbara, but the fact that you... well, you would need expert legal advice. My research indicates that your situation is extremely unusual, perhaps even unique, because when people have been declared legally dead after years of being missing, and then turned up again... on the rare occasions that has happened, it has been considered fraud.'

There was a collective gasp.

'Now, clearly, no one has directly benefitted. Though the Costello family, and the Costello Woods Foundation, could be thought to have benefitted from the mystery surrounding your disappearance.

'I would argue you should take legal advice here because... whose paintings are they? Did your husband own them, or was it you? You created them.'

'I'm not an expert here, of course,' said Rachel. 'But this sounds like the sort of court case that might last for years and cost an absurd amount of money. Money that Gloria has and we don't.'

Barbara put up her hand, palm facing out towards Rachel to stop her. 'Well, I don't want that money. They are welcome to it. Or those paintings. They are nothing to do with me. It's too long ago and from a time when I was bitterly unhappy.'

'But we might want it, Mum. It could help us!' Cathy shouted, shaking her head. 'And what about your grandchildren, what about their children? It's so difficult for young people these days.'

'No,' Barbara said sharply. 'We aren't poor, none of us is, we don't need it. Let them keep the money. If it's a foundation, maybe they are doing some good with it. I'll read up on them. But it's not ours, not yours. No.'

Rachel broke the silence, turning to Karen. 'You won't have seen what I bought on the internet.'

She passed over a glossy brochure with a black, white, and red photograph on the cover. Barbara sighed audibly. 'Not that awful painting,' she whispered, exasperated.

'It's a catalogue for an exhibition in 2007, *The Lost Women of Abstract Expressionism*, one that relied heavily on Gran's work.'

Before Karen could take a proper look, Barbara grabbed the brochure and recited in a sing-song voice, 'In recent years, her work has been reassessed through a feminist and art-historical lens with the Death/Life series now seen as expressing proto-feminist rage against women's oppression.'

She slapped it down on the table. 'They wouldn't have been able to write that if they thought I was still alive,' she said. 'I wish I could tell them how much I hated those paintings, that he made me do them. It wasn't to do with feminism.'

Rachel looked at her, shaking her head. 'But the curators of that exhibition weren't entirely wrong. You were full of rage, anyone would be, given that situation. And you still are angry. Angry with Johnny for making you paint what you hated and deciding that you were a bad mother. You *should* have been furious about it, too, because he made your life impossible. Times were different then, but people were still meant to be kind and loving to each other. Weren't they?'

Karen felt she should interject, but wasn't sure how, or with what. But before she had a chance to respond, there was a chiming from Barbara's laptop, which had been an unexpected present from Nick to help her keep in close contact with all these rediscovered relatives. It was Elle on Skype, looking more sombre than they had seen her before.

'Hello, everyone,' she said, as Barbara angled the laptop on the table so the others could see her.

Elle's eyes were dark and wary, sad. 'I don't know how to say this.' She visibly swallowed and ran her hands over her hair. 'I'm sorry to be the bringer of bad news. I needed to double-check but unfortunately, I am right.' She smiled ruefully.

'Finally, I got around to doing the same DNA test as Lynne. I could have done the more complicated route of uploading my results to other sites like Meredith did, but it was too damn hard to understand. Well anyway, I took the test. So...'

She spoke fast, nervously.

'I looked for you, Lynne, as a match. I expected there to be a "close family", "first cousin" or something, the sort of connection Lynne has with Nick and Cathy. But there wasn't. We are fifth to eighth cousins. I have more shared DNA with Meredith.'

Elle blinked twice, before tears snaked down first one cheek, then another.

'I'm sorry, Lynne, so very sorry. You aren't my sister after all. We are distantly related somehow but we don't share a biological parent. Whoever it is, Johnny can't be your father.'

And all of them, every single one, turned to gape at Barbara as the colour drained from her face and she whispered, 'Oh my God.'

CHAPTER THIRTY-ONE

With her arms extended, Jean held the photograph, tilting it this way and that as she lay back on the couch. Gary was wearing the cutest red dungarees, the bib up high to the neck, with a blue and yellow striped T-shirt visible underneath. He looked up at whoever was holding his hand: Johnny, presumably. Not that it was possible to tell for sure, because the only glimpse of the adult in the picture was a pair of legs in denim. Oh! But the photograph shone bright as could be, colour flashing so intensely that it might be advertising the latest photographic processes. Glossy too, as though the paper had been coated in plastic.

Gary's little face seemed serious as he gazed upright. But was it? She had no idea. Jean was a disposable individual whose absence was far preferable to her presence. Could she have fought more to keep him? She had not fought at all and the thought sickened her. Jean had barely gone beyond complaining. What right did she have to call herself his mother?

She brought the picture up closer to her eyes. It was six months since she had seen Gary and his appearance had already changed. He was scarcely a baby anymore, must be properly walking, perhaps saying recognisable words. Daddy, for instance. The need for Gary made her physically dizzy, and she swung her feet onto the floor, folding her body over her knees.

Johnny seemed to expect she would be grateful and satisfied with an occasional photograph, or the odd message from her parents that they had seen their grandson and he was very happy with their gift of a stuffed elephant. She was not allowed to meet him because he needed stability and calm.

And she had agreed to that. Agreed. That, in itself, made her unworthy.

But Jean would do something about it. She stood up sharply, slotting her feet into canvas shoes. She needed to be with Gary this very minute. It was Sunday, when Johnny took him to the park. Jean grabbed her purse and her jacket, clattering down the stairs, and slamming the door behind her.

The sun outside was weak but warm enough to feel pleasant. It wasn't far, but she would get there quicker in the car and she needed to get there immediately. A few minutes later, she had parked, and Jean got out to stand behind a tree. She leaned against its rough bark. On the other side of the clubhouse, with his back to her, Johnny sat smoking on a wooden bench. She stood just far enough away that he could not spot her or sense her presence, but she shuddered as she saw him. In front of the bench, Leonore pushed Gary on the baby swings. Only her son's back, and his small hands clasping the metal chains that held the swing in place, were clear from her view behind the tree, but she heard him giggling. Suddenly he stopped and started to wail. Leonore slowed the swing and put her arms around him, while Johnny didn't move at all. His gaze into the middle distance seemed not to change.

Leonore scooped up Gary from the box-shaped swing and stood him on the ground. Could Johnny really be replacing her with his daughter? A ripple of fury went down Jean's body from top to bottom. Gary first toddled in Johnny's direction, then ran unsteadily, wrapping his arms around one of his father's legs. Johnny looked down briefly. Leonore picked up a beach bag and took hold of Gary's hand. They headed for the clubhouse.

This was her chance, thought Jean. Gary's diaper needed changing. She edged into the building before they spotted her.

Inside the sports changing room, Leonore laid Gary down on a wooden bench. She tugged his dungarees over his knees then noticed a shadow looming over her. She looked up suddenly.

'Oh,' she gasped. 'Oh. Jean. Oh.'

Jean was scarcely aware of Leonore, she thought only of Gary and how he was there, right in front of her. She sat down on the bench by his feet and stroked his cheek.

'Hello, darling,' she said. Oh, the wonder of it! But Gary didn't look happy, he looked confused.

Leonore stared at her anxiously.

'I don't think... shall I get Dad?'

'No,' Jean snapped. She glanced up at her stepdaughter, the girl's dark braids dangling almost to her waist as she bent over. Leonore wore a cotton dress and ankle socks, she was no more than a kid herself. What was Johnny thinking?

Leonore sat down next to Jean and pulled Gary onto her lap to change him.

'Can't I even do that?' Jean asked, but she made no move to stop Leonore. Gary started to cry, and Jean began stroking his cheek more rapidly as Leonore carried on with the changing. That finished, Jean picked him up and held him to her shoulder as he wriggled and wailed. Jean moved back and forth as she breathed a tuneless lullaby. He would not be comforted and neither would she. It felt hopeless.

She did not notice her unhappy stepdaughter had left the room until she returned, Johnny in tow.

'Jean,' he said quickly, taking Gary out of her arms before she even realised what was happening. His smell, his baby shape, all gone. Then he handed Gary to Leonore.

'Take him back to the swings,' he said. 'I'll be with you in a minute.'

Leonore held the boy tightly to her chest and walked towards the door, but she turned round to Jean as she did so, pity and fear playing together on her face.

'Right,' said Johnny, as the door banged shut.

'I thought we had this agreed,' he said coldly. 'You would stay away. You can't be a mother, you're useless at it. So listen, and listen good. You will not contact either of us again. You will not show up, try to see Gary, gawp at him from a distance, have anything to do with him. If you do, I *will* have you committed. Do you understand?'

Jean stared at him. 'He's my son,' she said quietly.

'And he's mine. If you want him, sue me.'

He stared at her with contempt. 'But you can't, can you? Because you have no money, because your parents don't think you're a fit mother, because you just weren't up to it. I am going to bring him up and do a real good job of it. You...' he scoffed. 'You are a lost cause. Every time Gary sees you, it damages him.'

He pushed her into the pale blue concrete wall, pressing her hard by the shoulders.

'Stay away.'

Then he was gone, the door swinging aggressively behind him.

The changing room smelled of old sweat and fresh urine, of bullying and failure. Jean sat heavily on the wooden bench. She could not begin to describe the depths of her misery, the words for it all gone.

She walked outside slowly and, looking around, she found no sign of Gary, Johnny or Leonore. But all around, children were laughing and playing. She saw no reason for her existence. She was no longer a mother; no longer an artist either. She felt a sudden hatred for art almost as strong as her hatred for Johnny. What a waste of her life, she thought. And of Gary's. Everything should have been different.

Jean walked towards her car and sat in the driver's seat. What now? She rested there blankly, unaware of time passing.

From time to time, resting there, a new and terrifying truth struck her. No matter how she tried to avoid it, she had to admit she was pregnant; the period she seemed to have had six weeks before was just one of those things. Her pregnancy scare wasn't a false alarm; that was the bleeding. Now she had something else that Johnny would take if she let him. But he didn't know. She had told no one, not given away the slightest hint that this unreal thing was real after all.

As she sat there, her mind wandered and then she caught sight of them, Helena and Mike with Billy and Bobby. All walking down the road and happy, each parent holding a child by the hand. Which kid was which? She had no clue. Would Gary look like this in a year? She would not be allowed to know.

And they were all laughing, more and more loudly, their mirth leaching out of them. Helena mocked her with her ability to do what Jean had not, to create and be a mother too. Somehow. Mike, how she hated him, stared at her with disgust. He looked her right in the eyes as he drew his finger under his throat. You're dead, his expression said.

Back and forth they rocked hysterically, she heard them cackling loudly, terrifyingly, like the grotesque woman in the funfair, that red-haired plaster model called Laughing Sal she had seen in Playland on her very first time in San Francisco. The day she knew she would come to the city, be an artist, live this sort of life. The experience destroyed her and she must destroy something in return.

Jean tried to start the car. She wanted to mow down the four of them, to kill them, make sure they were dead by running them over again and again. Her fingers trembled as she tried to turn the key in the ignition. But it wouldn't work; she couldn't grip it properly. Nor would her foot stay on the gas pedal. She couldn't make her body do what her brain thought it wanted.

She gazed down at her lap, taking a sharp breath, before looking up at her friends. But they had gone, turned into the park. She watched them walk towards the tennis courts, carefree, the sun filtering joyfully through the unfurled leaves on the trees all around. They were living in a fairy tale. Surrounded by magic, by hope.

As she sat there, moments and hours rolling by, she began to realise it hadn't been them after all. Her pain had conjured them up. Helena and Mike, Billy and Bobby, were not in the park, mocking her with their happiness. That was some other family. But whatever the truth of it, whoever they were, she knew for sure that she had intended to kill them.

The time to leave the city was now. Immediately. This very minute, before her brain forced her body to act.

CHAPTER THIRTY-TWO

For the past few months, Barbara's laptop had followed her from room to room, was next to her when she went to visit any of her children, and even on her rare visits to the wellbeing centre – she had stopped her yoga teaching, saying it didn't matter anymore – she made Lynne put it in her backpack.

Barbara spent many hours on it talking to Gary, looking at him, trying to reconcile the tiny child she'd left, with a man at the beginnings of old age. Gary had scanned a lifetime's worth of photos for his mother. There he was, a sad-faced child; a glowering teenager; a hippy, with wire-framed glasses; a serviceman in uniform; a middle-aged university graduate; and the round, ruddy man of today, his hair short and grey, salt and pepper stubble on his small double chin.

Such a tangled web of guilt. And regret over Gary's life. He should have grown up with the mother he deserved. Barbara had spent more than sixty years refusing to think about what might have been, now she wasn't wasting another second. There would be no more yoga teaching as she spent what energy she had on Gary. His immediate forgiveness was surely temporary; she dreaded the day he became distant or angry. Besides, she was ninety. There was so little time left.

In the end, Nick had been the first in the family to make contact with Gary, both of them bewildered and awkward, although Nick's emotional advantages lurked in the back of both their minds.

Elle had prepared them all for what to expect from Gary. He, too, became estranged from his father after he went back to live with his grandparents in his teens. He joined the army, mainly to work with dogs and much later, he became a book dealer, buying and selling first editions on the internet. Very gently, especially to Barbara, Elle tried to break the depths of his rejection and disappointment. But in the end, her warnings were unnecessary. Gary overcame a lifetime of hurt very quickly, or so it seemed from his words and actions.

But all of them, Barbara especially, knew that this was not the end of things. Was this dementia, she wondered, that she couldn't remember what had happened. If Johnny wasn't Lynne's biological father, then who was? There wasn't a long list of men to choose from. Of course, she could be wrong. There could be circumstances, men, who had slipped her mind. All those strange pills, the electric shock treatment, the sheer horror of that time. Something must have happened then. Perhaps she was better off forgetting after all. Yet every step of the way she had done the best she could, even when that seemed like almost nothing, and that she was incapable of doing anything right. Maybe she would be dead before any other horror would emerge and her children would have to sort it out. That was almost a relief. She would not torment herself over it. What she, what they, had now was enough.

However, just a few months after this realisation, Lynne's email had pinged: *New discoveries for Lynne Pendleton*. She opened the website and reeled at the link's message. *You and Robert likely share one parent*, it said. Another half brother, along with Gary. Lynne could not believe it; when would all this end?

'So, Mum,' Lynne began quietly. 'Does the name Robert Prior mean anything to you.'

Barbara screwed her face up a little, confused.

'I don't think so. I'm... not sure.'

'He'd be around my age, it's not clear from the site, but a similar generation.'

'Why do you want to know?'

'He's coming up as my half-brother. There's an outside chance it could be another relationship, but as he's my generation some of those options are ruled out, and he's not a missing relative on your side, because Larry's daughters aren't connected to him, but he is to me. And Meredith too. Remember that Prior name in the cease and desist letter?'

Lynne's nervous babbling over, they both fell silent.

'That means Robert and I share the same father. Who was he, Mum? Please tell me.'

Barbara laid her head against the chair and stared at the ceiling. After a few moments, she straightened her head once more. Lynne could see the unfamiliar emotions on her mother's face. Guilt? Embarrassment? Confusion? Lynne clasped her hands, hoping her mother could not see how much they shook. Barbara took them, trying to quell the shaking in her own.

'I'd forgotten her surname,' Barbara said after a few moments. 'When I saw her on that video, I thought something wasn't quite right. She had two surnames during the time I knew her but the one she used on the video was different.'

'What do you mean? I don't understand.'

'Women change their names so readily, even if they are only married for five minutes. It's hard to keep up sometimes. I mean, how long did you stay married?'

Lynne tutted in fury. 'For heaven's sake, Mum, what does that matter! WHO are you talking about?'

'It was a truly horrible time of my life. Not that he was horrible; I was. So I ran away. He wasn't a bad man at all, he was much nicer than Johnny. I was the one at fault.'

'Mum! Surely it can't have been that awful?' Lynne perched on the arm of the chair and hugged her mother.

'I knew that he was distantly related to Johnny. Second cousins, something like that. Their grandparents fell out over something a hundred years ago but we weren't interested. We never discussed the subject, it didn't occur to any of us. If you hadn't said Robert Prior, I wouldn't have remembered him at all.'

'Remembered WHO?'

'Mike, your biological father. He is, was, called Mike Prior. And he was married to my dearest friend Helena.'

Family Tree: Costello-Woods 2019

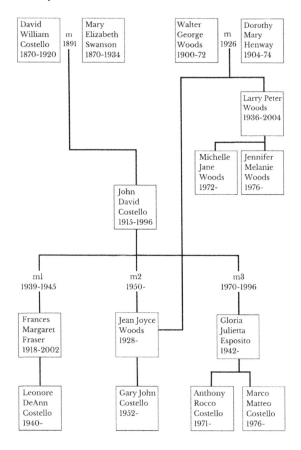

David William Costello 1870-1920 — m 1891 — Mary Elizabeth Swanson 1870-1934

Walter George Woods 1900-72 — m 1926 — Dorothy Mary Henway 1904-74

Larry Peter Woods 1936-2004

Michelle Jane Woods 1972-

Jennifer Melanie Woods 1976-

John David Costello 1915-1996

m1 1939-1945

m2 1950-

m3 1970-1996

Frances Margaret Fraser 1918-2002

Jean Joyce Woods 1928-

Gloria Julietta Esposito 1942-

Leonore DeAnn Costello 1940-

Gary John Costello 1952-

Anthony Rocco Costello 1971-

Marco Matteo Costello 1976-

Family Tree: Prior-Swanson-Costello 2019

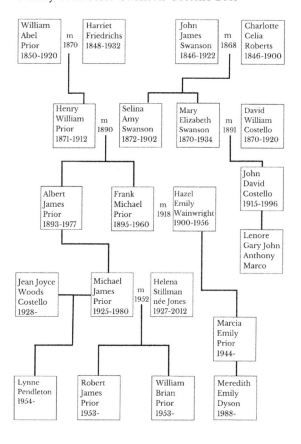

Epilogue

The experience was like watching someone else's home movie, while simultaneously taking part. Karen observed the film from a distance, viewing the action playing out on screen.

There they all were, generations of Barbara's descendants and extended family, gathered together in the cool breeze of the garden. Her ninety-first birthday party was a noisy occasion, with everyone talking and laughing at once, commenting on the extraordinary changes that had happened over the course of the year.

Karen was warmly welcomed, embraced, given prosecco and elaborately iced cake, but she wasn't the star attraction of this event. That remained Barbara herself. She was not required to do anything in particular except eat and speak from time to time. Karen smiled at Danny chasing his baby niece January, Barbara's first great-great-grandchild. Janna was perfecting her ability to walk and considered breaking into a run the most amazing fun. She shrieked and giggled loudly, while her uncle doubled up with laughter. Janna's pregnant mother, Amber, watched with amusement, holding nothing stronger than a glass of water. Barbara stared at Amber, clearly bemused by everything about her. Expecting again, and so soon! Perhaps she would name this new child September.

There was Lynne, still fussing over Barbara, but more relaxed than Karen had seen her before. And Cathy, still arguing with Lynne. There stood Nick, loving the idea of having a brother. As for Rachel, maybe she would sit on the board of the Woods Costello Foundation. No one else wanted to do it. Though negotiations with Gloria and her sons remained in progress, all parties realised this would be a positive outcome. Gary, who had only recently arrived in England, stood on the edge of the festivities. Gazing across the garden, he found the whole thing hard to believe. So that was his mother, the person he had missed his entire life.

For months after they had discovered that Johnny was not Lynne's biological father, Karen had felt defeated, sick with herself and ready to give up on her third career. If only she had waited until they received concrete proof that Lynne's paternal DNA was an exact match to Gary's. She'd been too impatient and as a result, she had compromised her professional reputation before it had even been established. It wasn't the first time that the need to act right this minute had got her into trouble, and it probably wouldn't be the last. Nevertheless, the family had been gracious. They had enough to deal with now and would put genealogy aside for the moment. But then Robert Prior had taken a DNA test...

This birthday party marked the end of Karen's involvement; she had done her job, and it turned out that it was a good one after all. There was relief and professional satisfaction in that. She felt touched to have been invited to this celebration, to have reunited a group of people who had been divided by... circumstance. But whose fault was this separation? Was Johnny to blame? Sure, in many ways. But what about Barbara's parents, who could have helped her and didn't? The mores of the time, to which she could not adhere? Or Barbara herself? And her own neurology, or hormones, or illness, however you wanted to look at it.

On the train going back to London, Karen wondered how it would all turn out, whether Lynne rued the day she had sent her initial email, or Rachel and Danny wished they had given entirely different Christmas presents. And what about Robert Prior, not known as Bobby since his twenty-first birthday, or his twin brother Bill? How were they coping with a half-sister and the knowledge their father had been unfaithful with their mother's closest friend? So far, none of them appeared unhappy or regretful, quite the reverse, that all of this had been forced into the open.

But Karen didn't know for sure; how could she? What seemed right for now, this afternoon, might prove trickier to negotiate in the long run. The end of Karen's involvement marked – for the Woods, Costello, and Pendleton families, and all their many descendants – just the beginning.

Banging shut her front door, after a journey involving the train, tube and bus, Karen flung herself onto her bed. She felt worn out, with the kind of satisfying exhaustion that follows the conclusion of a big piece of work, relieved to be on her own at last. They were not her family, her place. She belonged here, between her four beige walls, her chosen family – small, imperfectly formed and not all legally related – at the end of the phone.

After lying down for a few moments, she pulled herself up again, unscrewing a bottle of red wine and tearing a thin cellophane cover from a takeaway salad. Karen opened her laptop and logged onto all the familial DNA sites. Each of them took its own sweet time to launch, and she forked leaves into her mouth as she waited.

Someday, Karen's obsessive internet searching would benefit her too. Her son, the baby snatched away by her own mother, would upload his DNA onto one of those sites.

Then, surely, he would look for her. She would be there, as she had been for so many years, just waiting to be found.

HELP ME SPREAD THE WORD

I'm so pleased you read *DNA Never Lies*. If you liked it, I'd greatly appreciate you posting a short review on Goodreads, Amazon, or anywhere else you get your books.

Publishing is a very competitive market, and authors like me need readers to tell their friends and family about books they've enjoyed. Support from people like you can make all the difference to a novel's success.

Thank you

Sue

HEAR MORE FROM SUE!

I really hope you enjoyed this book and want to know more about the new novel series featuring Karen Copperfield, investigative genealogist.

The next book in the series, *Lie By Lie*, will be out soon, and there's some more about it on page 318.

So if you'd like to keep up to date on this and future novels, as well as find out more about the use of DNA to reveal family secrets, and the extraordinary histories of ordinary people, just sign up at the link below. There won't be too many emails: promise! We'll never share your email address and you can unsubscribe at any time.

You'll also receive a free ebook novella, *Lies Behind Her*, which looks at the mystery behind Karen's mother Marian.

Sign up now at www.suegeorge.co.uk/newsletter

ACKNOWLEDGEMENTS

This book is a work of fiction, and none of the characters is based on any individual, living or dead. However, some of what happens to them arises from real events and beliefs common at the time the action takes place. In particular, the depiction of Jean/Barbara's life was inspired by the difficult and painful choices faced by many women of that time.

The portrayal of San Francisco in the 1940s and 1950s, including that of the art world, is based in fact. But while there was rivalry between different art schools in San Francisco, loosely based on whether they supported muralists/surrealists or the beginnings of abstract expressionism, none of the rivalries were exactly as portrayed in the book and the colleges mentioned in this novel are fictional. There was also, however, a sense from some that the presence of 'too many' women at art school was lowering the standards. Fortunately, artists such as Jay DeFeo and Joan Brown proved them wrong.

Lake View is wholly fictional, a combination of several rural Californian towns.

The British and Commonwealth Games took place in Vancouver in 1954, and the race between Roger Bannister and John Landy can be seen on YouTube.

However, no one like Victor Pendleton was there as a coach. Mother and baby homes were established institutions in many countries during the 1950s, including Canada. Elizabeth House was not one of them.

When Jean/Barbara drives into Canada, she is heading for the squatter community of Dollarton, in the area around Maplewood Mudflats. The novelist Malcolm Lowry had lived there until the early 1950s. The shacks where the community lived were eventually destroyed by the City of Vancouver in 1971.

For my knowledge of DNA, I began with my own tests. The online course in genealogy from the University of Strathclyde, Glasgow, gave me the basics of how genetic genealogy works. Facebook groups such as DNA Detectives and the International Society of Genetic Genealogy have helped extend this knowledge.

Thanks to Luca Fossum and Aimee Walker, who were hugely helpful in reading and providing in-depth comments on earlier drafts, and to Melanie Underwood for her meticulous editing.

For my interest in genetic genealogy, I want to thank my sister Julia George. Not only does she know all about our own family tree, and remembers who is related and how, but she gave me and my son Alexis Ancestry tests one Christmas. As predicted, there weren't any DNA surprises in our own close family, but it set me wondering: what if there had been?

All mistakes are my own.

Lie by Lie
First her, then him, then all of them

2015: Heather and Andy always suspected they were siblings: it was a standing joke in the area where they grew up, something they were bullied about from their earliest school days. But Heather had been adopted, and Andy's mother and stepfather flat-out denied there was any connection. Still, they looked so alike, that the rumours persisted for the next thirty years, until DNA tests finally proved they were right. But the question remained: who were their biological parents?

1971: She's only 15 but she really wants to keep the baby. And why shouldn't she? Why were her parents so stupid? She wouldn't be in this mess if they had just kept their mouths shut.

2021: Investigative genealogist Karen Copperfield gives most of her extended family a very wide berth. So when her cousin Phoebe shows up on her doorstep she wants to run away far and fast. But then Phoebe makes her an offer she can't refuse...

ABOUT THE AUTHOR

When Sue George's first novel was published, a very famous writer called her 'a born storyteller'. But life got in the way, and despite publishing a couple of books, Sue's storytelling took a back seat. Instead, she spent years writing and editing on various publications, including a long stint at the Guardian newspaper.

Her historical interests led to a Masters' degree in Life History Research from Sussex University, but because her mother and sister had already drawn up extensive trees for many branches of the family, Sue's involvement in genealogy came later. Her own DNA tests have so far led to no big surprises, welcome or otherwise.

Sue lives in London, where she is happy to divide her time between the peaceful green spaces of Epping Forest and the boundless creativity of the city.

Find Sue on:
Facebook at SueGeorgeAuthor
Twitter @suegeorge
www.suegeorge.co.uk

ALSO BY SUE GEORGE

Fiction
Death of the Family

• • • ● ● • ● ● • • •

Non-fiction
Women and Bisexuality

Printed in Great Britain
by Amazon